UnDeRcOvEr Kitty

A SECOND CHANCE CAT MYSTERY

Sofie Ryan

BERKLEY PRIME CRIME
New York

BERKLEY PRIME CRIME
Published by Berkley
An imprint of Penguin Random House LLC
penguinrandomhouse.com

Copyright © 2021 by Darlene Ryan
Excerpt from *Curiosity Thrilled the Cat* by Sofie Kelly © 2011 by
Penguin Random House LLC

ISBN: 9781984802354

First Edition: January 2021

Printed in the United States of America
1   3   5   7   9   10   8   6   4   2

Cover art by Mary Ann Lasher
Cover design by Katie Anderson

Titles by Sofie Ryan

The Whole Cat and Caboodle
Buy a Whisker
A Whisker of Trouble
Telling Tails
The Fast and the Furriest
No Escape Claws
Claw Enforcement
Undercover Kitty

UnDeRcOvEr
Kitty

Chapter 1

"Elvis?" I said. I folded my arms over my midsection and frowned to emphasize how preposterous I thought the suggestion that Rose Jackson had just made to me was.

"Yes, dear," she replied with the same patient tone in her voice that a kindergarten teacher might use with a five-year-old still learning to tie their shoelaces.

"You want *Elvis* to do a cat show?"

Rose pursed her lips and studied the pale blue tablecloth that she had just spread over a chrome kitchen table. She looked at me over her shoulder. "I think those woven place mats would look better, don't you?"

So we were changing the subject. Okay. I was used to her doing that.

The retro table and chairs she was looking at, which dated from the early 1960s, were in excellent condition. "You're right. They would be a better choice," I said. "Potential buyers will be able to see what good shape the top of the table is in."

Rose had already pulled the cloth off the table. I

moved to grab one end and we folded it, working in unison the way we had dozens of times before. When we were done, Rose hung the cloth over her arm and smiled at me. "Thank you, Sarah," she said. She gestured in the general direction of the storage space under the stairs leading to the second floor. "I'm going to look for those place mats."

"Hang on a minute," I said. "You didn't answer my question."

Rose Jackson was tiny, barely five feet tall depending on which shoes she was wearing. Arguing with her was like arguing with a bear over a picnic basket. There was no way it was going to end well for you. She looked at me now with guileless gray eyes—not that I was fooled for a second by her innocent gaze. "I'm sorry. I thought the answer was obvious. I wouldn't have asked you if I weren't serious. I haven't gotten that feeble yet." She smoothed a wrinkle out of the tablecloth. "And it's two shows."

"Rose, I just don't think Elvis is really a . . . performer."

"Nonsense!" she exclaimed, waving away my words with her free hand. "He has looks. He has charisma. He has talent. He has star quality." She gestured toward the white molded chair by the front window where Elvis was sprawled, a clump of dust clinging to the top of his head, one foot seemingly keeping time with a rhythm only he could hear.

He seemed to be ignoring our conversation, which didn't surprise me since he was a small black cat and *not* a beloved music icon. To be fair, *my* Elvis did command attention when he walked into a room, although in the cat's case it wasn't his swivel hips and sexy sneer, it was his adorable head tilt and scarred nose.

"Sarah, we need Elvis for this case," Rose said, her tone matter-of-fact. "We can't work it without him."

Elvis sat up, bent his head, gave a quick wash to the thick black fur on his chest and then looked expectantly at me. It was as if he'd understood the conversation.

Rose, along with her friends Liz French and Charlotte Elliot and Rose's beau, Alfred Peterson—Mr. P.—ran a detective agency known as Charlotte's Angels, the Angels for short, out of the sunporch of my store. Although I'd been skeptical when they'd decided to go into the investigation business, they had turned out to be surprisingly good at it. As Rose had explained, "No one really pays any attention when old people ask questions. Most of the time they don't pay any attention to us at all."

It didn't hurt that between the four of them they knew pretty much everyone in North Harbor—probably everyone in this part of the state of Maine. To borrow one of Rose's expressions, they were all as sharp as tacks. And they weren't above roping anyone (me) they needed help from into their cases.

Just then, two men came in the front door of the shop. One looked to be in his twenties, the other in his fifties: Father and son, I felt certain. They both had the same vivid blue eyes and dimples. They looked around as though they'd come with a purpose.

"I'll take care of these two." Rose handed me the tablecloth.

"This conversation isn't over," I said.

"Of course not." She smiled and patted my arm.

Anyone with any sense would have realized that she was just humoring me.

She headed toward the two men, turning that smile on them. "Welcome to Second Chance," she said. "Are you looking for anything in particular?"

Second Chance was a repurpose shop, part second-hand store and part collectibles shop. We sold furniture, dishes, toys and some musical instruments—mostly guitars. Many things had been repurposed from their original use, like the teacups we'd turned into planters or the church pew that had become verandah seating.

Our stock came from a lot of different places: yard sales, free piles, flea markets, abandoned storage units, people looking to downsize. I bought things fairly regularly from a couple of trash pickers. We'd been hired a number of times to sort through and handle the sale of the contents of someone's home—usually because they were moving into something smaller. I'd even waded into a ditch once after a chair.

I headed for the workroom, stopping to give Elvis a scratch on the top of the head and pluck off the dust bunny. He leaned sideways to take a look at the two customers. Elvis was as much a part of the staff as anyone else. Most people were charmed by his friend-liness and the way he seemed to have an opinion on what they were thinking about buying, often walking around an item with his head cocked thoughtfully to one side and then signaling his okay with a mrrr of approval.

I hung the tablecloth on the portable metal cloth-ing rack that Mac had scavenged from a curbside pile a couple of weeks earlier. He had also come back with two folding wooden chairs, a large wicker basket and a beautiful round mirror with a bevel edge. "It looked like whoever lived in the house had moved out," he'd said as he pulled the tarp off the bed of his truck so I could look at his "finds."

On paper, Mac was my second in command; in practice, he was much more than that. I owned Second Chance, but Mac was a big part of the store's success. He could fix just about anything. He had a good sense of what would catch a customer's eye and he seemed to have an unending number of ideas for ways to give old things new life. Over the past year and a half that the store had been open, Mac had become more of a partner than an employee and now that connection had spread to our personal lives—with a little nudge forward from Rose and her merry band of matchmakers.

I walked over to the workbench where Mac had left a selection of paint cans for me. I was in the process of converting a long, low bookcase into a set of cubbies that I could envision in a mudroom or by a back door. I'd told Mac I was thinking about painting the outside of the piece some shade of gray with two different colors—I was leaning toward blue and red—for the interior. There was enough blue and red paint left over from other projects and I thought the shades of both would go well with gray, but there wasn't enough of the latter in any permutation, including a pretty blue-gray I'd used for a games and electronics cabinet. I set the blue-gray paint, which was called Winter Sky, aside. Before I bought any more of it, I wanted to try swatching it next to the red and blue.

I also had a sketch I'd done of what I was thinking

about for shelves for the cubby that I wanted Mac's opinion on. I'd changed the spacing three times now. I decided to check on Rose and her customers and then head out to our workshop in the former garage space.

Rose was just coming in the front door with a very self-satisfied smile on her face.

I looked around the shop. "What did you sell?"

"Those two nightstands," she said as she walked over to join me. She gestured toward the bare area on the floor. "A birthday gift."

"I just put them out yesterday," I said. I had stained the two pieces midnight blue. The tops had been painted black and there were brass pulls on the drawers.

"Do you remember the woman who came in about half an hour after you brought them in from the workroom?"

I nodded. "I really thought she was going to buy them."

The woman had walked around the nightstands, looking at them from every angle. "What do you think?" she'd said to Elvis, who had made three of the four circuits with her. He had meowed his approval and I was certain we had a sale, but she'd left without buying anything.

Rose brushed off the front of her apron with one hand. "She did, in a sense. She went home and hinted pretty broadly, from what I could gather, to her husband and son."

"And that was them." I waved a hand in the general direction of the parking lot.

"I suggested they might want to come back in a couple of weeks and look at that tall dresser Mac has been working on. That would look lovely in a room with those two nightstands." She raised one eyebrow. "I might have pointed out that Christmas isn't that far away."

"Rose Jackson, is there anything you can't sell?" I teased.

"Fruitcake," she replied, taking my question way more seriously than I'd intended.

I knew Rose well enough to know that pursuing *that* comment could take us down a conversational detour that might take the rest of the morning to get through, so all I said was, "Good to know."

I looked at the empty space where the two nightstands had been. "So what should we bring in from the workroom?" I asked.

"Has Avery finished that trunk you got from Cleveland?"

Avery was my youngest employee, a smart, creative, quirky teen who was also Liz French's granddaughter. Cleveland was a picker I bought from regularly. A couple of weeks ago he'd shown up with a 1930s vintage theatrical trunk with both of the original trays inside. It was grimy, which made sense when he explained he'd found it in the basement of an old house that was slated to be torn down, but it seemed to be surface dirt and not anything deeply embedded. The price Cleveland had named was so good I didn't dicker and I didn't think twice about not paying it. Avery had spent hours meticulously cleaning the trunk, even using a toothbrush in some spots. We'd set the trunk out on a tarp during an unseasonably mild and sunny day a week ago and that had gotten rid of the last bit of mustiness that the kitty litter we'd left inside for several days hadn't removed.

"That's a good idea," I said.

Rose's gaze narrowed thoughtfully. "We could open the lid, drape a couple of quilts over it and fill the inside with those pillows Jess made."

"And what if we bring out that side table?" I asked. "The one with the pull-out shelf. We could put two or three vases on the top and fill them with branches I could get Mac to cut from those bushes next to the workshop."

"And maybe one or two of the teacup planters on that shelf."

"That would work," I said. "It would catch people's attention."

Rose beamed at me. "I'll look for some vases and I'll get those place mats as well."

I looked around. Elvis had disappeared, probably gone upstairs to sprawl on my desk and shed cat hair on every single piece of paper on it. "We didn't finish our conversation," I said.

"I don't know what more I can tell you," she said. "We have a new case and we need Elvis."

"Who's your client?"

Rose nudged her glasses up her nose. "We've been hired by the organizers of the Atlantic Coast Cat Shows. Chloe and Will Hartman."

"Atlantic Coast Cat Shows?" I said. "I've never heard of them."

"They're affiliated with the AFA, the American Feline Association. It's a fairly new group. They promote breed registration and responsible breeding, but they're far more business-oriented than, say, the ACFA, the American Cat Fanciers Association."

Business-oriented. In other words, they were looking to make a profit. "So you don't need to report to the AFA board?"

Rose waved away my words. "No. The shows are completely autonomous. The Hartmans are our clients and we report directly to them. Chloe Hartman is related to Stella Hall somehow. It's either second cousin once removed or first cousin twice removed."

We had cleared out Stella's brother's home after his death and sold much of his furniture in the shop. We'd discovered a Marklin model train set in excellent condition . . . and a dead body in the kitchen. The latter had turned into a case for the Angels.

"Why did they hire you?" I couldn't imagine why a cat show would need detectives.

"Someone had been trying to sabotage recent shows in New Hampshire." Rose shook her head. "They don't want a repeat of what happened there at the Maine shows."

I remembered seeing a poster about the cat shows in the library. "One of those shows is here in North Harbor, isn't it?"

"Yes. And the other is in Searsport."

Elvis was just coming down the stairs as if somehow he'd known that we were talking again about something that involved him. He came over to me and I bent to pick him up. "What do you mean by sabotage?" I asked. Elvis turned to look at Rose as though he wanted to hear the answer, too.

Rose straightened the front of her apron. "It's mostly

been nuisance things so far. Someone set off the fire alarm and the sprinklers in one venue during the show setup. Luckily there were no cats in the building at the time. Some of the show cages have been damaged. A sound system suddenly stopped working. It's really just been vandalism up to now, but it's escalating."

"Escalating how?" I wasn't going to put Elvis into a situation where he might get hurt, even though the scars he had suggested that anyone who tried to tangle with him would have a fight on their hands.

She took a moment before she spoke. "At the most recent show a cat ended up with a pinched paw because the door of a cage had been tampered with."

Elvis nudged my chin with his head. I felt as though he was trying to tell me we had to do something. I let out a breath as he shifted in my arms. He did his head-tilt thing and I realized that Rose was doing the same thing. "For the record, the two of you can't always use your collective cuteness to get your way," I said, my finger flicking between the two of them.

"We're not trying to get our own way," Rose protested as Elvis meowed loudly in agreement. "We need your help. We need to be part of the shows, part of that culture, to find out exactly who's trying to sabotage things. Showing Elvis is our best way in." Her gray eyes and his green ones stayed fixed on my face.

I was the first one to look away. "I don't know anything about how to show a cat," I said. I knew I was beaten. Elvis was purring. A smile was starting to spread across Rose's face. They knew I was beaten, too. We were just negotiating the terms of my surrender. "And Elvis isn't a purebred anything."

I didn't know anything about the cat's history. The first time I'd seen Elvis he was eating eggs and salami in a booth at The Black Bear pub. The cat had been wandering around the harbor front for at least a couple of weeks before that. No one seemed to know where he belonged.

When I'd left that day Elvis had followed Sam, who owned the pub, and me out to the curb, jumped onto the front seat of my truck and settled himself on the floor on the passenger side, where I had wedged a guitar case.

I had a cat, whether I wanted one or not. And while he might not have had a pedigree that went back generations Elvis was smart. He loved the TV show *Jeopardy!* and he had an uncanny ability to spot a lie. I didn't have an adequate explanation for either of those quirks.

"Elvis doesn't need to be a purebred, and *you* don't have to do anything," Rose said, waving a hand like she was shooing away a fly. "There's a household pet category in each of the shows. Elvis will ace it."

I stifled a grin at one of Avery's expression's coming out of Rose's mouth.

"I see you trying to swallow that smile, missy," Rose said. She was trying to look annoyed, but it wasn't working. "I've seen the competition and he is head and shoulders above them—no offense to the other cats, but Elvis has the *it* factor."

I held up a hand. "I'm just going to take your word for that."

"And you should." She softened her words with a smile. "You don't have to worry about a thing. I have everything worked out."

That was exactly why I *was* worried.

"You and Alfred can register Elvis as co-owners and Alfred will deal with showing him and everything else."

Elvis gave a murp of agreement as though this was something they had worked out in advance—which, for all I knew, they had. I wondered if Rose had cleared all of this with Mr. P., but I knew it didn't matter because he would do anything for her. Just like all the rest of us.

"Fine," I said. "But if Elvis misbehaves or doesn't cooperate, that will be Mr. P.'s issue to deal with."

"Nonsense," Rose said. "Elvis is a very well-behaved cat." She reached over to stroke his dark fur. "Aren't you?" He nuzzled her hand and purred even louder.

Elvis *was* a well-behaved cat—for the most part. He was also as single-minded as Rose was. "You've been warned," I said. "This is my due diligence."

Rose patted my cheek. "Honestly, dear, you worry too much. What could go wrong?" With one last smile for Elvis she bustled away to get the place mats from under the stairs.

What could go wrong?

Pretty much everything.

Chapter 2

I grabbed my coat and headed out to our main workshop in the former garage, leaving Rose and Elvis working, and likely conspiring, in the store. We had no snow, but it was cold, typical weather for early November in Maine. Once we had some snow it would be busier in North Harbor. We were close to a couple of popular ski resorts. Tourists came to town during the spring and summer for the beautiful Maine seacoast. In the fall and winter months it was the nearby hills with the spectacular autumn colors and skiing that brought them in.

Mac had built a workbench for the old garage space and he was seated at it, in front of a window on the end wall, taking apart a chandelier so Avery could clean the tear-shaped pedagogues which, I had learned, was the correct name for the dangling crystals. I had bought the chandelier on impulse and instinct at an auction in Camden the previous weekend. It was circular, made of brass with descending tiers of the crystals. The brass showed only the lightest of wear and my cursory examination, paired with past experience, had told me that the pedagogues weren't scratched, just coated with years of grime.

There was something about the simple, classic, midcentury design that suggested to me that the fixture was worth more than the opening bid of fifty dollars. In the end I'd spent over three hundred dollars for the light and as I loaded it into my SUV I crossed my fingers that I hadn't—as Rose would put it—bought a pig in a poke.

And I hadn't.

After a more detailed look at the chandelier, and a little online research, Mac had discovered that it had been designed by Christoph Palme in the early 1960s and would probably bring between six thousand and sixty-five hundred dollars. Roughly twenty times my investment.

Mac smiled at me. "Hi," he said. He was tall and fit, all lean, strong muscle. He had light brown skin, brown eyes and close-cropped black hair. And he smiled like Ivory soap and peppermints.

I smiled back at him. "Hi," I said.

He set down the pair of small, needle-nose pliers he'd been holding. "So what did Rose want to talk to you about?"

I leaned against the end of the workbench. "She wants to put Elvis in a cat show in Searsport."

He raised an eyebrow. "New hobby?"

"New case." I explained about the Angels being hired to find out who had tried to sabotage the earlier shows.

"So she pretty much played on your sympathy."

"Pretty much," I said sheepishly. I did hate the thought that a cat could have been seriously injured because of the vandalism.

"You do know the show starts tomorrow, right?" Mac said. "A couple of customers were talking about it yesterday."

I shouldn't have been surprised. It was exactly the kind of detail Rose tended to leave out. I let out a frustrated breath and pushed my hair behind one ear. "Rose forgot to mention that. I thought I had some time to get Elvis ready."

I could see a smile dancing around Mac's eyes. "Get him ready how? Is there a talent component to the show? A swimsuit competition?" The smile had made it all the way to his lips.

"No," I said. "I just thought I could . . . I don't know, brush his fur, give him a supplement to make his coat shinier." I picked up the tiny set of pliers Mac had been using and opened and closed them a couple of times. I wished I could use them to snip out the parts of this case that were already giving me grief. I looked over at Mac. "Is this a mistake?"

He shook his head. "I don't think so. If you can describe a cat as charming, then that's what Elvis is. He likes people and he likes attention. He'll be fine."

"So, so many things could go wrong," I said.

Mac reached over and took the pliers out of my hand. "Or they could go right."

I rolled my eyes at him. "I'm trying to worry here and you're making it difficult."

He laughed. "Hey, for all you know Elvis just might win and all that worrying will have been wasted." He caught my hand and gave it a squeeze. "It's a cat show, Sarah. Not brain surgery. Seriously, what could go wrong?"

Rose had said almost the same thing. I was pretty sure their words had already jinxed us.

The plan for Saturday was that Mac would open Second Chance and I would drive Elvis, Rose and Mr. P. to Searsport for the show. I'd drop them off and return late afternoon to pick them up. But as Elvis and I ate breakfast—cat food for him, Brussels sprouts, bacon and egg bake for me—I realized I wanted to go to the competition, or at least stay for a little while and check the place out.

I picked up my phone and called Mac.

"Yes, I can take care of the shop for a while," he answered instead of saying hello.

"How did you know what I was going to ask you?" I said.

"I know you." I could hear the smile in his voice. "I knew you wouldn't let Rose and Alfred get involved in this case without checking things out yourself."

I propped an elbow on the counter and leaned my head against my closed hand. "Every time they have a new case I say I'm not getting involved and then I do."

"It's your process."

"My what?" I asked, picking up a bite of bacon and holding it out to Elvis.

"Your process," Mac repeated. "You know, the way hockey players stop shaving and grow a beard during the playoffs. A lot of them have their own little rituals throughout the whole season—taking the same number of practice shots in warm-up, putting on their gear in the same order every game."

"So me saying I'm not getting caught up in one of the Angels' cases and then doing it anyway is the equivalent of a playoff beard?"

"Exactly."

Elvis put a paw on my knee and then looked pointedly at my plate. I snagged a tiny bit of egg and fed it to him. He licked his whiskers and started to wash his face. "I think I need a new process," I said.

Mac laughed. "No, no, no. You can't change the process. That would be bad luck. That would be like shaving your playoff beard or washing your jersey before the last game in a seven-game series."

I grinned even though he couldn't see me. "Well, the last thing I need is bad luck."

"So take your time," he said. "Avery and Charlotte and I can handle the shop."

"Cleveland will probably be by sometime this morning," I said. "If you see anything that interests you, there's an extra sixty dollars in petty cash."

"Is it okay with you if I let Avery take a look? She has a pretty good sense for what will and won't sell."

Avery had an eye for color and a way of looking at things that had translated into some very unique and popular designs for the front window of the shop. People still commented about her Valentine's window featuring four mannequins dressed up as members of the band KISS. She lived with her grandmother, went to a progressive half-day school and worked at Second Chance in the afternoons and some part of most Saturdays.

"Go ahead," I said. "She's going to do another window display and she has a list of things she's looking for. She went with Rose and Mr. P. to a flea market last weekend. Rose bought a teapot, Alfred got more reels for his View-Master and Avery came back with a crystal ball."

"What does she have planned for the window?" Mac asked.

I gave Elvis another bit of egg. "I don't know. All I know is it has something to do with Thanksgiving." The holiday was just three weeks away. It was also the first major holiday since Mac and I had become a kinda-sorta couple and I wasn't sure what to expect—or what was expected of me.

I went over the short list of things I wanted Charlotte and Avery to take care of and Mac urged me to take my time at the cat show. I told him I'd call if I was going to be longer than the morning and we said good-bye.

Searsport is a small town at the head of Penobscot Bay, about forty minutes from North Harbor. We often had tourists who were staying in Searsport come into the shop. History buffs loved the town. Some of the grand sea captains' homes had been turned into bed-and-breakfasts and many of the businesses in the downtown looked the same as they had a hundred and fifty years ago.

"This is such a pretty place," I said as we drove

through the town on the way to the resort where the cat show was being held.

"Searsport flourished during the Age of Sail," Mr. P. said from the backseat of my SUV.

I glanced in the rearview mirror at him. He was wearing a dove gray beanie that Rose had knit for him and a few tufts of his hair—almost the same color as the hat—poked out from underneath it.

"Where were the ships going?" I asked. "China, I'm guessing."

"And India," Rose said. She had been a teacher and knew a lot about the history of New England in general and Maine in particular. "There were shops and factories to make all the goods those ships carried."

"Close to three hundred sea captains sailed out of Searsport in its heyday," Mr. P. added. "Imagine how many cats there would have been."

I frowned. "Cats?"

He smiled. "Oh yes. Cats were often carried on trading ships to control rodents. Many sailors believe cats bring good luck. Especially black cats."

I looked at Mr. P. in the rearview mirror again. Elvis was on the seat beside him, preening as though he'd understood the old man's words.

"But black cats are supposed to mean bad luck," I said, making a left turn at the sign for the Captain's Rest, which was where we were headed.

"Not among sailors," Mr. P. said. "It was believed that cats could protect ships from bad weather."

"Cats react to changes in barometric pressure," Rose added. "Their inner ears are very sensitive to even small changes."

I thought about how restless Elvis got when a storm was headed our way.

"And the pressure often drops before a storm," I said. "So they could warn a ship's crew about bad weather ahead."

"Exactly," Rose said, smiling like I was a student who had just aced a quiz.

I saw another direction sign for the resort up ahead. Its logo was a ship's wheel.

"Tell me about the Captain's Rest," I said. "It doesn't seem like the kind of place to host a cat show."

"The Captain's Rest was originally a sea captain's home," Mr. P. explained. "It's been converted to an inn with all the amenities and the former carriage house on the property is now used as meeting space. It's the right size for this type of event."

"And since they've just opened, having the show here is a perfect opportunity to generate some interest in what they offer," Rose said.

I could feel her gray eyes on me. I shot her a quick look. "What?"

She shook her head. "Nothing, really. I was just thinking how lovely all the rooms are. The inn would be a lovely place for, say, a romantic getaway."

Rose was about as subtle as a backhoe parked on the front lawn.

"I'll keep that in mind if anyone happens to ask for a recommendation," I said.

She reached over and patted my leg. "You do that, dear," she said.

I knew she wasn't done trying to orchestrate a romantic evening for Mac and me. Not by a long shot.

* * *

The Captain's Rest inn overlooked Penobscot Bay and even surrounded by leafless trees the former sea captain's home was picture-postcard perfect. It was painted a creamy, buttery yellow and all the ornate trim was white including the widow's walk surrounding the rooftop cupola.

"Wow," I said as Mr. P. directed me to the carriage house, which was located to the left of the inn itself.

"Built in 1874 by Captain Joshua Graydon for his wife, Caroline," he said.

The carriage house was equally impressive, painted in the same yellow and white color scheme.

"I'm guessing this building was constructed at the same time as the house," I said as I pulled into the parking area to one side of the carriage house. It was two stories high and then some, with its own cupola sporting a copper roof and weather vane. A Juliet balcony was centered above a row of tall, multipaned windows. A build-out on the ground floor had more windows, two large square banks of them on either side of the entrance, which I guessed by its size and shape had originally been windows as well. A large signboard to the right of the doors welcomed visitors to the Searsport Cat Show.

Rose had given me very few details about the show so I didn't really know what to expect. A few minutes on my laptop had gotten rid of the idea that "showing" Elvis meant Mr. P. would be leading him around on a leash. Other than that I wasn't really sure what the cat show was going to look like. I had asked if they needed to practice anything, but Mr. P. had assured me that both he and Elvis were ready.

We signed in at the registration desk and received our participant ID badges from a woman wearing a cat ears headband studded with faux pearls. "This is Elvis?" she asked, indicating the cat carrier I was holding.

I nodded. "It is."

She leaned over the table and smiled. "Hello, Elvis," she said.

The cat meowed a "hello" and tipped his head to one side as he looked at her through the mesh panel on the top of the bag. He was already turning on the charm. Maybe Rose was right. Maybe Elvis would turn out to be a natural at this kind of thing.

The woman handed Mr. P. some paperwork and directed us toward another set of doors. We showed our badges and then made our way into the cat show proper. The setup was devoted to everything cat. Numerous large vertical banners hanging from the high ceiling featured cats of all colors, shapes and sizes.

There were booths selling everything from cat toys and scratching posts—the latter that Mr. P. had custom made for Elvis was as nice as anything I could see for sale—to bubblers and food delivery systems. There was a stall offering custom-made cat carriers and another with two artists who would paint your cat dressed and posed as King Henry VIII or some other historical figure like Paul Revere or Queen Elizabeth I.

There was so much going on and so many people around I didn't know where to focus my attention. I was like the proverbial kid in a candy store.

"I had no idea a cat show was like this," I said.

"Then this is a good learning experience for you," Rose said. I was pretty sure I wasn't imagining the slight reprimand I could hear in her voice. Mr. P. gave me a sympathetic smile.

The commercial booths rimmed the space and the center seemed to be devoted to the cats that were taking part in the show. Since Rose seemed to know where we were going I just followed behind her and Mr. P.

Each cat contestant had its own small section, a kind of staging area to wait and get ready for the judging. And their spaces held more than just a carrier bag. Most of the areas were outfitted with what looked like miniature tents of every color and design you could imagine. There were soft blankets or towels in the bottoms of the tents. They all had mesh windows so their inhabitants could see what was going on around them. Several had music playing and I saw white noise machines set up at three different stations.

All the spaces were personalized, many with photos and ribbons won, I was guessing, at past shows. Some of the cats we passed looked a little apprehensive. Some seemed more relaxed and curious. A few seemed to be ignoring everyone and taking a nap. The people with them were working on their computers, checking their phones, talking to passersby or to their cats. Everyone seemed busy.

I glanced down at Elvis. He was happily looking out the mesh window of the bag. As usual he wanted to see everything around him.

Rose continued to lead the way down the long aisle

of tables, walking with a purpose, smiling at everyone. She didn't seem lost at all and since Mr. P. was content to follow without asking any questions I did the same. But as we passed cat after cat, I began to feel a niggle of worry.

Mr. P. spoke to several people, all of whom smiled and said something back to him. Was there anywhere he went that he didn't make friends? I wondered, although I already knew the answer.

The level of activity was a little overwhelming. Mr. P. looked over his shoulder at me and slowed his pace so I could catch up.

"I didn't know it was going to be like this," I said in a low voice.

He looked up at me, nudging his glasses up his nose. "What did you think it would be like?" he asked. There was genuine curiosity in his voice. He was the least judgmental person I knew.

I shrugged. "I don't know. Just not this." I looked around. "We don't have any of the things other people have. Will Elvis be okay?" I felt a bit foolish realizing I didn't want Elvis to look out of place, as though the other cats might snub him. I pulled a hand back over my hair.

"We have everything we need, my dear," Mr. P. said.

"All I brought was the litter box, some food and water and a copy of Elvis's vaccination records."

He smiled. "That's all you needed to bring."

Ahead of us, Rose had stopped in the aisle and turned to look back at us. She wasn't impatiently tapping her foot, but her body language, arms crossed, chin up—told me she wanted Alfred and me to pick up the pace. We hurried to join her.

"We have a lot to do," Rose said. "Let's get Elvis settled."

The cat murped his agreement from the carrier bag.

I looked around at where we were standing. We were at the end of the row. A large black and purple tent was sitting on the table. A soft purple towel had been folded in the bottom and a similar-colored blanket had been draped over the top. To the right of the carrier was a tray with dishes for water and food. To the left it looked as though some kind of grooming station had been set up. There were several brushes and combs and two more large towels, these a paler shade of purple than the fleece blanket.

"I think we're in the wrong place," I said. I could feel Elvis moving restlessly in the carrier slung over my shoulder, impatient to get out.

"No, this is us," Rose said as she bent down to rummage in her ubiquitous giant tote bag. "One oh four."

She pointed her elbow at the table and I finally noticed sign number 104: ELVIS, "THE KING," OWNED BY SARAH GRAYSON AND ALFRED PETERSON.

"Where did all this come from?" I asked.

Mr. P. smiled again. "I got us all set up yesterday morning. I thought purple was appropriate, given that it was the King's favorite color." He gestured at the carrier. "May I?" he asked.

Before I could answer Elvis gave a loud meow.

I nodded. "Go ahead."

Mr. P. unzipped the bag and lifted Elvis out. My shoulders involuntarily tensed. Would he try to bolt?

Elvis made no effort to jump out of the old man's arms, but he did crane his neck to look around. He seemed curious but not the slightest bit unsettled. Rose had been right about one thing: Elvis had the right kind of temperament for a cat show, for any large group of people. He was the most sociable cat I had ever seen; although to be fair, I hadn't actually been around a lot of cats.

I slipped the bag off my shoulder and took a good look at the setup Mr. P. had created. In addition to the eating area and the grooming space, there were several toys next to the cage. There was even an iPod connected to a small speaker that I knew Mr. P. had bought from Teresa Reynard, one of the other pickers we regularly dealt with. I had no doubt that if I checked it, the iPod would show a playlist of the "other" Elvis's music.

"The litter box can go under the table," Mr. P. directed. He had created a screened-off area using three-sided poster board. "For Elvis's privacy," he explained.

I recognized the artwork on the cardboard—curved lines and shapes that on closer examination were line drawings of cats. Dozens of them.

"Did Avery do this?" I asked.

He nodded.

It seemed as though everyone had been in on getting Elvis ready for the show.

I turned to Rose. "Now that you've infiltrated the show, what exactly are you watching out for?"

"Anything that could disrupt things," she said. "At the shows in New Hampshire, both the sound system and the sprinklers were tampered with and several of the show cages were damaged, so we'll be watching out for that here."

"Being participants also means that we'll have the opportunity to gather information without arousing suspicion," Mr. P. added.

In other words, they'd be able to get all the behind-the-scenes gossip. Rose, especially, was very good at that kind of thing. She was one of the smartest people I knew, but she wasn't above letting people think she was a slightly ditsy old lady if it served her purpose.

"Do you need to check in with your clients?" I asked.

Mr. P. smiled. He and Elvis were checking the banners hanging from the rafters overhead. "I've already spoken to them. Don't worry. Everything is going according to plan."

I hoped that was a good thing. I gestured at Elvis. "So what does His Majesty do next?"

"All the cats, including Elvis, wait until it's time for their category to be judged."

I looked around again. "Where does that happen?"

Rose gestured to an area near the long back wall of the room. It was divided into five separate sections by what looked to be moveable wall panels. Each section was open in the front and closed in on the three other sides. An inverted-U of tables held several cages. In the center of the space were two more long tables arranged in a T-shape and covered with bright red tablecloths. A sign suspended from the ceiling in each area indicated which judging section it was: Ring 1, Ring 2, etc. I could see that the sign for Ring 2 also read "Household Pets." That was probably where Elvis would be judged.

"Okay, so Elvis is in the household pet category," I said. "How many other categories are there?" It was clear there was a lot more going on than I had anticipated.

"Seven," Rose said. "Household pet, of course." She smiled at Elvis who seemed to smile back at her. "Kitten. Championship. Premiership. Veterans. Miscellaneous. And Provisional."

"So they all have different criteria?" I asked.

She nodded. "Kitten is pretty obvious. These are cats between four and eight months old. The other designations are a little more complicated. The Championship category, for example, is for unaltered, pedigreed cats over eight months of age."

I thought of all the different cats I'd seen when we'd come in. "And pedigreed means the cat is a specific breed, not a bit of everything like Elvis. How do they make the distinction?"

Rose tipped her head to one side and studied me. "What do you know about the structure of these shows?" she asked.

"Nothing," I said, feeling my cheeks get warm. I should have done more research.

"This is an AFA-sanctioned competition. American Feline Association."

I nodded. "I remember you saying that, and I saw their logo on the paperwork I filled out about Elvis."

Mr. P. had finally set Elvis inside the tent. He was walking around on the fluffy purple towel, sniffing to see if it met with his approval.

"That's right," Rose said. "The AFA is an organization that registers cats for show and keeps track of their lineage—their family tree, so to speak. They also keep track of judges and things like the standards for the various recognized breeds. But each show is run independently by its organizers."

"How many recognized breeds are there?"

"In an AFA show, forty-two."

I looked down the long aisle of tables. Had we passed anywhere close to that many different cats? "Forty-two?" I'd been expecting Rose to name a number closer to two dozen.

"Forty-two," she repeated. "Five cages down on the other side, did you notice a stocky gray cat with really thick fur?"

"Yes," I said. "It reminded me of a teddy bear for some reason."

"That's a British shorthair," Rose said. "There's also Ragdoll, Maine coon, Siamese, Russian Blue and Abyssinian." Rose was ticking them off on her fingers. "Bengal, Persian, Scottish fold. Would you like me to list them all?"

"No, thank you," I said. "I get the picture."

Elvis seemed to be satisfied with his temporary accommodations. He had stretched out on his side and was washing his face with his right paw. Mr. P. zipped the door closed and joined us.

"Rose was just explaining about the judging categories," I said. "But what happens during the actual process? What does Elvis do?" I knew Alfred would know.

Mr. P. gestured in the direction of the judging areas Rose had indicated before. "There will be judging happening in several different rings at once," he said. "Every cat has a number. When we're called, we'll take Elvis to a cage in his ring. He doesn't really have to do anything other than be himself. The judge will take each cat out one at a time, inspect it and decide where it places compared with the other cats."

"That sounds easy."

Mr. P. nudged his glasses up his nose. "It is and it isn't. In Elvis's category the cats aren't judged by breed standards because they aren't purebred. That makes it a little harder to be objective. The judge will be looking at things like the cats' physical condition, their attractiveness."

I grinned. "In other words, the cat version of the swimsuit competition."

Rose gave a soft sigh and shook her head.

Mr. P. simply smiled. "That's one way to put it. The judge will also be looking for cats with personality and presence."

"Elvis definitely has personality," I said. I turned to look at the cat. At that moment his personality would best have been described as laid-back. He was sprawled out on his back, eyes closed.

"What if he doesn't behave the way he's supposed to?" I asked.

"He just has to behave like a cat," Mr. P. said. "Everything will be fine. There's nothing to worry about."

Looking around, I could think of lots of things to worry about. I slipped one hand behind my back and crossed my fingers. Just in case.

Chapter 3

By the time the first cats in his category were called almost an hour later, Elvis had had a nap, a snack and a bath, *and* I had brushed his fur until it gleamed. Mr. P. carried Elvis to the judging ring and settled him in one of the cages.

"Behave," I whispered.

There were several rows of chairs in front of the judging area, with about three-quarters of the seats filled, but Mr. P. moved to stand at the back of them where we had a better view.

Elvis was sitting up in his cage, looking around with curiosity but no apprehension. When a ginger-colored cat was placed in the cage to his left he looked at the newcomer with interest. The other cat in turn regarded Elvis in the same way. The two cats seemed intrigued, not combative in any way.

I realized I'd been holding my breath. It didn't matter how well Elvis performed. What mattered was catching the person who had been sabotaging the shows before a cat—or a person—got hurt.

It occurred to me then that Rose had disappeared more than half an hour ago to do what she called some "fact finding" and hadn't come back. I scanned the area. Off to the left a bearded man holding a beautiful, longhaired white cat seemed to be arguing with a pretty blonde woman. Behind them, a very muscular man with a sleeve of tattoos covering his left arm towered over the crowd. He wore a T-shirt that read *Cats Are People Too* and was carrying a tiny black and white kitten with deep blue eyes. There were a lot more people moving around now than there had been earlier, which made it harder to spot Rose. Not that she would be easy to find. She was so tiny it was easy to lose sight of her in a crowd.

"Rosie is fine," Mr. P. said as though he'd read my mind. "She knows what she's doing."

I didn't have the heart to tell him that was exactly what worried me.

I turned my attention back to Elvis, who was still watching the big cat in the cage next to him, who in turn was giving a last pass to his face with one paw.

"That's a red cat," Mr. P. said in a quiet voice. "They are more commonly known as a ginger or marmalade tabby."

"He's beautiful," I whispered.

The judge for Elvis's category was a man somewhere in his midfifties. He wore a gray tweed jacket with a blue shirt and a gray tie. I found myself wondering if he'd chosen the jacket because the pattern meant it wouldn't show cat hair. He had a thick head of snowy white hair, dark-framed glasses and a warm smile. I squinted, trying to see the nametag he wore. *J. Hanratty*, it read. I wondered what the J stood for.

Elvis seemed to be watching the proceedings with interest. When Mr. Hanratty lifted him out of his cage he bobbed his head in seeming acknowledgment and he appeared to be playing to the audience seated in front of us. The judge pointed out the cat's thick, shiny fur, his green eyes and his easy disposition. Elvis alternated looking at the man and making eye contact with onlookers.

"He's doing very well," Mr. P. whispered.

When the judge noted the scar on Elvis's face and speculated about what might have happened, the cat obligingly cocked his head from one side to the other and meowed with enthusiasm when the man commented that he had a certain rakish charm. Mr. P. and I exchanged smiles and I realized, to my shock, I cared about where Elvis was going to place. I didn't want him to come dead last. I could imagine how Rose would crow if she knew what I was thinking.

I looked around again. There was still no sign of her.

The judge was returning Elvis to his cage.

"What a charmer," the woman standing on the other side of Mr. P. said. She was about five foot five, an inch or so shorter than I with olive skin, dark eyes and dark curls that just brushed her shoulders.

He turned to look at her. "Thank you."

"Oh, is he yours?" she asked.

"Ours." Mr. P. gestured to me then offered the woman his hand. "I'm Alfred Peterson and this is Sarah Grayson." He dipped his head in the direction of the cat cages. "And that's Elvis."

"Debra Martinez," the woman said. "He's going to finish in the top three, you know."

"That's nice of you to say so," I said, "but I don't think so. This is Elvis's first show."

"Well you'd never know it," Debra said, brushing a clump of cat hair from her burnt orange sweater. "He's going to do well. He has the 'it' factor."

The "it" factor. I didn't know how to reply to that. Luckily I didn't have to.

"What about your cat?" Mr. P. asked.

Debra smiled. "His name is Socrates. He's a Blue British shorthair."

One of the purebreds, I realized.

"He's the current front-runner in the points race, isn't he?"

She nodded.

Alfred looked at me. "From what I've heard, Socrates is the favorite to win in the Championship category."

Debra's smile grew wider. "Yes, he is." She held up one hand, her middle finger crossed over her index finger.

The judge had been consulting his notes, but now he looked up and the audience in front of us grew quiet.

Debra leaned in front of Mr. P. "Just watch," she said to me, raising her eyebrows. "'It' factor."

To my amazement, she was right. Elvis came in second—the marmalade tabby took first—which meant both cats moved on to the next round.

I collected Elvis. "Good job," I whispered as I picked him up. He seemed quite pleased with himself, as though he'd understood my words. And who was to say he hadn't?

Debra was still talking to Mr. P. "Hello, Elvis," she said when the cat and I joined them.

"Mrrr," he replied, his whiskers twitching. He ducked his head, which meant *you may scratch the top of my head*. Debra of course spoke cat and in a moment Elvis was purring happily.

"Where's your station?" Debra asked, glancing over her shoulder at the rows of tables.

"Down at the end." Mr. P. pointed and we started walking, dodging people with and without cats.

"So are we," she said. "I think we might be neighbors. What number are you?"

"One oh four," Mr. P. said.

Debra smiled. "We're right beside you. I like to be down at the end. Socrates can get a little hyper if he's in the middle of all the action." She was very friendly and it occurred to me that she'd be a good source of information about the goings-on at the show. Not that I was going to get any more involved in the case than I already was.

"How long have you been showing Socrates?" I asked.

"This is his third year," she said. "But before Socrates I had Plato. He was Best Cat three years in a row. Both Plato and Socrates share a family tree so I'm hopeful that Socrates will do as well." She stepped sideways to dodge a man with a Siamese cat on his shoulder. "And before you ask, yes, all my cats were named after Greek philosophers. Before Plato there was Thales."

Mr. P. nodded approvingly. "One of the Seven Sages of Greece."

I hadn't taken any philosophy courses in college, but I had no doubt he was correct.

Elvis was looking over my shoulder now. Something had caught his attention. Probably food.

"I have to ask," Debra said. "Why Elvis?"

Mr. P. smiled and hiked up his pants. They were almost up to his armpits already. "Sarah, I'll let you take this one," he said.

"It's kind of a long story," I said, "but I'll try to condense it for you."

I explained how Elvis had just turned up one day along the downtown waterfront. Over the next several weeks it seemed almost everyone saw the friendly black cat with the scar across his nose.

"One night he managed to slip inside the door at The Black Bear and he stayed there for one entire set the house band was playing, all Elvis Presley stuff."

"I love their turkey chili," Debra interjected. Then she held up both hands. "I'm sorry. I interrupted you. Keep going."

Elvis had shifted in my arms as if he somehow knew we were talking about him. I scratched behind his left ear and he gave a small sigh of happiness.

"The next morning he showed up in the alley when Sam—Sam Newman owns The Black Bear—was taking out the recycling. Sam named him Elvis since he seemed to like the man's music."

I remember how Sam had shrugged when I'd asked about the name. "He doesn't seem to like the Stones, so naming him Mick was kinda out of the question," he'd explained.

"So how did you end up with Elvis?" Debra asked.

"I stopped in to see Sam and the two of them walked me out. Elvis jumped into my truck and wouldn't get out and all of a sudden I had a cat."

Right on cue, Elvis meowed loudly as though to say, "Lucky for you."

Debra laughed. "It looks like things worked out well for both of you."

I nodded. "They did."

It was slow going through the crowd of people. Several times we were stopped by someone wanting to exclaim over Elvis. He ate up the attention with his usual good nature. I had to admit Rose had been right: Elvis was a great show cat.

I looked ahead and was happy to see that Rose was waiting for us, standing in the aisle with her tote bag at her feet, talking to a woman with cropped blonde hair and red-frame glasses. It was the same woman I'd seen arguing with the bearded man right before the judging started.

"That's my friend Christine," Debra said, indicating the blonde woman. "She comes to all the shows with me and helps with the setup. My kids think I'm a crazy cat lady. Not that I care." She looked around. "And Tim is here somewhere. He comes to quite a few of the shows, too. We all went to high school together."

As we came level with Rose and Debra's friend, Debra stopped. Her dark eyes narrowed as she stared at the older woman.

"Rose Jackson," she said and her dark eyes lit up.

Recognition spread across Rose's face followed by a smile. She took two steps toward us and caught both of Debra's hands in her own. "Debra Martinez. It's so good to see you."

"You two know each other," I said.

"We took a class together," Debra said. "Instructional methods. It must be what, Rose? Eight years ago now?"

"At least," Rose said.

Debra turned her attention to me for a moment. "Rose did the most innovative presentation about using contemporary music to teach high school English. She used the music of Aerosmith. It was the best presentation in the class. The rest were so dry and dull."

Mr. P. and I exchanged a glance. He pressed his lips together; trying to stifle a smile, I was guessing. Rose was a huge Aerosmith fan. She'd taken my friend Michelle and me to one of their concerts when we were teenagers and, to my undying mortification, had danced in the aisle with Stephen Tyler. He gave her one of his scarves. She gave him a kiss that lasted way, way too long, as far as teenage me was concerned.

Elvis yawned. He wasn't that interested in conversations that weren't about him or food. Mr. P. raised an eyebrow and I handed the cat over to him.

"Do you have a cat in the show?" Rose asked Debra.

She nodded. "Yes." She gestured at the tent behind Christine draped with a pale green gauzy scarf. A beautiful gray cat was watching us all with curiosity from inside the tent. "This is Socrates."

"He's very handsome," Rose said.

Socrates had a stocky build with a thick coat of fur. His most striking feature was his beautiful copper eyes.

Rose and Debra continued to talk. They seemed to have a lot of catching up to do. Mr. P. was feeding a sardine to Elvis and talking to him in a low voice. A post-show debrief perhaps.

I smiled at Debra's friend. "I'm Sarah Grayson."

"Christine Eldridge." She smiled back at me. "How would you feel about a cup of coffee?" She had deep blue eyes, and three piercings in one ear and two in the other. She inclined her head toward Rose and Debra. "Trust me, this is going to take a while."

"I would feel very happy about a cup of coffee."

She pointed to the far corner of the space. "Come with me," she said.

I touched Mr. P.'s arm. "I'm just going to get coffee. Do you want anything?"

He shook his head. "I'm fine. Thank you."

"Let's go this way," Christine said, pointing in the opposite direction from which I'd just come. "It won't be quite so crowded."

I followed her and we made our way around the waiting area to the outer edge of the room, where the commercial booths were located. She was right: There were fewer people.

"I'm guessing this is your first show," she said.

"Did the fact that I didn't know where the coffee was give me away?" I asked.

She laughed. "That wasn't what I was thinking of, but yes, it does."

"So what gave away my first-timer status?"

"Debra," she said. "You just met, didn't you?"

I nodded.

"Deb knows every cat and every owner in the show. Since you just met, I knew it had to be your first show. And by the way, how did your cat do? Elvis, right?"

"Yes. He was second in his group."

"Excellent," Christine said. "That should shake things up a little."

"Is that good or bad?" I asked.

"Depends on who you talk to."

The cheeky grin on her face suggested this was someone who might be an even better source of information than Debra Martinez—whom Rose was no doubt grilling in her own gentle way—right now.

"How long have you been coming to the show?" I asked.

"Debra roped me in after her second one. Turned out it was fun. I've met a lot of really nice people. They always have decent coffee and I like the cats—especially Socrates. He's a very good judge of people."

The coffee booth was just ahead. I could smell the wonderful aroma of the coffee and I recognized the logo of one of Mr. P.'s favorite roasters. There were several small tables in front of the booth and not all of them were occupied. I couldn't let this chance pass, I told myself.

"So what do I need to know?" I said to Christine. "And I'm buying."

Fifteen minutes later I'd enjoyed an excellent cup of coffee and I'd learned a lot more about the behind-the-scenes machinations at the various New England cat shows. Debra was well-liked by the other competitors and it seemed everyone would prefer her to win the national title over a man named Jeffery Walker, who was new to the show circuit and was seen as an upstart.

"Jeffery is nice enough, but he can be a little aloof," Christine said, wrapping both hands around her coffee cup. "His cat, Nikita, is a purebred white Persian with copper eyes and he's inching closer to the top of the overall points standings with each show. He has a real shot at being both Maine and Atlantic Coast champion and could be national champion as well."

The bearded man I'd seen her arguing with earlier was probably Jeffery Walker, I realized.

She took off her glasses and rubbed the bridge of her nose. "I know this probably sounds petty, but I think he's cheating."

"Cheating how?" I asked.

"I think he's using a catnip spray to calm his cat before judging. It has a faint minty smell, at least to me, and I'm certain I've smelled it on him and Nikita more than once. But I can't prove it and I don't want to make things difficult for Deb."

"But I thought catnip was a stimulant."

Christine put her glasses back on. "Most of the time, when it's inhaled, it is. But some cats just get all mellow and relaxed. I'm pretty sure that's how Nikita reacts. Jeffery's not playing fair." She shrugged. "Deb says I have an overdeveloped sense of right and wrong."

As we were walking back we passed a young man on a ladder hanging a sign to signify the judging area.

Christine looked up at the banner and made a sound of exasperation. It was backward, I realized. The arrow at the bottom was pointing away from the judging rings

"I need to make sure this gets fixed," she said. "Can you find your way back?"

"I can." I was pretty sure I could see the top of Mr. P.'s head from where we were standing.

"Thanks for the coffee."

"Thanks for the conversation," I said.

Christine was already moving toward the young man, who was making his way down the ladder. "Anytime," she said over her shoulder.

When I got back to our section in the staging area, Elvis was sitting on the table with one of Rose's dishtowels held around his neck with a clothespin while Mr. P. brushed his teeth. The cat didn't look that happy about the process, but he didn't look miserable, either. I decided this was one of those things I wasn't going to question.

Debra and Socrates were gone and Rose was poking around their area while trying to pretend she wasn't.

I walked up behind her as she was casually nudging a cardboard box under the table with her left foot. "Looking for something?" I said.

She started and swung around, putting one hand on her chest when she realized she'd been busted by me. "Heavens!" she exclaimed. "Why are you sneaking up on people? You could have given me a heart attack!"

"Your resting heart rate and blood pressure are lower than mine," I said.

She waggled a finger at me. "That's because you use too much salt. If you used more herbs and spices when you cook you could cut back on the salt. Next time you make carrots, try roasting them and adding a little fresh dill. And it wouldn't hurt you to drink a little more tea and a little less coffee."

I could see the conversation was going to get way off topic the way it had a tendency to do when Rose was involved.

"Why are you spying on Debra?" I asked. The direct approach seemed to be the best way to get things back on track.

"I'm not spying," Rose retorted with just the right amount of indignation in her voice. However, her gaze slipped away from mine and her cheeks were slightly flushed.

"You're a terrible liar," I said.

"Most people would consider that to be a good quality."

"It is a good quality." I stepped closer to her and lowered my voice. "What are you doing?"

She glared at me. "I'm doing the job we were hired to do, Miss Nosy Pants. I'm trying to find out who's been sabotaging these shows and make sure it doesn't happen again."

"You think Debra is a suspect? Seriously?"

Her gray eyes narrowed. "Everyone is a suspect, Sarah," she said.

"But you know her."

"I know a lot of people. It doesn't mean they get a free pass."

Out of the corner of my eye I could see Mr. P. rinsing Elvis's teeth with a squirt bottle. "What would Debra have to gain?"

"She has genuine competition for the first time in several years. There's a Persian that's beaten Socrates several times."

"Nikita," I said. "Christine told me about the cat and its owner. She seems to think he might be cheating."

"You mean the catnip spray."

"Debra told you."

Rose nodded.

"I still don't see how disrupting the shows would help Debra—or anyone else, for that matter."

A woman carrying a gray tabby in her arms moved past us. Rose smiled at both of them. "If the sabotage keeps up, it's possible the last shows could be cancelled. If those happen to be shows that Nikita might have won, that would benefit Socrates in the points standings."

I rubbed the back of my neck. I'd only just met Debra, but I found it hard to believe she'd do anything that might lead to a cat getting hurt. I thought about how she'd talked to Elvis and scratched behind his ear and how she'd smiled at every cat we'd passed. "Well, then what about Christine? She seems to be Debra's best friend. Maybe she's the one behind the vandalism out of loyalty to her friend."

"She's a suspect, too," Rose said. "And Debra's friend Tim." She looked around, then inclined her head in the direction of a tall man with sandy hair about half a dozen staging spaces away from where we were standing. He was wearing a chocolate brown sweater and I could see the strap of a camera around his neck. "That's him, over there. He's a mechanical engineer. I'm keeping a close eye on him."

"An engineer would be more than capable of messing with a sound system or damaging some cages."

"And Socrates doesn't like him," Rose said as though that was what really mattered. "Debra admitted that."

"I thought everyone in this building was a cat person," I said.

"Not Tim Grant."

"Rose, is there any possibility the vandalism was just a cluster of accidents and bad timing?" I asked. I realized I should have asked the question before I'd agreed to let Elvis take part in the show.

She shook her head. "No. Alfred looked at one of the cages. The damage to the door was deliberate. And he talked to the technician who worked on the sound system. The man said it didn't stop working by accident. Someone tampered with it." She looked around the space. "I think one of these cat people is in fact a snake in the grass."

Chapter 4

There wasn't much else to say. I said good-bye to Elvis, whispering a reminder for him to behave himself, and headed back to Second Chance with a promise that I'd be back to pick them all up.

When I got back to the shop I found a six-foot-high mannequin sitting on the workbench. It reminded me of a giant Ken doll down to its lack of anatomical correctness. I looked around. There was no sign of a matching Barbie.

I stepped into the shop. Mac and Charlotte were putting a bed frame together. Or to be more accurate, they were standing next to the pieces of a bed frame, staring at them.

Charlotte caught sight of me and smiled. "How's Elvis doing?" she asked.

"Believe it or not, second in his first round of judging."

"I'm not surprised at all," she said. She studied me for a moment. "You didn't have any lunch, did you?"

"I had a cup of coffee," I said. "And one of those butterscotch drops Rose always has in her bag."

"A cup of coffee and a butterscotch candy is not lunch."

I held up a finger. "Actually now that I think about it, it was two butterscotch drops."

Charlotte laughed. "You're incorrigible," she said. She brushed off the front of her apron and came and kissed the top of my head. "There's half a spinach quiche in the staff room. I'll warm up a slice for you."

"Thank you," I said.

She looked at Mac. "As soon as I do that we'll take another shot at that bed."

He nodded. Charlotte headed for the stairs. Mac came over to me.

"So everything went well," he said.

"It did," I agreed. "Isn't this where you say *I told you so*?"

He shook his head. "No, that's kind of obvious."

"Really?" I said.

"Really."

I put one hand over the other on his shoulder and leaned my cheek against his arm. I could feel the warmth of his skin through his shirt.

"You know what else is obvious?" I asked.

He caught my left arm and pulled me in front of him so we were just inches apart. "What?"

I leaned in and kissed the side of his mouth. "You have the wrong set of side rails for the bed," I whispered.

Mac folded me against his chest, rested his chin on the top of my head and laughed. "Charlotte's right," he said. "You are incorrigible."

*   *   *

I got back to Searsport just after Elvis had gone through his second time in the ring. Once again he'd come in second. I found him happily eating a sardine while Rose spoke to the man she'd pointed out to me earlier, Debra's friend Tim Grant. I remembered what Rose had said—that the man wasn't a cat person— and as I studied his body language, I could see that she was right. Not only was Tim Grant standing back from the unzipped door of the tent where Elvis was licking the remaining half of his little fish, the top part of the man's body was leaning back slightly as though he was recoiling from the cat just a little.

"Perfect timing, Sarah." Rose smiled as I joined them. "This is Tim Grant. He's a friend of Debra's."

"Nice to meet you, Sarah," he said, smiling at me. He had pale blue eyes and pale, freckled skin.

"You, too," I said.

Rose put a hand on my upper arm. "I hope I wasn't overstepping, dear. I was just telling Tim how you wanted to look at the photos he's been taking of the show."

I did? I felt her grip tighten on my arm. I got the message. "Oh. Yes. I do." I nodded to show my enthusiasm. Maybe a bit too much enthusiasm. Rose shot me a look that made me think I might have looked a bit too much like a bobblehead doll.

"I do have some shots of your cat," Tim said. His long fingers played with the gold signet ring on his right finger, twisting it from side to side. "Rose mentioned you're looking for photographs of the show overall."

Rose's nails dug into the underside of my arm, her way of telling me not to mess up whatever scheme she was working.

"I am," I said. "This is Elvis's first show. I'd like the photos for . . . posterity."

"Okay," he said slowly. "Will you be here tomorrow?"

I nodded again. This time with a little less vigor. "Yes, I will."

Elvis had finished his sardine and washed his face. He stuck his head out through the open tent flap and meowed loudly at me. I reached over to stroke his fur, which meant Rose had to let go of my arm. Tim took another step backward.

"I'll uh . . . I'll bring my tablet and you can take a look at all the photos I have so far." He hiked the strap of his camera a little higher on his shoulder. Elvis was watching him, green eyes narrowed as though there was something about the man he didn't like.

"Thank you so much," I said. "And of course I'll pay for any photos I want."

Tim held up a hand and shook it and his head. "No, no. You're friends with Debra. I couldn't take your money."

"That's so kind of you," Rose said. She seemed to be doing her "sweet old grandmother" persona. I had no idea why.

"Okay then . . . I'll see you tomorrow," Tim said. He disappeared down the aisle before I could reply.

"Good heavens, that is a twitchy man!" Rose exclaimed.

"He's afraid of cats," I said.

"Merow," Elvis said, a disgruntled expression on

his face. That might have been because I'd stopped petting the top of his head and not because Tim Grant disliked cats.

"Then what on earth is he doing at a cat show?" Rose said.

I shrugged. "I don't know. He's been friends with Debra and Christine since high school. Maybe he has a thing for one of them." I raised one eyebrow and grinned at her. "Or both of them."

"Debra is *not* the kind of person to get involved in some kind of love triangle," Rose said firmly. She pushed her glasses up her nose and frowned at me. "And really, the best you could come up with was that you wanted photos of the show for *posterity*?"

"That's what you get when you throw me into the pool without checking to see if I can swim. I had no idea what I was supposed to say."

"Tim takes photographs all the time, according to Debra," she said. "Christine is a volunteer, so the three of them were here for the setup and they'll be here until takedown. Aside from an electrical issue at one of the booths, there haven't been any problems so far, but that doesn't mean our saboteur has given up."

"You think those photos could help you figure out who that is?"

"Alfred has a list of everyone who signed in to get things set up," Rose said.

Elvis looked at her and licked his whiskers, a not-so-subtle hint that he'd like another sardine.

"You're looking for anyone who isn't on that list," I said.

She smiled and reached up to pat my cheek. "I

knew you weren't just another pretty face." She reached past me and lifted Elvis out of the cage. "Millicent's mother is going to give me her recipe for sardine crackers. We'll be right back and then we can hit the road."

She slipped around the table before I could find out if Millicent was a person or a cat.

I looked around wondering where Mr. P. was. I spotted him standing several tables away talking to a man and woman I didn't recognize. They looked to be somewhere in their forties. She was tall, easily six foot, with hair brushing her shoulders and long side bangs. She wore black skinny jeans with chunky heeled boots and a long black sweater edged in white. And she had the kind of effortless good posture that made me think she'd been a model or a dancer. The man was wearing jeans, a white dress shirt and a burgundy wool sport coat. His hair was short on the sides, a bit longer on the top and more gray than brown, as was his closely cropped beard.

Alfred caught sight of me and gestured that I should join them. "This is our colleague, Sarah Grayson," he said as I walked up to them. "Sarah, please meet Will and Chloe Hartman, our clients."

So I was a colleague now. "It's a pleasure to meet you," I said, shaking hands with both of them in turn.

"You as well," Will said.

"Thank you for volunteering your cat as a cover," Chloe said. "I think for now it's better if everyone doesn't know that we've hired private investigators."

"We don't want anyone upset unnecessarily," Will added smoothly. His right hand tapped against his leg as though he were keeping time to music only he could hear.

"I understand," I said. Rose had said that Chloe was related to Stella Hall, but I could see none of practical, down-to-earth Stella in the woman in front of me.

Mr. P. smiled. "Don't worry, we're very good at flying under the radar, so to speak."

I looked around. No one seemed to be paying any attention to us.

"The last thing we need are these 'incidents' disrupting the pet expos that will be taking place in conjunction with the next several shows," Chloe said. She waved one hand through the air and I noticed that her nails were a deep shade of pink and as beautifully manicured as Liz's always were. "We have vendors coming in from all over the East Coast and we're expecting visitors from several states as well as Canada. People spent close to ninety-nine billion dollars on their pets in the past year. There's no reason some of that shouldn't be spent here."

I worked to keep my expression neutral. Ninety-nine billion dollars? I'd had no idea that pets were such big business. I could see that getting some of that business was very important to Chloe Hartman; not surprising, since Rose had said the AFA—which was sanctioning this show—had more of a money-making orientation than other cat associations.

"People want their pets to be happy," Will said. "We want to help them make that happen. We're animal lovers ourselves." Once again he'd stepped in to take the edge off his wife's words.

"We understand your concern," Mr. P. said. "We've

added extra security to the remaining Maine events, starting with this one. There will be cameras at all of the shows and all participants must have their ID badges to gain access to the floor before and after hours—no exceptions."

I nodded my agreement as though I knew what Alfred was talking about. He may have looked like the stereotype of a doting grandfather in his blue zippered sweater and hiked-up pants, but he was very smart and very resourceful, with computer skills that rivaled the best hackers a fraction of his age. I was both impressed by his confidence and a little concerned about where and how he'd gotten all the equipment. With respect to Mr. P.'s activities during a case, I'd learned that sometimes it was better not to ask too many questions.

Alfred went on to assure the Hartmans that the "security detail" would check the entire building after everyone had left and again before the building opened to show participants in the morning. "And I'll see you both in the morning for another check-in," he added.

Chloe and Will both seemed happy with what they'd heard. I repeated that it had been a pleasure to meet them and they left.

I waited until they were out of earshot, talking to the owner of a Siamese cat, before I turned to Mr. P. "We have a security detail?" I said.

He looked a little puzzled. "Of course. Did you think I was lying to our clients?"

"No." I pulled a hand over the back of my neck. It had suddenly knotted up on one side. I hadn't meant to imply that Mr. P. was being deceitful. I looked around fervently hoping the "security detail" wasn't just Rose and Elvis. "Are they here?" I asked.

Mr. P. looked around. "Right over there," he said, pointing in the direction of the main doors.

I leaned sideways for a better look. At first I didn't see anyone that I recognized and then . . . "Cleveland?" I said, my gaze swiveling back to Mr. P. "Cleveland is our security team?" It had taken me a minute to spot the trash picker since he wasn't wearing his ubiquitous plaid shirt and UMaine Black Bears ball cap.

Mr. P. smiled. "Of course not."

I felt the knot ease in my neck and then it occurred to me if the team *wasn't* Cleveland, did that mean it *was* Rose and my cat?

"Memphis is helping as well."

I looked across the space again. Cleveland's younger brother, Memphis, was in fact standing beside him. Cleveland and his many siblings had all been named after American cities. Memphis caught sight of me looking in their direction and raised a hand in hello. I waved back at him.

"You look skeptical," Mr. P. said.

"It's not that I don't trust your judgment," I began. I stopped. That was exactly what it was. I took a deep breath and let it out. Alfred must have had a good reason for hiring the brothers. "Why Cleveland and Memphis?"

"You know Cleveland was in the army?"

I nodded. "I know. He was one of the people who came to help when we painted the veterans' drop-in center." I'd learned a lot about the man that weekend just watching him interact with people.

Mr. P. took off his glasses and cleaned them with a little cloth he took out of his pocket. "Cleveland was army intelligence. He's smart and resourceful, which is more than enough reason to work with him. But he also has skills and experience that I believe will help us stop any more sabotage." He smiled and folded the little piece of fabric back into a perfect square. "And as for Memphis, he's never met an electronic device he couldn't figure out. He's renting us the cameras we're using."

About six weeks earlier we'd taken on the job of clearing out a house at the opposite end of the street from Second Chance. We'd been hired by the grand-daughter of the owner. She'd convinced him to move closer to her in the Boston area. She'd stepped into the house, taken one look around and called us at the sug-gestion of Glenn McNamara, who owned the sand-wich shop and bakery, where she'd gone to hide out with a giant cup of coffee while she figured out what to do.

The old man had been a paranoid conspiracy theo-rist with a home security system that included cam-eras, motion detectors and an alarm that sounded like an air horn, all connected to a laptop with a password he had refused to divulge to his granddaughter. A password Mr. P. might have been able to crack if he hadn't been out of town at the time.

It was Mac who had suggested I ask Cleveland if he knew anyone who could help. "Cleveland is the only person in North Harbor who probably knows more people than Rose and her cohorts," Mac had said.

"We can take care of it," Cleveland had said as we'd stood in the parking lot next to his old truck. "Memphis and I."

In the time that I'd known the man he'd been true to his word. I'd had no idea how they'd disable the security system, but I knew Cleveland had a better chance of accomplishing it than I did. Cleveland and his brothers had installed solar panels on the roof of his house and his ancient truck ran in even the coldest weather. All I'd managed to do with that security system was get shocked twice and probably damage my hearing permanently.

They had somehow disabled the system and removed the cameras, wires, motion detectors and whatever device it was that delivered a small electric shock to anyone who tried to open the garage door.

Now I had a better idea why they'd been so successful. I looked up over my head. Out of the corner of my eye, I could see Cleveland and Memphis coming toward us.

"You won't find the cameras," Mr. P. said. "He's that good."

The men joined us before I could answer. Cleveland was wearing black trousers and a long-sleeved gray T-shirt. His dark hair threaded with gray had been cut shorter than he usually wore it. He generally had a couple of days' worth of stubble, but today he was clean-shaven. Liz would have said he cleaned up well.

Memphis was a couple of inches shorter than his big brother. He was dressed in all black, his thick hair pulled back in a ponytail. Where Cleveland was still and steady, there always seemed to be a current of energy running through Memphis.

Cleveland smiled. "Hey, Sarah," he said. "How's Elvis doing?"

I smiled back at him. "So far, so good. No surprise, he loves the attention."

"He wasn't the slightest bit shy during the judging," Mr. P. said with an edge of pride in his voice.

"'Shy' is not a word that comes to mind when you think about Elvis," I said. The cat's personality had charmed more than one customer in the shop.

"Sarah, do you have any clue where Elvis was living before he showed up in town?" Memphis asked.

I shook my head. "He has that scar across his nose and a couple of others that are covered by his fur so he got into some kind of a fight at some point in his past. Other than that, the vet said he seemed to have been well taken care of. Whoever he lived with had to have been good to him. He likes people." I gestured with one hand. "He's in his element here."

I noticed that while Cleveland seemed to be listening to the conversation his eyes had done a quick scan of the space.

"Any problems so far?" Mr. P. asked.

Cleveland shook his head. "Nothing unexpected. A few people trying to get in early without their passes. A couple of complaints when we wouldn't let anyone park in the fire lane."

"The cameras are working," Memphis added. "And we've been checking the judging areas regularly. So far so good." His right thumb tapped a rhythm against his leg.

"We'll do one last walk-around before we lock up tonight," Cleveland said to Mr. P. "I don't expect any problems. I'll be in touch if there are."

Mr. P. smiled. "Thank you," he said.

Memphis held up a hand, fingers crossed. "Good luck tomorrow."

"Thanks," I said. I watched the two men walk away. I'd been a bit too quick to judge Mr. P.'s decision to hire them, I realized.

I turned to him, tucking my hair back behind one ear. "I'm sorry," I said. "I underestimated you. I should know better."

He smiled. "Apology accepted. And it's nice to think I still have a surprise or two up my sleeve."

I smiled back at him. "That you do."

There was a young woman making her way toward us and I realized she was trying to get Mr. P.'s attention.

I touched his arm. "I think someone is looking for you," I said.

He turned to look in the direction I had indicated and smiled. "That's Jacqueline."

Before I had a chance to ask who Jacqueline was, the young woman had joined us. She was tiny even wearing black ankle boots that added a good three inches to her height. The boots were paired with matching black tights and a green floral wrap dress. Her long red hair was pulled back into a high ponytail.

"Sarah, this is Jacqueline Beyer," Mr. P. said to me.

"She's the Hartmans' social media director. And she knows the real reason we're here."

"Hi, Sarah," Jacqueline said. She had a strong handshake. Her nails were clipped short and unpolished, not unlike my own. "I hear Elvis caused a bit of a shakeup in the companion category. He's already generating a bit of a fan base online."

"Really?" I said.

She nodded. "I got a great close-up shot of him during the judging. He's looking at the audience and his head is tipped to one side. So cute!"

She turned her attention to Mr. P. "I've been posting photos from the show all day and we've been getting a lot of comments. There hasn't been a single thing said about any vandalism, just the usual trolls being nasty about the usual things."

She turned away and sneezed twice into her elbow. I noticed her eyes were a little red.

"I'm sorry," she said, giving her head a little shake. "I'm allergic to cats. And yes, I know how weird it is that I'm working at a cat show." She looked at Mr. P. again. "Tell Rose I tried the Neti pot. I think it's helping."

"I'm glad to hear that," Alfred said.

Jacqueline reached into her pocket and pulled out a flash drive. "Here's a copy of all the photos I took." She glanced at me. "There are maybe a dozen shots of Elvis. Download a copy of anything you want to keep."

"Thank you," I said. Elvis was going to end up with more professional photos than a runway model at this rate.

"Anything else you need?" she said to Alfred.

"Not a thing," he said.

Jacqueline sniffed a couple of times. "I'll keep monitoring all of the accounts. If anything comes up, I'll text you. Otherwise, I'll see you tomorrow."

"That's fine," he said.

"Nice to meet you, Sarah," she said, smiling at me again.

"You, too," I said.

She headed back the way she came.

"Poor child," Mr. P. said. "She really loves cats."

There was a meow then behind us. Rose and Elvis were back. The latter smelled even more like sardines than he had before.

"I take it you got the recipe you were after," I said.

"Merow!" Elvis answered.

Rose smiled. "We did. And that's not all we got." She had that cat-that-swallowed-the-canary look— pun intended—that always made me nervous.

"What else did you get?" I asked.

She and Elvis exchanged a look. "A clue!"

Chapter 5

"What do you mean, you got a clue?" I said. Elvis leaned toward me and breathed sardine breath on me. I made a face at him and it seemed to me that he grinned.

"After Elvis tried the crackers—and don't tell me he didn't need to do that because how would I know if it was worth making the recipe unless I knew he liked them."

The cat gave me a smug look. I narrowed my eyes at him before turning my attention back to Rose. "I'm not going to say that," I said.

"Fine." She squared her shoulders and lifted her chin, showing me she didn't think she'd done anything wrong regardless. "So anyway, I got the recipe and we were talking and Junie told me that there's a couple—Suzanne and Paul Lilley—who are trying to start a new cat registry."

I held up one hand. "Hang on a minute. Who's Junie?"

"Millicent's mother," Rose said, an edge of annoy-

ance creeping into her voice. "I told you she was going to give us her recipe for sardine crackers. Weren't
you listening?"

"I was listening," I said, a little defensively. I still
had no idea whether Millicent was feline or human. It
didn't seem like the right time to ask. "Why is this
new registry important?"

"The American Cat Fanciers Association is the
largest registry of pedigreed cats and the American
Feline Association is number two," Mr. P. explained.

"There's been talk that the two groups may merge
and that kind of thing always leaves disgruntled people on both sides," Rose added, "especially since the
AFA is far more interested in running the shows to
make a profit."

"So this couple are trying to step in and convince
people on both sides who don't want the merger to
register with them," I said.

Rose nodded. "Exactly."

Mr. P. hiked up his pants. "The Hartmans mentioned the possible merger. They didn't say anything
about anyone trying to start another registry."

"Maybe they didn't know," Rose said.

Elvis leaned sideways, resting his chin on Rose's
arm so he could get a better look at something in the
next aisle that had attracted his attention.

"What would be the advantage of starting another
registry?" I asked.

Rose arched an eyebrow. "In a word, money. According to Junie, the Lilleys plan to offer a menu of
expensive—and profitable for them—DNA tests to

help establish cats' bloodlines. That sounds like a motive for trying to sabotage the AFA shows."

I nodded. It did to me, too.

"And it seems they were here," Rose said.

"Are you sure?" Mr. P. asked.

She nodded. "Suzanne Lilley was wearing a wig—not a particularly good one—and her husband had on a ball cap and dark glasses. Junie was not fooled."

I wanted to meet Junie. She sounded like she didn't miss much.

Rose was holding her cell phone. Elvis ducked his head, butting the edge of the case.

"Yes, thank you for the reminder," she said. She swiped a finger across the screen, tapped it several times and then held up the phone so Mr. P. and I could see. "Junie took their photo."

I leaned in for a better look. The photo was of a man and a woman standing next to a booth that sold coats for cats. The blonde bob on the woman was obviously a wig, not to mention not-very-good-quality synthetic hair.

"She's wearing something to make herself look heavier." I pointed at the screen. "See how her torso is out of proportion with her much smaller arms and legs."

Mr. P. nodded. "I see what you mean," he said.

The man's sunglasses covered a large portion of his face, as did the brim of his cap. They looked like they were trying not to be noticed, which ironically just made them stand out more.

Rose shook her head. "Their looks are amateur

night. For heaven's sake, Avery could pull off a better disguise than that."

As much as the idea gave me a headache, Rose was right.

"Good work, Rosie," Mr. P. said, beaming at her.

Rose smiled back at him. "I had a good teacher."

He gestured at the phone. "I need to get that photo to Cleveland."

"I'm sending it to you now," she said, swiping at the screen of her phone as Elvis poked his nose in to "help."

In a moment Alfred's phone chimed. "Thank you," he said. He looked at me. "I'll be about ten minutes, if that's all right."

"Of course it is," I said. "Take your time."

He made his way down the aisle toward the entrance. I licked the tip of my index finger, briefly touched Rose's shoulder and made a hissing sound. "You're hot today," I said.

Rose gave me a sly grin. "Yes, I am," she said.

We packed up everything we were taking back with us and Elvis got into the carrier bag without much fuss.

Mr. P. returned just as we finished up. "Cleveland and Memphis are up to date," he said.

We headed out to the SUV. I set Elvis on the backseat next to Alfred, who leaned over and unzipped the bag so the cat could climb out. Rose settled herself on the passenger side of the front seat with her tote bag at her feet.

"I'm curious," I said as I fastened my seat belt. "Do either of you know why Cleveland's whole family is named after different cities?"

Rose and Alfred exchanged a look.

"What?" I said.

He cleared his throat. "Their mother named all the children after the cities she was living in at the time they were born."

"She got around," I said and immediately regretted my choice of words. I noticed a patch of pink high on each of Mr. P.'s cheeks.

Next to me, Rose gave a snort. "What Alf is diplomatically trying to say is that she named each of the children after the place they were conceived."

Mr. P.'s face got even pinker.

"I get that," I said.

"Well, I wasn't sure," Rose replied.

We drove in silence for a few minutes then Rose spoke again. "It's been a long day. Why don't you join us for supper?"

"Thank you," I said, putting on my blinker to turn right. "But I already have plans."

"Real plans or pizza in front of the TV with Elvis?"

A loud meow came from the backseat.

"Like Elvis just said, real plans. Right about now Mac should be in my kitchen making lasagna rolls."

Even out of the corner of my eye it was hard to miss the grin on Rose's face. "We don't have to leave that early in the morning," she said, "if for instance you happen to be having a sleepover."

I held up my right hand but kept my eyes glued to

the road. "Number one, there are *not* going to be any sleepovers whatsoever. And number two, I am not having this conversation with you."

"Fine," Rose said in a quiet and contrite voice.

We drove on in silence.

"What size pajamas do you wear?" she asked after a long pause. "I want to get you a pair."

"It's not Christmas for weeks," I said. "Why do you suddenly want to get me pajamas?"

"I know it won't be Christmas for a while," Rose said. "It's just that given those stretched-out, faded pajamas I've seen you wandering around in early in the morning, it's no wonder there aren't any sleepovers happening."

"And we're going to listen to the radio now," I said, reaching for the knob. I was pretty sure I could hear Mr. P. laughing softly in the backseat over the music.

I caught the scent of onions and tomatoes and other good things when we got home and stepped through the front door. Elvis looked up at me and licked his whiskers. Rose reached up and smoothed a stray strand of hair from my face. She leaned in to adjust my scarf and whispered, "Mac is lucky to have you, sweetiebug." Then she headed purposely down the hall with Mr. P. trailing behind her. He smiled as he passed me. "Have a wonderful evening," he said.

I stepped into my apartment and gave a little sigh of happiness as I kicked off my shoes. Supper was cooking and a gorgeous man was smiling at me from the kitchen. "Welcome home," he said.

Elvis meowed loudly and headed for Mac.

"He thinks you mean him," I said.

Mac opened the refrigerator door and took out a small dish. "I meant both of you," he said, setting the dish on the floor.

Elvis eyed the contents, sniffed it and then gave a murp of thanks before bending his head to eat.

"Poached chicken," Mac explained.

I hung up my jacket as he made his way over to me. He wrapped his arms around me and kissed me. "What happened at the show?" he asked.

The show . . . right, the show. I gave my head a little shake. My brain had been focused on repeating that kiss. "You're looking at the current holder of second place in the Household Pet category. Elvis. Not me."

"Very impressive," Mac said. He kissed me again, this time on my forehead, which didn't make my brain short-circuit the way the first kiss had. "I need to take a look at supper."

I trailed him to the kitchen. He turned on the oven light and peered through the glass, seemingly satisfied with what he saw.

Elvis was still happily eating. "You spoil him," I said to Mac, who was now checking out something in my refrigerator.

I leaned over and peeked at the pan of fat noodles, spinach and sauce in the oven. The cheese was making a golden, delicious crust on the top. My stomach gurgled. "You spoil me, too," I said.

Mac grinned at me over his shoulder. "I like spoiling you." He closed the refrigerator door and for the first time I got a good look at the chef's apron he was wearing. It was denim with the word *Spicy* across the chest in red letters.

I laughed. "Where did you get that?"

"Would you believe Liz gave it to me?"

"Actually I would. Liz, Rose, Charlotte—even my grandmother—they're not exactly subtle with their matchmaking."

Mac leaned against the counter and folded his arms over his chest so all I could see were the *S* and the *P* from "spicy." "I won't tell you what Liz suggested I wear . . . or not wear . . . with it."

I felt my cheeks get red. "What happened to the stereotype of a cookie-baking, sweet, little gray-haired grandmother whose romantic advice consists of asking when you're going to meet a nice boy and settle down?"

He gave a snort of laughter. "If Liz lives to be a hundred she won't let her hair go gray. Your grandmother has been stringing your brother along for weeks, letting him think she buys this subterfuge he concocted that he's dating Jess. And Rose may bake the best chocolate chip cookies I have ever eaten, but she fits no one's stereotype of a grandmother. It is the twenty-first century. Grandmothers have lives beyond cookies and rocking chairs."

"I have no trouble with them having lives," I said. "I just want them to stay out of mine."

He leaned forward and caught my sweater, pulling me against him again. I was getting to like having Mac in my kitchen. Then he kissed me again. Yes, I definitely liked having him in my kitchen.

"You are kind of spicy," I said, "but maybe that's just your lasagna."

He kissed me again. Slowly. "Or maybe not," he whispered.

Over dinner we talked about the show. I told Mac what we'd learned about Suzanne Lilley and her husband.

"Do you think they could be behind the vandalism?" he asked.

I set my fork down and shifted a little in my seat so I was facing him. "Honestly? No. The so-called disguises they wore today—a bad wig and a baseball cap with sunglasses—wouldn't and didn't fool anyone who knew them. I can't see how they could have disabled a sound system or tampered with the latches on the cages without being noticed dressed like that." I reached for my water glass. "And would a cat person do anything that could possibly hurt a cat?"

Mac shrugged. "Money makes people do all sorts of things."

After dinner we curled up on the couch to watch a movie. Mac had never seen a single Star Trek film. I had started him with *The Wrath of Khan* and now we were moving on to my favorite movie in the Trek universe, *The Voyage Home*.

Elvis was lounging on his cat tower, sprawled on his stomach, all four legs hanging limply down as though he was too exhausted from his day to do anything else.

"What are you doing tomorrow?" I asked. "Once I

drop off Rose, Alfred and the furball, I'm going to check out a flea market."

"Tempting," Mac said. "But I'm going to Rockport with a sailing buddy to look at a boat."

"Who buys a boat in November?" I asked.

"Someone who's looking for a winter project."

I leaned my head against his shoulder. "And will this winter project involve you?"

"That's what I'm hoping." Mac's long-term plan had always been to have his own boat. I hoped one of these days he'd be the one with a winter project.

"Text me when you get back or if something dramatic happens," he said.

I knew Rose would be watching for the Lilleys, which meant something dramatic happening was a real possibility.

The next morning Rose and Mr. P. were waiting in the hall when Elvis and I came out.

"How was your evening?" Rose asked, a tiny smile pulling at her lips.

"Very good," I said. "You need to try Mac's lasagna rolls. He made his own sauce."

"It did smell good," she said. "Do you know what he used for spices?"

I shook my head. "No, but I'm sure he'd share the recipe with you." I looked from her to Mr. P. The latter looked a little tired. "How was your evening?"

"We had a very nice night. We opened the bottle of wine your father made."

My father—stepfather, if you wanted to get technical—was a professor and former journalist who still did some writing. He'd gone on a winemaking retreat as research for a story. Months later he'd given us all a bottle.

"I'm surprised the two of you can stand upright this morning," I said as we walked out to the SUV. I still had my bottle unopened, but I'd had a glass from the bottle Dad had given to my brother, Liam. One glass had been enough.

"I had a little from the bottle Peter gave to Liam," Mr. P. said, "the night he came to the poker game. So I was circumspect how much I drank and Rosie has a tolerance for alcohol that belies her size."

I gave him a side eye as I opened one of the back doors of the car so Elvis could climb in. "Was that the poker game where you won every hand and Liam tried to bet his boots?"

"Every hand but one," the old man said with a smile. "And sadly my feet are not the same size as your brother's."

Once Elvis and his entourage were settled at the cat show, I headed to the flea market on the other side of Searsport. The building, a huge former barn, was packed with people. It was the first time I'd been at this site and I could see that it was a popular spot. I did a circuit of the space, just looking for things that seemed like they'd work in the shop and getting a general sense of what was for sale. Then I started around again, looking in earnest. In the end I found several treasures and I was happy with how much money I'd spent.

I bought a metal stool, a Chinese checkerboard, a

half a dozen vintage soda bottles, two very worn quilts that I knew from experience could find new lives as pillows and a wire crab cage. I was confident that Mac could turn the Chinese checkerboard into a seat for the stool. The one it had now had a massive dent in the middle, which meant I'd gotten the stool for an excellent price.

Everything fit easily into the back of my SUV and I drove back to the show hoping nothing "dramatic" had happened in the couple of hours I'd been gone.

Mr. P. was brushing Elvis, Debra and Christine were laughing about something and Rose was passing around a tin of brownies when I rejoined them. I grabbed one because I knew from experience they wouldn't last long.

"We're celebrating," Rose said with a big smile. "Elvis and Socrates are both in the finals in their respective categories."

"That's great," I said. I smiled at Debra. "Congratulations!"

"Thank you," she said. She looked at the round metal tin Rose was still holding. "I think I need to do a bit more celebrating."

Christine leaned forward and grabbed another brownie. "I know I do," she said, waggling her fingers at me. "A lot more."

Since I was in public, I brushed the few remaining chocolate crumbs off my fingers instead of licking them away, then went over to see Elvis and Mr. P. "Good job," I said to the cat, scratching behind his ear. He nuzzled my hand.

"How was the flea market?" Mr. P. asked.

"Very successful," I said. I told him about my idea for the stool and the Chinese checkerboard. "I used to play Chinese checkers with Gram when I was a little girl. I was pretty good."

"We played the game a lot when I was a boy." He studied me for a moment. "Perhaps we could play a game or two before you start work on that stool."

"I think that could be arranged," I said. "I meant what I said, though. I was pretty good."

A confident smile spread across his face. "There is no honor in winning against a lesser opponent."

That was about as close as Mr. P. came to saying, "Game on!"

I glanced over my shoulder. Rose was talking to Christine, probably about the brownie recipe, based on her hand gestures.

"Have the Lilleys shown up?" I asked Mr. P., lowering my voice a little.

"Not as far as I know," he said. "But Cleveland found them lingering in the parking lot last night. Suzanne Lilley said she had dropped a glove and they were looking for it. But he thought she might have been filming people with her phone."

"Not a very creative excuse."

He gave a slight shrug. "From what I've seen, they don't seem to be particularly creative people."

"Do you think they caused the problems at the other shows?"

He hesitated.

"It's too easy, isn't it?"

He nodded. "Yes, it is. And in my experience things seldom are that simple."

*   *   *

Tim Grant came by about an hour later. He was carrying his camera; a black nylon and canvas messenger bag was slung over his shoulder. "Hi, Sarah," he said with a smile that was a little warmer than it had been the day before.

Rose had just come back with a cup of tea. "Oh, hello, Tim," she said. "Are we going to look at your photographs?"

He nodded and pulled an iPad from his bag. He tapped and swiped the screen and after a few moments set the tablet on the end of the table about as far as he could get from Elvis, who was inside his tent, looking in Socrates's direction. The big gray cat made a low murp and seemed to glare at Tim. Elvis looked over his shoulder at the man as well and then made a soft meow. I eyed them for a moment. It almost seemed they were talking about him. Elvis had always been a good judge of people and it seemed Socrates might be as well.

"Tim offered to let Sarah look at the photos he took yesterday," Rose was telling Debra, who had walked over to join us. "We got so caught up in everything we forgot to take any."

"That's really nice of you," Debra said, bumping her friend's arm with her shoulder.

"It wasn't a problem," he replied with a smile. He glanced at me. "I went through all the photos last night and found several good shots of your cat."

"Thank you," I said. His attention had already shifted back to Debra.

I noticed how Tim seemed to light up around her. Rose and I exchanged a look. She'd seen it as well.

Tim showed me how to swipe through the various images and how to tag the ones I was interested in. I slid sideways so Rose could see as well. Tim stepped away from us to talk to Debra. Christine had taken Socrates out of his cage and was slowly brushing his fur. Tim made sure to stay well away from the cat, who in return gave him a look that could only be described as disdain.

"Oh, look at that one," Rose exclaimed over a black-and-white shot of Elvis with the judge. The cat's head was cocked to one side in his usual I-am-so-cute pose and they looked as though they were having a conversation.

In the end we decided we wanted all the photos of Elvis and there were three crowd shots that included the Lilleys that Rose thought we should also have. In one they looked to be checking out the main entrance.

"Do you think they were trying to figure out what we put in place for security?" Rose whispered.

"Maybe," I said, keeping my voice low so we wouldn't be overheard. "Or they could have just been looking for ideas for running their own show."

When Tim came back, I showed him which photos I'd tagged and he emailed copies to me. I thanked him and once again offered to pay for his work.

He shook his head. "I'm not a professional," he said. "I just enjoy being here and taking photographs of the cats."

Debra had joined us again. She looked at the photo of Elvis with the judge that was currently on the iPad's screen. "That's gorgeous," she said. She looked over at Socrates, who was still with Christine. "Socrates hates having his picture taken. He's either looking at his feet or his eyes are closed."

I wondered if what the cat really disliked was the person taking the photograph.

Rose's brownies were good, but we still needed lunch so at about twelve thirty I pulled on my jacket again. Charlotte had told me about a small sandwich shop in town. Rose and Mr. P. decided they wanted some kind of soup. That sounded good to me, too.

"Maybe vegetable," Rose said. "Or tomato."

"Or split-pea," Mr. P. added.

"Could I bring you back anything?" I asked Debra and Christine. I explained where I was going.

"I'd love a chicken salad sandwich," Debra said.

Christine abruptly jumped to her feet. "Would it be okay if I tagged along?"

"Sure," I said. "I could use an extra set of hands."

"I'm ready," she said, grabbing her coat.

We headed out to my SUV. "I'm at the far end of the lot," I said, pointing to the left. "I had no idea there would be so many cars—or people here—today."

Christine smiled. "The last day of a show is always the busiest."

We found the car without any problem. Christine immediately turned around in the passenger seat to look at my flea market finds. "Is that a Chinese checkers board?" she asked.

I nodded. "It is."

She craned her neck for a better look. "And a crab cage?"

I nodded again and fastened my seat belt.

Christine turned back around in her seat and did

up her own belt. "I can't wait to see your store," she said with a smile.

"Come by anytime," I said. "Elvis and I will be happy to show you around; although I should warn you, he has some strong opinions around quilts and pillows."

"I'll keep that in mind," she said as I backed carefully out of our parking spot. "By the way, thanks for letting me tag along. I confess I had an ulterior motive."

"If it has to do with coffee or cookies, I'm in." A woman in a red minivan gestured for me to go ahead of her. I waved a thank-you.

Smiling, Christine shook her head. "No coffee or cookies, but I like the way you think." She hesitated. "You can keep a secret, right?"

I nodded, eyes fixed on the road. "Absolutely. More than once I've kept the secret that there was leftover coffee cake in the staff room."

She laughed. "Well, that makes you sound very trustworthy."

"So what's your secret?" I asked.

"I ordered a custom-made carrier for Socrates as a surprise for Debra. I saw the partner of the man who's making it talking to someone down the aisle from where we were and I was afraid she'd see me and come to say hello. I didn't want her to ruin the surprise, so I asked to tag along with you to avoid her."

She paused for a moment. "Debra has been an incredible friend. She—and Socrates, too, as crazy as that might sound—were there for me when my husband died almost two years ago. And Debra was my number one cheerleader when I decided to go back to get my master's degree. I wanted to do something to show how grateful I am." Her voice caught on her last few words.

I shot a quick glance in her direction again.

She put a hand to her chest. "I'm sorry," she said.

I shook my head. "Don't apologize. I know how you feel. I have a friend like that—more than one, actually—and a bunch of sometimes-meddling quasi-grandmothers who love me like crazy."

Christine cleared her throat. "We're lucky."

"We are," I said. "Rose has a saying for that kind of friend: 'Good friends don't let you do stupid things . . . alone.'"

She laughed. "That's Debra, for sure."

I saw her glance in my direction. "New friends can be good, too."

I nodded. "Yes, they can."

We found the sandwich shop and our timing was good because it wasn't very busy. I got pea soup for Mr. P. and chicken vegetable for Rose and myself. The soup came with a fat buttermilk cheese biscuit. Christine ordered the pea soup for herself and two chicken salad sandwiches. "One of them is for Tim," she explained as we got back into the SUV. She set the take-out bag on the seat as she fastened her belt. "You probably noticed he has a bit of a crush on Debra."

"It's kind of hard not to notice," I said.

"Well, Debra doesn't seem to see it. Honestly, sometimes I just want to shake him and tell him to move on." She blew out a breath. "On the other hand, he came to the rescue at a show about three weeks ago when there was a problem with several of the judging cages. Socrates was stuck in one of them and it was Tim who patiently unjammed the latch and got Socrates out of his cage and two other cats out of theirs."

"He's an engineer, right?" I asked as I started the car.

Christine picked up her take-out bag and balanced it on her lap. "Yeah. He's some kind of consultant. If it's mechanical or electronic, he seems to be able to fix it. Not me. I blew up the vacuum cleaner the time I tried to fix that and knocked off power the length of my street."

Since we were still in the parking lot I could turn my head to look at her. "You can't tell me that and not give me details."

She laughed and shifted her body toward me a little. "I'll warn you, it's a long story."

"I can drive slowly if I have to," I said.

I didn't have to drive slowly, but I did laugh most of the way back to the show. Still, in the back of my mind what Christine had said about Tim wouldn't go away: *If it's mechanical or electronic, he seems to be able to fix it.*

After lunch I did a little exploring around the cat show venue and found a bracelet for Avery with a tiny enamel black cat charm that reminded me of Elvis. I wanted to do something to thank her since I'd learned from Mr. P. how much the teen had helped him get everything ready for the show.

At the end of the day, Elvis came in second overall in the Household/Companion Pet category. We got a ribbon and a trophy.

Alfred had some sardine crackers to celebrate—for

Elvis, not for himself. I began to gather the cat's things. Rose stopped to speak to someone and then she joined me, rolling the purple towels we'd used into fat cylinders and stuffing them into one of her canvas carryalls.

"I'll wash these tomorrow," she said.

"You were right, you know," I said as I crouched down to fold the screen Avery had made for the litter box.

"About what?" Rose asked.

I glanced up at her. She looked genuinely perplexed, a tiny frown wrinkling the space between her eyebrows.

"You're the one who was certain Elvis would behave and do well. You said he had the 'it' factor. You *were* right."

She leaned down and planted a kiss on the top of my head. "And I could just as easily have been wrong."

Cleveland waved to us as we headed out.

"Cleveland and Memphis are staying until the show has been dismantled," Mr. P. said.

"I take it everything went well today," I said.

He nodded, pushing his glasses up his nose with one finger. "There were no issues at all. I'm happy to be able to say this show was sabotage-free."

Rose waved at someone across the parking lot. "It may be a coincidence, but there was no sign of Suzanne or Paul Lilley."

"I'm not convinced they are our culprits," Mr. P. said. "But it's important not to jump to conclusions, so we're going to look into both of them before the North

Harbor show. Just because things went well here doesn't mean we should get complacent."

I knew in Mr. P.'s case that looking into the Lilleys meant scouring the internet and in Rose's it meant using all the real-world connections she had.

"While you're doing that, maybe you could take a look at Tim," I said.

Rose stopped in her tracks and turned around. "Tim? Tim Grant, Debra's friend? Whatever for?"

I explained what I learned from Christine, about how Tim had come to the rescue when Socrates and the other cats had been stuck in the cages that had been tampered with.

"So you think Tim could have engineered the vandalism so he could play the hero?" Mr. P. asked. I recognized that gleam in his eye. He was considering the idea.

I shrugged. "People have done stranger things in the name of love."

Chapter 6

November was usually a quiet month at the shop, but anyone who came by Second Chance during the week that followed the cat show wouldn't have thought so. We had four bus tours full of Canadian and international tourists stop in, all on their way to Patriots or Bruins games in Boston, not to mention five carloads of a family reunion on their way to New Hampshire. Mac made the shelves for my cubby project and I managed to settle on the paint colors, prime everything and put on two coats of the final colors. By the time Monday of the following week rolled around I was happy to have a quieter morning. The North Harbor Pet Expo and Cat Show was starting on Wednesday and I knew the end of the week would be busy.

The entire event was planned to last for four-and-a-half days. The pet expo would start on Wednesday and continue through Sunday. The cat show was scheduled to last from Friday afternoon setup to Sunday. They were both being held at the Halloran Arena complex.

The arena had just been named in honor of the family of retired Judge Neill Halloran. The Hallorans had been in North Harbor since the town's early days more than 250 years ago. My grandmother had known the judge since high school and she'd been very vocal about seeing that the Halloran family's contributions to the town be recognized.

Neill Halloran had been instrumental in getting the complex built several years ago. He'd not only worked tirelessly at fund-raising, he'd also quietly made a very large donation himself. The center had an ice surface and two gyms in two connected buildings. The cat show was being held in the smaller gym and the pet expo in the larger one. Once again Cleveland and Memphis were providing security.

Neither Mr. P. nor Rose had unearthed any incriminating information about Suzanne and Paul Lilley. There was nothing to suggest the couple had been behind the problems at the earlier shows.

Mr. P. was at his desk in the Angels' office—my former sunporch. I tapped on the frame of the open door and he gave a little start. "Sarah," he said. "I'm sorry. I didn't see you there."

"I didn't mean to startle you. I brought you a cup of tea." I stepped into the office and set the tea on his desk, well away from his laptop.

"Thank you," he said. "I was just thinking I'd like a cup." But instead of taking a sip, he took off his wire-framed glasses and adjusted one earpiece.

"Something's on your mind," I said. "Is it something to do with the case?"

He sighed and slipped his glasses back in place. "I'm not sure."

I leaned against the edge of the desk. "Tell me what's bothering you." I gave him a little grin. "You know what they say about two heads."

"They make it impossible to wear a turtleneck sweater?" he said, deadpan. Then he smiled.

I laughed. "That, too." I inclined my head toward his computer. "You found something that didn't sit right with you. What is it?"

He took a sip of his tea before he answered. "Why did Suzanne and Paul Lilley use such cartoonish disguises at the show?" He slid his laptop closer, lifted the top and clicked a few keys. Then he beckoned me closer.

I leaned in for a good look. A photo of the Lilleys was centered on the screen. It looked like it had been taken at some sort of business function. Paul Lilley was in a gray suit and his wife wore heels and a slim-fitting black-and-white plaid dress.

"If the Lilleys were trying to cause some kind of problem at the Searsport show, why were they dressed in such a way that they'd stand out?" Alfred asked. "The terrible wig, the oversized sunglasses; they didn't disguise the Lilleys or help them blend in. So why were they dressed like that?"

I straightened up. "I don't know," I said. "You're right. It doesn't make any sense."

Mr. P. took another sip of his tea. "I could be heading off on a wild-goose chase."

The old man was smart; he was very aware of the nuances of human behavior and he had good instincts. "Or you could be . . ." I hesitated, frowning. "What's the opposite of a wild-goose chase?"

"My late mother used to say it was chasing a bear with a basket of apples." There was a gleam in his eyes that told me I was walking into a setup, but that didn't stop me.

"No disrespect to your mother, but chasing a bear, let alone a bear who's just swiped a basket of fruit, sounds kind of dangerous. And what if you caught up to him? Then what? Would you say please give me back my apples?"

The twinkle was still there. "You're right," he said. "Chasing a bear with a basket of apples does sound dangerous, however my mother always called that scenario a 'fruitful pursuit.'"

I groaned at the play on words and the old man smiled. I pushed away from the desk and gestured at the computer. "So go see if you can catch a bear," I said. "Or at least a basket of apples."

He inclined his head slightly. "I'll do my best."

Since Alfred Peterson's best was ten times better than anyone else's, I knew he'd get to the bottom of what the Lilleys were up to.

I was dusting our collection of guitars about half an hour later when Christine and Debra walked into the shop. Elvis, who had been helping Mac with a customer, made a beeline for the two women.

"Hi, Elvis," Debra said with a smile, bending down to pick him up. The cat murped a hello back at her.

"Surprise," Christine said, holding out both hands.

"A good one," I said, walking over to join them.

"I hope it's okay we stopped in without calling first."

I nodded. "Of course it is."

Elvis and Debra seemed to be having a conversation. She reached out and gave my arm a quick squeeze.

Christine looked around the room, the smile on her face getting bigger. "I love your store." Her eyes lit on the musical instruments. "I didn't know you sold guitars," she said.

"Do you play?" I asked.

She made a face. "Not very well. I know a few chords and a few songs."

"She's a lot better than she's letting on," Debra chimed in.

"If you'd like to look at what we have, go ahead," I said. "No pressure. I promise."

Christine looked over at the wall again. "I kind of do. But there's somewhere we have to be in about half an hour. The reason we stopped by is Debra and I were hoping we could lure you and Rose out for lunch."

My gaze flicked over to Mac, who was helping a customer looking at the bed he and Charlotte had set up on Saturday. He gave an almost imperceptible nod.

"I'd love to have lunch," I said. "I don't know what Rose's plans for the day are. She's out back. Give me a minute and I'll go get her."

Rose was in the Angels' office talking to Mr. P.

"I'm sorry to interrupt, Rose," I said, poking my head in the open doorway. "Debra and Christine are here. They've invited us to lunch."

Mr. P. laid a hand on her arm. "Go," he said. "I have everything under control."

Rose looked at me. "What about you, Sarah?"

I smiled. "Mac can handle things here."

She walked back out to the shop with me. Mac's

customer was gone and, based on the satisfied smile on his face, he'd sold the bed. Debra and Elvis were checking out a bookcase and Christine kept shooting little glances over at the guitars.

"I'm so glad the two of you came in," Rose said, beaming at her friend.

"The thanks should go to Christine," Debra said. "The little house I've been renting for years in Rockport has been sold and I have to move on very short notice. Christine has invited me to stay for a while and I said yes. So I'm here to figure out what I should bring and what I should put in storage."

"Where is your apartment?" Rose asked Christine.

She pulled her attention away from the guitars and named a street at the far end of town that ran along the shoreline where it curved down toward Rockport and Camden. She had to live fairly close to Clayton McNamara, I realized. We'd cleared out and sold a lot of furniture and collectibles from his house, part of the efforts of the old man's daughter and his nephew, Glenn.

"The big brick building?" Rose asked.

Christine nodded.

"The one you like so much at the end of Clayton's street," Rose said to me. "With that lovely verandah on two sides and the high windows."

"That's it," Christine said.

"I have a thing for old houses," I said. "I have one myself."

"I've been there about six months and I really like it," she said.

"It's very kind of you to invite Debra to live with you," Rose said.

Christine seemed a bit embarrassed by the praise and brushed away the compliment. "It's not a big deal. My landlord is a cat person so Socrates will be welcome and I'll enjoy having the company. Plus this might be the push I've needed to clean out my spare room." She turned to me. "Any chance you'd be interested in a collection of old LPs? It's mostly '60s rock."

"Absolutely," I said.

Mac was at the cash desk and I'd seen his head snap up at Christine's question. We sold old vinyl records about as fast as we got them in. Our customers were split pretty evenly between baby boomers and music lovers under the age of twenty-five.

"Maybe once the show is over you could come take a look at what I have," Christine said.

"Tell me when and I'll be there," I said.

We set a time for a late lunch and agreed to meet at McNamara's. The sandwich shop and bakery was quiet enough that we'd be able to talk and the food was excellent.

Liz came in about half an hour later with Charlotte. It turned out that Liz was driving Rose and Mr. P. to the arena complex for a quick meeting with Cleveland and Memphis about security, so Charlotte was covering for Rose.

"I've finished the plan for the backyard," Charlotte said to me.

I wanted to make some changes to the landscaping

around my house and Charlotte, who seemed to have a magic touch with plants, had offered to help.

"When can I see it?" I asked.

"Can you come for supper tomorrow night? Nicolas will be there and I'm making scalloped potatoes."

"I like both of them," I said with a grin. "I'll be there." Nick was one of my oldest friends. Rose, Liz and especially Charlotte had hoped for a romance between the two of us, but in the end our relationship was more like that of siblings.

"I could have dropped off Rose and Alfred," I said to Liz.

"Why should you have all the fun?" she said. Liz and Rose had been friends forever. They might needle each other from time to time, but their loyalty to each other ran bone deep.

Elizabeth Emerson Kiley French had been married twice and widowed twice. She could be very charming unless you made the mistake of getting on her bad side or keeping her from something she'd set her mind on, and then she became a formidable enemy. She was smart, beautiful and not afraid to say exactly what she was thinking. More than one woman after meeting Liz had said, "I want to grow up to be her," including me. The majority of men, even those a lot younger than she was, tended to lose their ability to think straight in her presence.

"I have to get my jacket," Rose said, heading for the stairs. She looked over her shoulder at me. "I'll meet you at McNamara's if that's all right."

"Okay," I said. I turned back to Liz, wrapping my arms around her shoulders.

"And what do you want?" she asked, turning her head to eye me suspiciously.

"What makes you think I want something?" I asked, trying to sound innocent. "Can't I just give you a hug because I'm happy to see you?"

"You can," she countered, "but you're not." She poked me in the ribs with her elbow. "Spit it out, snookie. I don't have a lot of time."

"Could you ask Elspeth what she knows about Chloe Hartman?" Elspeth was Liz's niece and owned a successful spa in town. I had a feeling Chloe's perfect nails might have been done there.

She frowned. "The new client?"

I nodded.

"And what makes you think Elspeth would know anything about the woman?"

I explained about noticing Chloe Hartman's professional-looking manicure when I was introduced to her. "There aren't a lot of places to get one that good in this area."

Liz nodded. "What are you looking for?"

I shrugged. "I don't know. Whatever Elspeth can share will help."

"I'll see what I can do," she said. She waved her hand in a shooing motion. "Now, go hang all over someone else. I have places to go and people to see."

I could see a smile tugging at her eyes and mouth and I knew she didn't really want to get rid of me. "Thank you," I whispered as I stepped back.

Rose and Alfred left with Liz. Charlotte came downstairs wearing her favorite blue apron. "What do you need me to do first?" she asked.

"There are two lace tablecloths up in my office that need to be packed for mailing," I said. "But you don't have to do that right now."

Charlotte nodded and I realized her attention had gone elsewhere. She was looking at a round table that had been in the shop for several weeks. There were several pieces from our collection of vases on the tabletop. Avery had added bare branches she'd found behind the garage workshop and in her grandmother's backyard, interspersed with stems of tiny yellow artificial flowers.

"Sarah, would you mind if I changed the display on that table?" Charlotte asked. She walked over to it and eyed it thoughtfully, arms folded over her chest. "Thanksgiving isn't that far away and I think maybe it would draw a little more interest if we set it up with that theme."

The table had been in the shop for weeks and had generated no attention. "Go ahead," I said. "And if you'd like to use them, Rose cleaned all of that enamel-handled cutlery that I got from Cleveland." I gestured over my shoulder. "It's on the shelf right beside the chairs in the workroom."

"I only vaguely remember what it looks like," Charlotte said. "I'm going to go take a quick look if that's okay."

I looked around the store. It was empty except for the two of us and Mac over at the cash desk. "Go ahead," I said with a smile. "I think I can handle this."

Charlotte went out to the workroom trailed by Elvis, who apparently wanted to look at the knives and forks as well. I walked over to join Mac, who seemed to be making a list of some kind.

"You sold the bed, didn't you?" I asked.

He nodded. "And two of the quilts that were used to dress it. The woman who bought it is coming back with a half-ton, but I'm not sure the bed will fit so I was writing down the instructions for reassembling it." He gestured across the room. "What do you want to put in its place once it's gone?"

I looked over at where the bed was sitting. It occupied a large area of floor space. "What about bringing in that big china cabinet that came from the Winston house?" Since we'd started cleaning out houses and apartments for people who were downsizing we'd gotten some nice pieces of furniture in the shop. Many of those customers were seniors and sadly their children weren't interested in their parents' things.

Mac shook his head. "The doors still aren't closing properly. I think it needs new hinges."

He ran a hand over his hair. "This is going to sound a little . . . out there, but what if we brought in that wringer washer?"

I squinted at him in surprise. I hadn't expected him to suggest that. "The washer that Jess and I found on the side of the road? The washer that Jess had insisted 'needed to be rescued'? I thought we were just going to sell it for scrap or let Cleveland take it."

"We can still do that," Mac said. "I think it might sell. Avery cleaned it inside and out, the hoses are in good shape, and it works. Why not take a shot?"

He had a point. People loved items that reminded

them of when they were kids. Things like 1970s vintage lava lamps, for example, were snatched up as quickly as we put them in the store. And a mid-1960s collection of troll dolls had started a bidding war on our website. We'd sold a pink electric stove from the '50s at an auction for twice what my research had suggested it would bring. Why not give the washer a shot?

"Okay," I said. "And given how fast that theatrical trunk sold, I'd also like to bring in one of those blue steamer trunks that we found at that yard sale in Lincolnville back in September."

"And maybe the set of suitcases—the blue ones. There were a few marks on the outside that Rose cleaned up and they've been aired out—not that they really had a musty smell to begin with."

"That'll work," I said. A while back I'd bought the contents of a couple of storage units. The suitcases had been in one of them. So had a wooden casket. The casket was out in the garage workshop. I was still trying to figure out what to do with it.

The woman came back with the truck and we loaded the bed. As Mac had predicted, the frame had to be taken apart. The woman looked over the list of instructions for reassembling it that he'd written out and seemed confident that she could put it back together again. While Charlotte vacuumed the floor where the bed had been sitting, Mac and I went into the workshop.

The washing machine, which he estimated was from the 1960s, was on casters so I hadn't thought it would be hard to wheel across the parking lot. However, what I'd forgotten was that the lot sloped down to the street, which meant that was the direction the washer wanted to go. I had visions of it getting away and rolling downtown until it ended up in the harbor, but Mac and I managed to get the machine to the back door without it going rogue.

"How did you and Jess manage to get this thing loaded and unloaded in the first place?" Mac asked as we rolled through the workroom and into the shop.

With the back of my hand, I pushed a strand of hair that had come loose from my ponytail away from my face. "A very inventive—if I say so myself—improvised ramp, a lot of complaining, some bad language and the fact that Jess is freakishly strong. How does she get such strong arms from sewing?" I asked.

I remembered how pleased with ourselves Jess and I had been when the washer was secured in the back of Mac's truck—which we had borrowed for the morning—and we were on our way back to North Harbor. We were a couple of miles down the road before it occurred to both of us that we'd have to get the darn thing off the truck, too.

Once the washer was in place we went back for the trunk and the suitcases. "Would you like me to dress everything?" Charlotte asked. "I could pile a heap of pillows inside the trunk and maybe drape one of those plaid throws over the lid."

I nodded. "Please."

Mac and I went back out to the workroom so he could get the box of dishes Charlotte wanted to use on the small table. He handed the box down to me and I set it on the workbench. I checked my watch. I still had a few minutes before I had to leave for

McNamara's. Mac joined me, brushing dust off the front of his jeans.

"Are we still on for the jam on Thursday?" I asked.

Thursday night jam at The Black Bear pub was a tradition in North Harbor. Jess and I tried to never miss a week. Owner Sam Newman and his house band, The Hairy Bananas, played classic rock and anyone and everyone was welcome to sit in. Mac had only been to a Thursday night at the pub once, as far as I knew. Every time we tried to make it happen a second time something would mess up our plans.

"Absolutely," he said, reaching for my hand and giving it a squeeze. "Nothing is going to screw it up this time."

I took a step back in mock horror and held my index fingers up in the shape of a cross. "Don't say that," I warned. "You'll jinx us."

Mac laughed. "I don't believe in jinxes."

"Says the man who wears the same unwashed jersey all through the hockey playoffs."

"Like I explained, that's a process," he said. "A process is different from a superstition."

I folded my arms over my chest. "How?"

"A process plugs you into the energy of the universe. It's science."

I laughed and patted his arm. "You just keep telling yourself that," I said.

Chapter 7

I was the first to arrive at McNamara's.

"Hey, Sarah," Glenn said. Glenn McNamara was tall with broad shoulders and strong arms and still wore his blonde hair in the brush cut he'd had as a college football player. "What can I get for you?" He grinned. "The cinnamon rolls are still warm."

"I'm meeting Rose and a couple of friends," I said. "So for now, just a table, please, and that should not be construed as a hard no as far as the cinnamon rolls are concerned."

"I'll keep that in mind," he said. He showed me to a table in the corner. "Coffee while you wait?"

I laughed. "Do you have to ask?"

"I hear you have a prize-winning cat," Glenn said when he brought my coffee in a big stoneware mug to the table.

I laughed. "I know Elvis is just a cat, but I swear all that attention—not to mention Rose and Alfred spoiling him all weekend—has gone to his head. I came out of the bedroom this morning to find His Majesty sitting on one of the stools at the counter and when I put his food on the floor he complained long and loud."

Elvis had still been miffed at me when it was time to drive to work and he'd spent the ride muttering on the passenger seat next to me instead of doing his usual backseat driving.

I took a sip of my coffee. It was hot and strong and delicious.

"What about the case?" Glenn asked. "Were there any problems?"

He knew about the Angels' latest investigation, I remembered, because he'd suggested Cleveland and Memphis in the first place.

"None," I said. "And I'm hoping the show here is the same."

Glenn held up one of his huge hands with the index and middle fingers crossed over each other and went to help a man who had just come in the front door.

Rose arrived less than five minutes later. Debra and Christine showed up before Rose had a chance to take off her jacket.

Christine set her leather satchel on the floor by her feet.

"I like that bag," I said.

"Me, too," she said. "It came from a thrift store in Portland."

"ReBoot?"

She nodded. "That's the place." She leaned down and flipped the top flap. "You wouldn't believe how much it holds. I have everything for my class tonight in case I get a few minutes to study."

I gestured at the headphones poking out of the top of the bag. "I have the same ones. How do you like them?"

"They're not quite as good as the active noise-cancelling headphones which is what I used to have, but I'm not buying batteries all the time anymore."

"What she's not telling you is that she's descended from a long line of mole people," Debra said with a teasing smile.

"Mole people?" Rose asked.

Christine made a face at her friend. "Debra gives me a hard time because when I study I need to shut out all distractions. So I go into the bedroom, I turn off the lights and I put my phone in a drawer. Then I put on this big old Patriots hoodie, put on my headphones and pull up the hood so I can shut out the world."

"Mole people," Debra repeated.

After a little deliberation we all ordered Glenn's BLT sandwich. "I swear you won't be sorry," I told them.

"Vinegar coleslaw or dill pickle kettle chips?" Glenn asked. "The kettle chips are made just down the coast in Rockport."

"I've never met a carb I didn't like," Debra said, "and since Tim isn't around, I'll have the dill chips."

The rest of us chose coleslaw. Rose and Debra decided to share a pot of tea as well.

"It will only take a few minutes," Glenn said.

"Please feel free to tell me it's none of my business," I said, adding cream to the refill of coffee Glenn had poured for me, "but does your friend Tim have something against potato chips?"

Debra blushed and ducked her head. "Not exactly."

Christine was stirring her own coffee. "It really has nothing to do with potato chips and everything to do with the fact that Deb is just way too nice."

She glanced over at Debra, who looked a little embarrassed but smiled and said, "Go ahead and tell them."

Christine took a drink from her coffee and then wrapped her hands around the heavy mug. "When the three of us were in high school we went on a class trip to Nova Scotia in Canada. It turns out ketchup-flavored potato chips are a Canadian thing. This football player who Debra had the hots for liked those chips when no one else in the group did. No one." She jabbed her finger in the air for emphasis. "So Deb pretended to like them, too."

Debra's cheeks reddened again. She shrugged. "I was sixteen. What did I know?"

Rose reached over and patted her arm.

Christine smiled. "Deb kind of oversold her enthusiasm for those ketchup chips. Tim's father was in Toronto on business a month after we got back and Tim got him to bring back ten small bags of them."

"It was such a sweet gesture I didn't have the heart to tell him I really didn't like the darn things," Debra said, shaking her head. "After that it just kind of snowballed."

"See? Too nice," Christine said.

"How long did you go before you told him?" I asked.

Christine had just taken another drink of her coffee. She made a strangled sound halfway between a cough and a laugh. She put one hand to her chest but held up the other to show us she was all right.

"You did tell him, didn't you?" Rose said.

"I couldn't," Debra said. "Every day I waited, it got harder. And how can I tell him now? It would be way too awkward. I know how silly it sounds, but I rarely even order chips if Tim is with us, because he always says it's too bad they don't have my favorite flavor and then about a week later he shows up with a big bag of the darn things he ordered from some Canadian place online."

Rose gave her shoulder a squeeze. "You're a very kind person."

"Who has to feed ketchup potato chips to the squirrels to get rid of them," Christine said in a low voice beside me.

"I like that the three of you have stayed friends all these years," Rose said.

I had a feeling she was going on a fishing expedition. Maybe I could help. "Rose and my grandmother have been friends since grade school."

"I had cookies." Rose lifted the lid of the teapot to peek inside. "I wanted to be friends with Isabelle because she was tall and I wasn't, which meant I couldn't reach the top shelf of books in our classroom. And I'd read everything on the bottom shelves. So I walked right up to her and said, 'I'll give you a cookie if you'll be my friend.'"

I'd recently seen a photograph of Rose at around the age she was talking about. I could picture her with her crooked bangs and a fierce look of determination on her face marching across the playground to talk to Gram.

"Of course, Isabelle, being a pragmatist even then, wanted to know what kind of cookie I was offering," Rose continued.

I laughed. "That sounds like Gram. I'm guessing they were chocolate chip."

Rose smiled. "They were." She poured a cup of tea for Debra and one for herself. "How did you two meet?" she asked, looking from Debra to Christine. "And how did you meet Tim?"

"Chem lab!" they replied in unison.

"What did you do?" I asked. "Blow it up?"

"There's no shame in that," Rose said. "Sarah set her school on fire. Twice."

Christine turned slowly to stare at me. "You set your school on fire?"

"No," I said, realizing I sounded a little defensive. "I set one of the ovens on fire. In Family Living class. It was mostly just a lot of smoke . . . and a little water from the sprinklers."

"That wasn't your fault," Rose said, leaping to my defense. "Those sprinklers were not calibrated properly."

"I'm sure they weren't." Debra's lips twitched in amusement.

"And we were talking about you two, not me," I said, determined to get the conversation back on track. "How did you two meet?"

"And how did you meet Tim?" Rose added.

Christine reached for her coffee. "Like Sarah, it involved fire," she said.

"I was at one table with a lab partner who wouldn't let me do anything because he was afraid I'd mess something up and ruin his perfect GPA." Debra took a sip of her tea. "Christine and her partner were at the table beside us and Tim was on the other side."

"We were studying Charles's Law," Christine added. "And in our defense, who thought it was a good idea to let a bunch of sixteen-year-olds use Bunsen burners?"

"How did the fire start?" I asked.

Debra held up her hand. "In *my* defense, you'd think a guy who was worried about messing up his GPA would keep his textbook well away from any flames."

"So you set your lab partner's chemistry textbook on fire, and . . . ?"

"Tim tried to beat the flames out with his lab notes." Debra made a face. "Not a good idea, it turned out."

"So I threw a beaker of water on the whole thing," Christine said. "At least I thought it was water."

Rose's lips were pressed together and she was shaking with laughter.

"Mr. Medina put the whole thing out with a fire extinguisher," Debra said, "but not before he got the tiniest bit singed."

I stared at her across the table. "You set fire to your teacher?"

"No!" She looked offended at the idea. "And his wife only had to draw on *one* eyebrow."

I was laughing so hard I couldn't talk, imagining their poor teacher with one eyebrow gone probably feeling panicked that the three of them could have burned the school down.

"The whole class learned a lesson about the value of working smoke detectors and fire extinguishers," Debra added, squaring her shoulders a little virtuously.

"Mr. Medina made us clean the entire lab on a Saturday as punishment and that's how we got to be friends," Christine finished.

Debra grinned. "Somehow Tim got into the school PA system and we blasted Aerosmith the entire time."

Rose caught my eye across the table. Tim had gotten into the school's public address system and probably past some kind of security camera. I had a feeling we were thinking the same thing.

Our food arrived then and the conversation pretty much stopped except for Debra and Christine exclaiming over the bacon and the mayonnaise on their sandwiches.

"Glenn makes his own mayo and his recipe is top-secret," Rose explained. "I've tried to bribe him to no avail. He gets his bacon from a small farm near Camden."

Afterward, over cinnamon rolls—with more tea for Rose and Debra and more coffee for Christine and me—the talk turned to the upcoming cat show.

"You know, I was a bit nervous about the show in Searsport," Debra confided.

"Did something happen?" I asked.

"Nothing really serious, just a couple of incidents at a couple of the earlier shows. Several cages were damaged and a sprinkler system went off."

"Who would do something like that?" Rose asked.

Debra shrugged. "The general consensus seems to be it's either Paul and Suzanne Lilley—they want to start a rival cat registry—or a woman named Sorcha Llywellyn. She was suspended from competing for a year for lying about aspects of her cat's lineage. Some people get a little too caught up in the competition."

Rose picked up her cup, realized it was empty and set it back down again. "I confess that might have been me on one or two occasions."

I made a bit of a show of clearing my throat as I said, "One or two dozen."

Everyone laughed.

"Maybe it doesn't have anything to do with the cats," Christine said to me. "Maybe it's more personal."

"What makes you say that?" I asked.

She shrugged. "No reason, really. I was just speculating."

We talked for a few more minutes then made a promise to meet up at the show for setup on Thursday afternoon.

Rose hugged Debra. "I'm happy you're going to be living so close by. I hope I get to see more of you—both of you—and Socrates."

"I appreciate the offer to look at my dad's records," Christine said. "I've avoided dealing with them for too long."

"It's my pleasure," I said. "You may be surprised what they turn out to be worth."

"I could always use a little something extra to put toward tuition." She smiled. "I have a list somewhere. I'll look for it and email it to you."

Debra and Christine left to pick up some boxes from a friend so Debra could finish packing. Rose and I headed back to the shop.

"You didn't seem that surprised when Debra mentioned the Llywellyn woman," I said.

"That's because Alfred already looked into her. She was hundreds of miles away in Florida when the incidents happened at the other shows. And the young woman readily admitted what she'd done and didn't object to the one-year suspension. She had no reason to want revenge on anyone associated with the show. It wasn't her."

"Do you think it could be Tim Grant?"

Rose took a moment before she answered. "I would be happier if it isn't, but I admit it's possible."

"I feel the same way," I said.

"Alf told me about his suspicions with respect to the Lilleys."

"Do you think he's right?" I glanced over at her.

"I think his instincts are generally right," she said. "I'm just not sure how that's going to help us."

Tuesday was another busy day at Second Chance. A bus full of Japanese tourists on the way to Prince Edward Island stopped in late in the afternoon and it was half an hour past closing time before we'd rung up the last customer.

As I came in from the parking lot after carrying two quilts out to the bus, Mr. P. beckoned to me. I stepped into the sunporch. "I did a little digging into Tim Grant," he said.

"And?"

"There's a very small window of time during which the cages that were damaged could have been vandalized. He has an alibi for that time. And for the sabotage to the sprinklers."

"I take it you think it's a *good* alibi," I said, picking a clump of cat hair off my jeans.

"Are two firefighters and a police officer good enough?"

I stared at him in surprise. "Yes. What on earth was Tim doing?"

Mr. P. smiled. "A dog got its head stuck in a road grate. Tim stopped to help. There was a story in the *Portsmouth Herald*. He managed to turn the dog ninety degrees and get him out."

"That was a nice thing to do," I said, "and I'm glad Tim's not the person who has been trying to disrupt the shows. Debra and Christine would be hurt."

I dropped Rose and Mr. P. at the house about fifteen minutes later and left Elvis with them.

I expected to see Nick's vehicle when I pulled into Charlotte's driveway, but it wasn't there.

"Is Nick running late or am I early?" I asked as I stepped into the kitchen and kicked off my shoes.

"He just called to say he has to go in to work," Charlotte said. "A fire somewhere." She was rinsing a carrot under the tap.

Nick was an investigator for the medical examiner's office, but before that he'd been a paramedic and he still worked some fill-in shifts.

"I haven't seen him in more than a week." The kitchen smelled wonderful. "He didn't make it to the jam last Thursday night."

There were place mats and napkins on the table. I added the cutlery, salt and pepper shakers and a dish of Charlotte's mustard pickles.

Charlotte had started chopping the carrot. "He works too much. He needs a girlfriend."

"I know," I said, looking around to see what else I could do. "But it's not really something we can order online for him."

"That would be convenient," she said with a smile, "but it's not likely Nicolas would want a girlfriend his mother picked out."

That was true.

"You probably know him better than anyone."

"No. No. No," I said, shaking my head emphatically. "I am *not* playing matchmaker for Nick." He wouldn't like me playing matchmaker any more than he'd like his mother doing it.

"Do you want Rose to do it?" Charlotte asked.

I grinned. "It could be entertaining."

"Really?" she said. "So you thought it was entertaining when she tried to get you and Nick together?"

I made a face at her. In truth, it had been funny in the beginning. Later, Rose's efforts had made me a little anxious because while I loved Nick to pieces, I loved him like a brother and I knew she—and everyone else who wanted us together—was going to be disappointed.

"I'll think about it."

"Thank you." Charlotte scooped up the chopped

carrot and dropped the pieces into a pot. "I made devil's food cake for dessert," she said.

I leaned against the counter and managed to snag a chunk of carrot. "I know a bribe when I hear one," I said.

"Does that mean you don't want a piece?"

She had me. I hung my head. "No, it does not."

Charlotte tried to stifle a smile and failed.

"I'll see if I can think of anyone who's single that I might be able to introduce to Nick. No promises. And I can't make him go out with anyone if he's not interested."

She gave up on holding back the smile. "Thank you, sweet girl," she said.

I shook my head. "You're lucky I have no willpower when it comes to your devil's food cake."

Supper was delicious, as always, and the cake was devilishly good. Charlotte and I spent about an hour going over her ideas for the backyard, with her showing me the detailed plan she'd drawn out and pictures of the different plants she thought would work. I went home with a lot more enthusiasm for the project—and a large piece of cake.

When I stepped into the hall, Rose came out of her apartment. She looked somber.

"What's wrong?" I asked. My grandmother and her husband, John, were visiting my mom and dad. "Did something happen to Gram?"

Rose shook her head. "No. It's nothing like that. They're all fine."

I felt a rush of relief that made my knees go weak for a moment. I put one hand on the wall.

"Come in for a moment," Rose said.

"Okay," I said. I followed her into the apartment.

Mr. P. was seated at the table. Elvis was on his lap. He got to his feet, setting the cat on his chair. Like Rose, he looked troubled.

I felt my stomach flip-flop and drop. "Was there more vandalism over at the arena?" I asked.

Mr. P. shook his head. "There was a fire—not at the arena."

"I know," I said. "Nick didn't come for supper. He got called in to work. Do you know where it was? Was anyone badly hurt?"

"It was out near Clayton McNamara's," Mr. P. said.

Near Clayton's, he'd said. Not *at*, so the old man was all right. Then I remembered who else lived out that way. I put a hand on my chest and it seemed to me that I could feel my heart racing underneath it.

Rose took both of my hands in hers. I could see the gleam of unshed tears. "I'm so sorry to have to tell you this," she said. "But Christine is dead."

Chapter 8

For a long moment I just stared at her. I had to have heard her wrong. My brain must have scrambled up the words. I shook my head. "No. There has to be some kind of mistake. Christine can't be dead. We just saw her yesterday."

"It's not a mistake." Mr. P. put a hand on my shoulder. "I wish that it was."

"But we just had lunch," I said stupidly, as though that somehow made death impossible.

Rose pulled a chair out from the table. "Sit down," she said.

"I'll get you a cup of tea," Mr. P. said.

I sat down and Rose took a seat as well.

"What happened?" I asked. I patted my pocket, feeling for my phone. "I should call Nick."

Rose reached across the table and put a hand firmly on mine. "Not now," she said. "Nicolas is working."

I opened my mouth to argue and closed it again. She was right. Mr. P. set a cup of tea in front of me. He looked at Rose. "Would you like a little hot?"

She nodded and gave him a tired smile. "I would, Alf. Thank you."

"What do you know?" I asked after Rose had added milk and a little sugar to her cup.

"It looks as though the fire was contained just to Christine's apartment. I haven't spoken to Debra, but I know she and Socrates are all right. I wish I could tell you more."

Just then there was a knock at the door. Rose got up to answer it. It was Mac.

"I'm so sorry," he said, wrapping her in a hug.

She put a hand to his face for a moment. "Thank you."

I got to my feet and Mac came across the room and put both arms around me. I laid my head on his shoulder. "Are you all right?" he asked.

I nodded, swallowing hard a couple of times so I wouldn't cry. "I'm glad you're here. How did you know?"

"Alfred called me."

I turned my head to Mr. P. and mouthed the words "Thank you." He smiled back at me.

I let Mac go and sat down again. Rose moved over and gave her seat to Mac. He shrugged off his jacket and draped it over the back of the chair.

"Would you like a cup of tea?" Mr. P. asked. "Or how about a cup of coffee?"

"Actually I think I'll have the tea, please," Mac said. He turned toward the counter, but Mr. P. was already on his feet. "Sit," he said. "I'll get it."

"Thanks," Mac said. He sat down and reached for

my hand. "I don't know a lot," he continued, "just really a little more than the basics."

Rose nodded, while I frowned. "How do you know anything?" I asked, feeling I'd missed a detail or two somewhere.

"Remember I went to look at that boat?" Mac asked. I nodded.

"Kevin is a firefighter. He didn't work the fire—he was off—but I called him and asked if he could find out anything about what happened." Mr. P. set a cup and saucer on the table in front of him. "Thank you, Alfred," he said.

"What did your friend say?" Rose asked.

"He said the fire was contained to Christine's apartment. It's too soon to know how it got started." He cleared his throat and I reflexively tightened my grip on his hand. "At first no one knew she was inside because I guess she was supposed to be at a class at the university and her car wasn't there. It turned out the class had been cancelled at the last minute when the prof had a flat tire driving back from Bangor."

Rose closed her eyes for a moment. I pressed my lips together and blinked hard a couple of times. If it hadn't been for a stupid flat tire Christine would be alive right now.

"She was studying," I said.

Mac nodded. "That's what they think."

I looked at Rose who had opened her eyes again. "Remember how Debra teased her about being one of the mole people when she studied."

Rose nodded. "I do remember." She looked from

Mac to Mr. P. "Debra said that when Christine was studying she liked to shut out the world. She'd sit on her bed with the door closed and the light off. She'd wear a big sweatshirt with the hood up and put on her headphones."

Mac cleared his throat. "Kevin said the paramedics did all that they could. They worked on her for a long time."

I looked at Rose. "Nicolas," she said.

"He would do that." I swiped at a tear that slid down my cheek.

Mac and I stayed at Rose's for a little while longer. Finally she got up from the table and came around to me. She put a hand on the top of my head for a moment. "Go home," she said. "You're tired. We'll figure out in the morning what comes next. There isn't anything we can do now."

I got to my feet and put my arms around her. "I love you," I said.

She reached up to pat my cheek, a gesture she'd been doing as long as I could remember. "I love you, too."

"If I find out anything else, I'll let you know," Mac promised at the door.

"We'll do the same," Mr. P. said. "Sleep well."

I handed Mac my keys. He unlocked the apartment door and I followed Elvis inside.

I was tired and sad and I wasn't sure what to do next. I dropped onto the sofa. Elvis climbed onto my lap and nuzzled my face like he knew something was wrong.

Mac hung up his coat and sat beside me.

"What can I get you?" he asked.

"Nothing," I said. "Just sit here with me for a few minutes."

"I'll sit here all night if that's what you want." He put his arm around my shoulders and I leaned my head against his chest, one hand still stroking Elvis's fur.

I sighed. "I didn't know Christine that well, but I liked her. I think maybe we were on the way to being friends." I raised my head to look at him. "This feels personal, if that makes sense."

He nodded. "It does. When someone dies unexpectedly—even if you don't know them well—it's not just the person that's gone. It's the potential relationship you might have had with them that you've lost as well."

We sat there for maybe half an hour. I told Mac Christine's story, about how she and Debra and Tim Grant met.

He laughed. "I can see why you liked her."

"I keep thinking about how Debra must feel. They've been friends for so long."

"She has Rose. Which means in a way she has all of us and we'll help her any way we can."

I liked the sound of that.

Elvis shifted on my lap then and yawned, which made me yawn, too.

"You need some sleep," Mac said. "Go put on your pajamas." He looked at the cat. "You, too."

I followed Elvis into the bedroom and put on my flannel pjs. I realized Rose was right about them. They weren't particularly sexy or flattering, but they were comfortable and comfort was what I needed. And I knew Mac wasn't going to run screaming for the hills. He'd seen me look a lot worse.

I brushed my teeth and washed my face. Elvis took a few passes at his fur with a paw and called it a night. Then we padded out to the living room.

"I'm set," I said.

Elvis meowed his agreement.

Mac put his arm around me and walked me into the bedroom. I sat down on the edge of the bed. "I don't think I can sleep," I said. "My brain doesn't want to shut off."

He leaned down and kissed me. "There isn't anything you can do for anyone right now. Let the world turn without you for a little while. C'mon, lie down."

Elvis was already settled on the nearby chair that we'd both given up pretending he didn't sleep on almost every night.

I lay down mostly because I didn't want to argue with Mac. Once he was gone I could get up and do . . . something.

Mac pulled the quilt over me and sat on the edge of the bed. "I'm going to sit with you for a little while."

"I'd like that," I said. I didn't want him to go. But I wasn't going to go to sleep and there had to be something I could do, someone I could talk to. Nick might be home right now. I could call him.

"Close your eyes," Mac said.

I closed them, promising myself I'd stay there for just a minute and then I'd get up and send him home.

I didn't.

I woke up with a start. I wasn't sure how long I'd

been asleep. I sat up and rubbed my eyes. I felt disoriented. There was no sign of Elvis. I looked at the clock next to the bed. It was quarter to seven.

I got out of bed and stretched. I could go for a run, I thought. I could call Nick. He'd be up by now—unless he'd gotten in very late last night. I needed a cup of coffee first, I decided. I padded out to the kitchen.

Elvis was sitting on a stool at the counter. Mac was leaning against the counter. He held out a cup to me. "Coffee?"

I took it from him. "Uh, thank you," I said. I took a sip. It was hot and good and just what I needed. "What are you doing here?"

He gestured at the sofa. "I stayed last night."

"I can't believe I didn't hear you making coffee." I looked at Elvis. "I can't believe he didn't wake me up."

Mac smiled. "We're both very stealthy—like ninjas."

The cat bobbed his head as though he was agreeing.

"And you slept like you were hibernating. I could have been grinding coffee and singing opera out here and you wouldn't have woken up."

I smiled back at him over my cup. "Somehow I don't think I would have slept through the experience of hearing you sing opera." I brushed my hair back off my face and it hit me then that not only was I still in my less-than-flattering nightwear, I also hadn't brushed my teeth and who knew what my hair looked like.

There was a knock at the door then.

"Merow!" Elvis said.

Mac pushed away from the counter. "I'll get it."

It was Rose. She was wearing a flowered apron and carrying a tray. "Good morning," she said to Mac. She came in and set the tray on the counter. Elvis craned his neck for a look. "A breakfast bowl for each of you," she said. "They're hot, so you need to eat them now."

I tried to run my hand through my hair, but it was so knotted I couldn't. "Umm, thank you," I said.

When I didn't make a move toward the food, Rose made a shooing motion with her hand. "It's getting cold," she said.

I moved then, picking up a bowl and grabbing two forks from a nearby drawer. I handed one to Mac.

"Do you know anything more than we did last night?" I asked.

Rose shook her head. "Alfred and I will ride with you if that's all right. We have some things to do."

I nodded. "Of course it's all right."

"I'll see you in a little bit then," she said.

As she moved past me I caught her hand for a moment and gave it a squeeze. She gave me a small smile back.

Rose's breakfast bowl was a mix of egg, sweet potato cubes, red pepper, onions, mushrooms and zucchini with a dash or two of sriracha and some shredded cheddar. Like everything she made, it was delicious.

I sat down next to Elvis. He looked inquiringly at me. I fished a bite of egg out of the bowl and held it out to him. He licked his whiskers in anticipation and took it from me.

"This is good," Mac said. He walked over and leaned against the counter again with his breakfast. I pushed his coffee cup closer. "What do you need from me?" he asked. "I can open the store if that will help."

"I'm going to try Nick in a few minutes," I said. "I

don't know if I'll get him or not. And you heard Rose. She and Mr. P. are coming with me so I think I'm okay for opening." I blew out a breath. "The pet expo starts today. They're going to need to go out to the arena at some point, even with Cleveland and Memphis there. And Rose, at least, will probably want to see Debra." I rubbed the back of my neck. The muscles had knotted right above my shoulder. "Mostly, if you can just be around all day that would help."

"Of course I can," he said. He leaned over and kissed me. Then he reached for his coffee and drank what was left in the cup. He straightened up then. "I'm going to go home, have a shower and get some clean clothes. We'll figure out the day as it happens."

I moved to slide off my chair, but he put a hand on my arm to stop me. "Sit, Sarah. I know where the door is."

I reached up and grabbed the neck of his shirt, pulling him close enough to kiss again.

He smiled. "I'll see you in a little while," he said.

He pulled on his shoes and grabbed his jacket.

"I'm glad you were here," I said.

He nodded. "Me, too."

I finished my breakfast and a second cup of coffee. Then I tried calling Nick. I got his voice mail. I left a message asking him to call. I had so many questions. Why hadn't Christine gotten out of the apartment? What had taken the firefighters so long to get to her?

When I stepped out into the hallway, Mr. P. was just coming out of Rose's apartment. "Good morning, Sarah," he said. "Rose will just be a minute."

"That's okay," I said. "I'm running a little early." When I hadn't been able to reach Nick I'd called Jess. Talking to her had made me feel better. "Nick's probably asleep," she'd said. "You know he'll call you. Once you get some answers from him you can figure out what to do next."

I glanced at the door to Rose's apartment. "Is she okay?"

He nodded. "She is. She's sad and I know she's worried about Debra, but you know Rosie. She's strong." He studied my face for a moment. "How are you?"

"I'm all right. Sad because I was just getting to know Christine and I liked her. A little frustrated because I want to do something, but I don't know what."

"That's understandable, my dear," he said.

Rose came out of the apartment then, her coat buttoned, tote bag over her arm. "I'm ready," she said. "I'm sorry to keep you waiting." She looked around. "Did Mac already leave?"

I nodded. "He wanted to get cleaned up."

We went out to the SUV and I unlocked the door. Mr. P. opened the back passenger side so Elvis could jump up on the seat.

"Thank you for calling Mac last night," I said to Rose.

"I like him," she said.

For a moment I felt my throat tighten. Rose had tried so hard to get Nick and me together. It was the happy ending she'd thought would be perfect. It just wasn't perfect for us. I knew this was her way of saying if Mac made me happy that was good enough for her.

"Me, too," I said.

Rose didn't say anything else until we turned at the corner and headed in the direction of Second Chance. "I spoke to Debra," she said. "That's why I kept you waiting."

"How is she?" I asked.

"She's upset and she blames herself."

"It's not her fault," I said, shaking my head.

"She thinks she should have been there. Socrates got something sticky on his tail. She decided to take him to a groomer instead of dealing with it herself, otherwise she would have been at the apartment."

I gave an involuntary shiver as though an icy finger had just trailed up my spine. "If Debra had been there, she might have been trapped as well."

I saw Rose nod out of the corner of my eye. "Yes, she might have been, but Debra thinks if she'd been there *she* would have been in the living room and seen the fire in time."

"That's too much responsibility for one person to put on themselves," Mr. P. said.

"Do you think the fire could be connected in any way to the vandalism at the cat shows in New Hampshire?" I asked. "Socrates is one of the top cats and Debra was staying with Christine."

Mr. P. hesitated before he spoke. "I think it's too soon to speculate. We don't even know the cause of the fire at this point."

He was right. It was a bad idea to jump to conclusions when we knew so little.

"I'd like to go see Debra later," Rose said.

I glanced over at her. "I'll take you. Just tell me when."

She smiled. "Thank you, sweetie."

I looked in the rearview mirror at Mr. P. "When do you need to go to the arena?"

"Late morning," he said. "But Memphis is picking me up. If anything changes, I'll let you know."

Mac's truck was in its spot by the garage workshop and Charlotte was coming along the sidewalk as I pulled into the lot. She joined us as we got out of the SUV, hugging Rose and then me. "I'm so sorry about your friend," she said.

Seeing her reminded me that I hadn't heard back from Nick. I pulled out my phone. There were no new texts from him. Where was he?

We went inside and as soon as I stepped into the shop I could smell the coffee. *Thank you, Mac,* I said silently.

"I'm going to go make the tea," Charlotte said.

"I'll come with you," Rose said. She patted the side of her bag. "I have cake."

When something good happened Rose baked; whether it was Avery getting an A in chemistry, or Elvis not biting the vet tech when he got his teeth cleaned, we had cake to celebrate. Or pie. When something bad happened she also baked. When I injured my arm we had cake. When a tree fell on Nick's car we had cake. It was her way of saying she loved us.

Mr. P. touched my arm. "We need to have a meeting to talk about the case and everything else."

"That's a good idea," I said.

"Will ten o'clock work for you?" he asked.

I nodded. "It will."

I'd been at my desk about half an hour, collecting orders from the shop's website, when there was a knock on my door. "C'mon in," I said as I added the last item to my list. I looked up to find Jess standing there. "What're you doing here?" I said.

She held up a large canvas carryall. It was stuffed with pillows. "I wanted to drop these off and see how you were."

I got to my feet and came around the desk. "I'm better. Thank you for being the voice of reason earlier."

Jess wrapped me in a hug. "Yeah, that's me. The voice of reason." She narrowed her blue eyes. "Have you heard from Nick yet?"

I shook my head.

"Want me to go bang on his door and wake him up?"

I knew she'd do it and a tiny part of me wanted to say yes. But I didn't. "No, you don't need to do that," I said.

"Are you sure?" she asked, raising one eyebrow. "You must have a boom box somewhere out in the old garage. I could do my impersonation of John Cusack as Lloyd Dobler in *Say Anything* and play Peter Gabriel outside Nick's bedroom window."

I laughed. "Sadly, there are no boom boxes in any of our storage spaces, so even though I'm sure you'd do a wonderful Lloyd Dobler, I'm going to have to say no to that idea, too."

Jess dipped her head in a half bow. "If you change your mind I'm only a text away." She lifted her head and her eyes met mine. "For whatever you need."

I felt my chest tighten. Jess had been my best friend

since we'd met in college. She was up for any hare-brained idea I came up with. She was up for any hare-brained idea *Rose* came up with. It gave me a sense of a bit of the grief Debra was feeling.

"What would I do without you?" I blurted.

"You planning on running off to join the circus?" Jess said.

I shook my head. "No."

"Did you forget to mention you were heading up to the International Space Station?" She pointed a finger at the ceiling.

"Also no," I said.

She smiled. "Then I guess you're not going to find out."

I gave her another hug, thanked her for dropping off the pillows and she left after I promised I'd talk to her later. I sat down at my desk again and picked up my phone, hoping I'd somehow missed a call or a text from Nick. I hadn't. It didn't matter. Maybe I'd been hanging around Rose too much because I'd already made up my mind. One way or another I was going to find out exactly how Christine had ended up dead.

We gathered in the sunporch just before ten. Charlotte took a cup of tea and came over to me. "I'll hold down the fort and Rose will fill me in later," she said.

I smiled. "Thank you."

As I reached for my coffee it struck me that there seemed to be too many cups on the table. Then Nick and Liz walked in together.

Nick was dressed for work in a long-sleeved polo-style shirt and black pants with what seemed to be myriad pockets. He stopped to speak to Rose for a minute, taking one of her hands in both of his. Then he looked around. He spotted me and made his way over to where I was standing by the table.

Liz, meanwhile, was talking to Rose now, one hand on her friend's shoulder.

"Hi," Nick said. "I got your message. I was in a meeting, that's why I didn't call you back; and then I knew I'd see you here."

"Rose called you," I said.

He gave me a wry smile. "It seems I'm part of the team."

"There are advantages to that, you know."

He gave me a skeptical look. "And they would be?"

"All the cake you can eat and there's a rumor we're getting team T-shirts."

He laughed, then his expression grew serious. "Mom told me you and Rose knew the woman who died. I'm really sorry."

"Thank you," I said. "We met Christine at the cat show in Searsport. She was funny and kind and I'm sorry I'm not going to get to know her better." I cleared my throat. "I hear you went above and beyond to try to save her. You didn't want to give up."

He pulled a hand across his mouth. "We did everything we could think of. It was too late."

"I know," I said. For a moment I didn't say anything more, but then I asked the question I wasn't sure if he'd answer. "Nick, what do you know about the cause of the fire?"

"Only what I've heard, which isn't much." His expression grew wary. "Last night I was focused on the victim . . . I'm sorry, on your friend. I didn't see much."

"I'm guessing the cause of death was smoke inhalation."

He didn't say anything, just looked away for a moment.

"C'mon, Nick," I said, making sure I kept my voice low. "You know Mr. P. can find out."

"It looks that way," he finally said.

I set my cup on the table. "How long before they know what happened?"

"I don't know." He held up a hand. "I really don't. The medical examiner's office will be working with the arson investigator. I'm going over to the scene when I leave here."

I took a step closer to him. "What aren't you saying?" I asked. He was sticking very tightly to just the facts—more so than he usually did. Something, some instinct told me there was more.

"I don't know what you mean."

"I mean you're not telling me something."

The muscles along his jawline tightened. "I can't give you information about an ongoing investigation, Sarah. You know that." His eyes flicked away from mine once again.

"I'm not asking you to do that," I said, struggling to keep the growing frustration I was feeling out of my voice. "But I know you. I know you paid attention to everything you saw and heard last night because that's who you are and there's something you're not telling me. What is it?"

I kept my gaze locked on his, almost daring him to look away. "It isn't anything concrete," he finally said. "It's just a gut feeling and for all I know it was the leftover cold pizza I ate on the run and not any kind of insight. It looked like the fire could have started on the sofa. Maybe a light tipped over. Maybe. People are careless. Accidents like that happen all the time, sadly."

I nodded but didn't say anything.

"The very first death I investigated was fire-related. Guy knocked over a lamp on his way out. A pillow caught fire. His grandmother ended up dying from smoke inhalation. There was just something about the burn pattern on the sofa last night that triggered that memory. It doesn't mean this fire was your friend's fault, which is why I didn't want to tell you."

The Christine I knew—I'd known—didn't strike me as the type of person who would leave an over-turned lamp on the couch. There had to be another explanation. "Thank you," I said.

Mr. P. clapped his hands then. "Please take a seat, everyone," he urged.

We all found chairs except for Nick, who leaned against the wall and Mac, who stood behind Mr. P., arms folded over his chest.

"I talked to our client a little while ago. Nothing has changed with respect to the show and the pet expo, except that there will be a mention of Christine's death when the show opens and it will be dedicated to her memory."

Mr. P. went on to talk about the plans for the show—Cleveland and Memphis were taking care of security including adding our extra cameras to the arena's system. Both buildings would be checked carefully for any issues after everyone was gone for the night and again in the morning before things opened.

"By now you all know that we have a couple of suspects that we're investigating. And we'll keep working on unearthing any others." He reiterated the details of the pet expo and the cat show. Then he looked around the room. "Is there anything else we need to talk about?"

No one said anything. I kept turning three words Nick had said over and over in my head: *People are careless.*

No. I didn't believe the fire was Christine's fault.

I stood up. "There is something we all need to talk about," I said.

Mr. P. smiled at me. "By all means. What is it?"

"I would like the Angels to take on a new client."

Rose was across the table from me. "Who?" she asked.

"Me," I said.

Chapter 9

For a very long moment no one spoke. They all just stared at me. I could see Nick out of the corner of my eye shaking his head. "Don't do this," he said in a voice so low I was certain I was the only one who heard him.

My mouth was suddenly dry and I swallowed a couple of times. Across the room I could see Mac looking at me. When he caught my eye and he gave an almost imperceptible nod, I felt the knot in my stomach untangle itself.

"And what would we be investigating?" Mr. P. asked.

"Christine Eldridge's death," Rose answered. She seemed to understand what had been going on in my head. Maybe because she'd been having the same thoughts?

"Yes," I said.

Rose focused her attention on Nick then. "Do you know something?" she asked.

I didn't want to put him on the spot. Before he could say anything, I turned to look at him and spoke first. Something had been itching in the back of my mind since I'd found Mac in the kitchen that morning and he'd joked about me sleeping through him singing opera. "Nick, did that apartment have a smoke detector?"

He thought for a moment. "There was one in the living room."

"Why didn't Christine hear it?"

"I believe that she was wearing noise-cancelling headphones," Mr. P. said.

I kept my attention focused on Nick. "I know which headphones she uses." I paused for a moment. "Used. They were in her bag when we had lunch yesterday. I have the identical ones. They don't have active noise-cancelling because Christine didn't want to keep buying batteries for them. They were *passive* noise-cancelling, which rely on padding. Even with headphones on, she should have heard the smoke detector. I've set the one in my apartment off more than once, so I know what I'm talking about. Why didn't she hear it?"

Something changed in Nick's expression. He straightened up. "Are you sure?"

"Absolutely," I said. "You can try my headphones if you want to."

"Nicolas, is it possible that fire was something other than an accident?" Liz asked from across the table.

Nick rubbed the back of his neck with his free hand. "I don't know. I only got a quick look at the scene last night. All my attention was on my patient.

It will probably be a few days before anyone knows for sure if the fire was an accident or . . . not."

"I don't want to wait for a few days," I said. "I want to start figuring out what happened now."

"That works for me," Mr. P. said.

I turned to smile at him.

"I'm in," Liz said.

Rose took a sip of her tea and set the cup down in its saucer again. "My vote is yes." She leaned sideways and looked at Mac.

"I get a vote?" he asked.

"Of course you do," she said as though her answer was obvious.

"Yes," he said.

Rose turned to Nick. I looked at him again as well.

"Can't you wait for just a couple of days until we know if there's anything *to* investigate?" he asked.

I shook my head.

Nick set his coffee mug on the table. "Why?"

I struggled to explain my thought process that I hadn't completely sorted out myself. I knew *I just have a feeling* wouldn't be enough of an explanation for Nick and I wanted him on board, although why I did was another thing that was hard to put into words.

"I don't like the math," I finally said.

"What do you mean?" Mr. P. asked.

"What are the odds the fire would happen on the one night of the week that Christine shouldn't have been home but was?" I looked from Alfred to Nick. "And what are the odds that the smoke detector wouldn't work on the exact same night?" I held up a hand to stop any objection Nick was going to make. "I know those headphones, Nick, and they wouldn't have blocked the sound. And what are the odds that also on that same night Christine's car wouldn't be in the parking lot in its normal spot? It would have alerted her neighbors that she *was* in that apartment a lot sooner and maybe have saved her life."

"Random things happen, Sarah," Nick said.

"Yes, they do," I said, struggling to keep my rising frustration out of my voice. "You find a quarter on the sidewalk. That's random. You get the cupcake with the most frosting. That's random. Your class gets cancelled and you end up dead is not random."

"What do you want from me?" he asked. I could hear frustration in his voice as well.

"Find out if the smoke detector was working properly last night. If . . . if you can show me it was then I'm willing to wait until we know whether the fire was accidental before we start digging in to what happened. If not, I'm the Angels' newest client."

He nodded and pushed away from the wall. "Done. I'll talk to you later."

Once Nick was gone, Rose got to her feet. "Where do you want to start?" she asked.

"I'm going to honor the deal I just made with Nick. For now we're going to concentrate on the case we have."

"We can do that," Rose said. I saw a look pass between her and Mr. P. She'd said "can," not "will."

Liz had also gotten to her feet. She came around the table to me. "You know how to liven up a meeting, kiddo," she said.

"I didn't plan it that way," I said. "It just kind of happened."

"Nicolas doesn't like losing." There was a bit of a devilish twinkle in her eye.

I shrugged. "He's going to have to get used to it this time."

Her expression grew serious. "I'm sorry about your friend."

"Thanks," I said. "I think you would have liked Christine. She was funny."

"I'm sorry I didn't get to know her." Liz held up one hand. She now had a pale pink French tip manicure.

"Very nice," I said.

"I fished all around that pond, and I talked to Elspeth, but the only thing I learned about Chloe Hartman is that she can be very single-minded."

I looked over to where Rose and Alfred were deep in conversation. "That isn't necessarily bad; Rose can be, too. And you."

Liz laughed. "If you think you're going to get me to say anything to incriminate myself you are out of luck, missy."

Mac joined us then. "I'm going out to the workshop," he said. "Come out when you're done here."

I smiled at him. "I will."

"You can walk me out," Liz said to Mac. "I have a lunch date."

I folded my arms over my chest and gave her the once-over. Liz always looked impeccable, but it seemed to me she'd taken extra pains with her appearance. She was wearing a black skirt with a coral sweater and a gray jacket. "Are you having lunch with Channing?" I asked.

Channing Caulfield was the former manager of the largest bank in this part of the state. Liz had called on his expertise more than once for one of the Angels' cases. He'd been happy to help because he'd been smitten with Liz for years. I teased her unmercifully about his unrequited crush, although I was beginning to think it might not be totally unrequited.

"That's none of your concern, Nosy Rosy," Liz retorted.

I leaned toward her and sniffed the air. "Spices, vanilla, patchouli. You're wearing Tom Ford Black Orchid. Very foxy."

"I am most certainly *not* foxy," she said emphatically. "And what I'm wearing is none of your business." She looked at Mac. "How do you put up with her?"

He smiled. "She's awfully cute."

"I have some photos of Sarah I'm sure you'd like," Liz said, giving me the same sort of smile I imagine the crocodile gave Captain Hook. "I'll find them for you."

I wrinkled my nose at her. "You're not my favorite anymore," I said.

She made a dismissive gesture with one hand. "Don't be ridiculous. No one's going to believe that." She started for the door, her high heels clicking across the floor. Mac grinned and followed.

"Tell Channing I said hello," I called after them.

I walked over to Mr. P. "Thank you for your support," I said. "I'm sorry for just dropping everything on all of you."

"You always have my support, my dear," he said. He slipped off his glasses and began the ritual of cleaning them. "May I ask what you're trying to learn?"

I put both hands on the top of my head, lacing my fingers together. "I don't exactly know."

"Do you think someone wanted Christine dead?"

"I . . . no. If someone wanted her dead why would they pick the evening she wasn't supposed to be at the apartment?" I sighed. "I don't think her death was something that was planned. But something just feels wrong about the fire. I can't exactly explain it and I realize I sound like Rose, but I just have a feeling."

Mr. P. put his glasses back on. "I trust Rosie's instincts and I trust yours. We'll figure this out."

"Thank you," I said. I glanced in the direction of the parking lot. "What time is Memphis picking you up?"

He checked his watch. "In about fifteen minutes."

"Call me if you need a ride back or anything else."

He nodded. "I will. And please let me know when you hear from Nicolas."

"I will," I promised.

There was no sign of Rose in the workroom. I realized she must be in the shop updating Charlotte on everything she had missed. It turned out Charlotte was with a customer. They were looking at a galvanized washtub that was filled with a collection of old soda bottles. I couldn't tell if the man was interested in the tub, the bottles, or both. I found Rose rearranging the pillows that were heaped in the blue steamer trunk. She had laid another plaid blanket over the open top, which made the whole arrangement look even cozier. She fluffed a fat blue pillow and came over to me.

"Am I wrong?" I said to her. I trusted Rose's judgment.

Rose didn't ask what I was talking about. She just shook her head and said, "I don't think so. I've had a bad feeling about the fire since I first heard what happened." She cocked her head to one side. "Does it strike you as odd that Christine wasn't supposed to be at the apartment but she was, while Debra was supposed to be there but she wasn't?"

I held up one hand. "Are you saying you think someone was after Debra?"

"Or maybe Socrates."

I stared at her without speaking for a moment. "So someone started the fire to hurt the cat?"

"I know how it sounds," Rose said. "I'm old, but I'm not daft, as Liz would say."

I'd never heard Liz use the word "daft" but it didn't seem like a good time to point that out.

"I don't think anyone was trying to hurt Socrates, but I do think it's possible someone wanted to knock him out of the competition."

"But it's a cat show," I said. "Nobody's going to take it that seriously, are they?"

"It's also big business; especially this year, where there's interest in signing the winning cats to endorsement deals for everything from pet food and supplements to products outside of the cat show market. There's even talk of a reality show, featuring the top cats in each category."

I raked a hand back through my hair. "I had no idea."

"Spending on pets in this country is a multibillion-dollar proposition. Some people will do anything to get a piece of that pie."

"Okay, let's say for a moment you're right. That means it's possible the fire and the vandalism at the previous shows are connected."

Rose nodded. "That had occurred to me."

"So what do we do?" I said.

"What we've been doing from the beginning," she said. "We keep working on the case we have and we wait to hear from Nicolas. But I also think we need to keep a close eye on Debra and Socrates."

"If someone was trying to hurt either one of them, they could try again."

"Do you think we could go see Debra after lunch?" Rose asked. "She's with Tim, over at the Hearthstone Inn. Tim wanted her to go back to Portland with him, but Debra didn't want to leave; and the Hearthstone takes pets, so that's where they went."

"Pick a time and I'll be ready," I said.

She smiled. "Thank you, sweetie."

"Are you going to tell her what you suspect?"

She let out a breath. "I don't know. She's already so upset. I don't want her to think what happened to Christine is her fault in any way, but I don't want anything to happen to her or Socrates, either."

I patted her arm the way she often did to reassure me. "We'll figure it out," I said.

Charlotte and her customer were carrying the galvanized tub still filled with bottles to the cash desk. It seemed the man wanted the tub and the contents. Or Charlotte had convinced him he did. She was very good at the soft sell.

My phone chimed then. I pulled it out of my pocket and checked the screen. The text was from Nick. Just two words:

No battery.

I remembered what Debra had said when she and Christine had told the story about the fire in their chemistry lab. She'd said the whole class had learned a lesson about working smoke detectors. I didn't see how Christine would have had one in her apartment that had no battery.

I turned the phone around so Rose could see the screen. She read the text. Then her gray eyes met mine and a look of resolve spread across her face.

I was the Angels' newest client.

Chapter 10

Rose promised that she would update Mr. P. I went upstairs for my jacket and a cup of coffee for Mac and then I went out to the workshop to tell him what was going on. I found him sanding the back of a teak patio bench, one of a set of two that Mac had bought from Cleveland. They had both been painted a glossy, disconcerting shade of hot pink. Mac had been working on the benches on and off for weeks now, coming back to them in between other projects for the shop. Now that most of the pink was gone, I could see the beauty of the wood underneath and I was considering keeping them for myself.

Mac turned off the sander when he caught sight of me and brushed off his hands and the front of his shirt before he pulled off his sanding mask.

I handed him the cup of coffee. "Thank you," he said. "This is dry work." He took a long drink.

"It's looking good," I said, walking around the bench to take a closer look. "I have to admit I thought you were crazy the first time I saw these two pieces. They were so, so pink."

He nodded. "I know. There were a couple of times I thought I was never going to get rid of that color, but now that I'm pretty much down to the bare wood I can see the quality of the craftsmanship." He gestured at a detail in the back of the bench. "Look at that join. This wasn't made on an assembly line. Both of these were hand-crafted by someone who knew what they were doing."

I ran my hand along the arm of the piece. "I'm glad you saw their potential under all that pink."

Mac took another drink of his coffee.

I wiped away the thin layer of dust clinging to my fingers. "I'm sorry I didn't tell you earlier that I wanted to look into Christine's death. I wasn't trying to hide anything from you. I didn't really know what I was going to say until I stood up and the words came out."

"It's okay," he said. "And for what it's worth, your reasoning makes sense to me."

"I heard from Nick."

"So now the Angels have two cases."

I smiled at him. "They do. How did you know that I was right and Nick wasn't?"

He folded his arms across his midsection, still holding on to his coffee cup. "Like I said, your reasoning made sense. The likelihood of so many coincidences happening just isn't logical; and let's face it, when Nick goes up against you and Rose it never goes his way."

I laughed. "So you were playing the odds."

He held up his thumb and finger about half an inch apart. "A little bit."

"To be fair, you know Nick will work this case as hard as anyone."

Mac nodded. "That's one of the things I really respect about him." He took another sip of his coffee. "You know, Nick and Rose actually are very alike. They're both intensely focused and they both don't give up easily."

I gave a snort of laughter. "Do not tell either of them you think that!"

"You don't agree?" he asked, his tone teasing.

I shook my head. "I'm not answering that on the grounds it will get me into trouble with both of them. The most I'm willing to concede is that each one thinks the other is stubborn."

Mac set his cup down on a nearby table, looked over his shoulder to see if anyone was in the parking lot and then pulled me toward him. "Would you also be willing to concede that since there's no one around it would be okay for me to kiss you?"

I put my arms around his neck. "Absolutely," I said.

I spent the rest of the morning updating the listings on the store's website. Avery arrived at lunchtime. She came in through the workshop, stopping to hug Rose.

"How were your classes?" Rose asked.

"They bite," Avery said as she headed for the stairs.

"Is that worse or better than 'like a dirt sandwich,' which was yesterday's answer?" I asked.

Rose smiled and shook her head. "I think it's too fine a distinction to make."

Avery disliked school. There had been issues at her previous school and the one before that and she butted heads with her parents over pretty much everything. Everyone had been surprised when Liz had suggested that Avery live with her and attend a private school that had only half-day classes. Avery was hardworking and creative and when I'd broached offering her a part-time job, Liz had given me a long look before saying, "Do you know what you're getting in to?"

"I think I do," I'd said. The truth was, I'd had a feeling that being around Rose and Charlotte and her grandmother would be good for Avery. Being around them had been good for me when I was her age.

I was rescuing my pen from under my desk a few minutes later when Avery knocked on the office door. I was pleased to see that she was wearing the bracelet I'd given her. I knew that meant she liked it. She wasn't the type of person to wear something she didn't like just to be polite.

"Is this a bad time?" she asked.

I brushed a dust bunny out of my hair and made a mental note to get Mac to help me move the desk so I could do a better job vacuuming underneath it. "No, it's fine," I said. "Elvis seems to think it's funny to knock all my pens off the desk."

"Yeah, he has a weird sense of humor," she said as though we were talking about a person and not a cat. She shifted somewhat uncomfortably from one foot to the other. "I, uh, just wanted to say I'm sorry that your friend died in that fire."

"Thank you," I said. I was touched by her words. Emotional situations weren't easy for Avery.

"Friends stick together, so anytime you feel bad you can come and hang with Nonna and me."

"I might just do that," I said.

Avery hesitated and then gave me a quick, awkward hug. I had to swallow against a sudden prickle of tears.

"I'll go get to work," she said, and she was gone.

After lunch Rose and I drove to the Hearthstone Inn to see Debra. The sky was gray and low and I wondered if we'd get snow or rain later. The inn was within walking distance of the downtown, overlooking the water at Windspeare Point, nestled among the trees overlooking West Penobscot Bay. Beyond the bay were Deer Isle, Swan's Island and the Atlantic Ocean. The inn itself was a three-story mansard-roofed Victorian built in the 1830s with high, narrow windows and intricate exterior details. The building had been painted three shades of gray, from a pale gray the color of early-morning fog on the clapboards to a deep charcoal on the mansard roof with accents of white, green and bronze on the cornices, moldings and other trim details. The front door was a deep, forest green.

Inside we were welcomed by a very friendly calico cat and a woman who looked to be in her midforties with gray hair in a chin-length bob, wearing a red plaid shirt tucked into black jeans. I was guessing she was one of the new owners of the Hearthstone.

"Rose, it's good to see you," she said with a warm smile.

It was no surprise that they knew each other. Rose had grown up in North Harbor; she'd spent her entire teaching career in town and she was the kind of person for whom a stranger was just a friend she hadn't yet gotten to know.

The cat was sitting on a wooden chair with curved arms and beautifully turned back spindles. I held out my hand. He sniffed it, narrowing his eyes in curiosity, then butted it with his head, a signal that it was okay to stroke his fur, which I did.

"It's good to see you, too, Maud," Rose said. She turned to me. "Sarah, meet Maud Fitch. She's the newest member of the library board and Maud and her wife are the new owners of Hearthstone."

"It's a pleasure to meet you, Sarah," Maud said, offering her hand. "I've been hearing good things about your shop. Rose says you may have some of the things I'm looking for."

"What do you need?" I asked. She had a firm handshake and the posture of a dancer.

"Among other things, I'm looking for several chairs for some of the bedrooms."

A smile spread across Rose's face.

I smiled as well. "I have a bit of a weakness for orphaned chairs and I'm certain there would be something you'd like."

"Good," Maud said. "I'll stop by the first chance I get." Her smile faded and she glanced over her shoulder. "You're here to see Debra Martinez."

Rose nodded.

"I was so sorry to hear that someone died in the fire."

"It was kind of you to offer a room to Debra and Socrates," I said.

"We're cat people," Maud said. She gestured at the

cat still sitting in the chair, now carefully washing his face. "You've already met Michelangelo, and Leonardo is around here somewhere." She held up one hand. "I swear they're named after the artists, not the Teenage Mutant Ninja Turtles—at least according to the shelter they came from."

She turned and indicated the hallway behind us. "Debra and her friend Tim are in the dining room. It's the second room on the left just around the corner."

We thanked her and moved down the hall.

"This is a beautiful old house," I said to Rose.

"It is," Rose said. "I'm so glad that Maud and her wife have bought the inn and are committed to a life here in North Harbor."

Debra was standing by the window, looking out into the side yard. She turned as we came into the room.

"I'm so glad you're here," she said. Tim was seated at the long rectangular dining room table. He got to his feet.

Rose wrapped Debra in a hug.

"I'm so sorry, Debra," I said. "Christine was a wonderful person."

"She was happy she'd met you. After we all had lunch she was so excited about finally, hopefully, being able to do something about her father's record collection. And she hoped she'd get to know you a little better, too."

I nodded, swallowing the sudden lump in my throat before I spoke. "I would have liked that."

Tim was hovering. I could see the worry etched on his face. "Why don't you sit down?" he said to her.

"I'm all right," she said. "Don't fuss." She gave him a small smile to soften her words as she turned back to Rose.

"Tim, how are you?" I asked. I felt a little guilty about suspecting him of being behind the sabotage at the New Hampshire shows when he'd really been helping save a dog.

He swiped a hand over his mouth. "I uh . . . I'm all right. Thank you for asking. I can't believe Christine is dead."

Maud came in then carrying a large tray. It held everything we needed for tea including a china teapot wrapped in a pink flowered quilted tea cozy, along with a plate of tiny cranberry muffins and a creamy cheese spread. "I'll be in the kitchen if you need more hot water," she said.

We took seats at one end of the table.

"Would you like me to pour?" Rose asked.

Debra nodded. "Please."

Tim cleared his throat. "I'm glad you came. Can you please convince Debra that the best thing to do right now is to come back to Portland with me? There isn't anything she can do here."

Debra looked across the table. Her hands were in her lap and I could see the right one was clenched into a tight fist. "I know you mean well, but I'm not going anywhere. I should have been at the apartment with Christine. And I'm not running off until I find out what happened."

Rose set a cup of tea in front of Debra, then she set down the teapot and put a hand on her friend's arm.

"What happened is not your fault," she said firmly. "If you had been there, we might have lost both of you."

"She loaned me her car," Debra said in a low voice, staring down at her lap. "I keep thinking if it had been in her parking space maybe someone would have figured out sooner that she was inside."

"And maybe someone else would be dead, too," Tim said. "The firefighters went inside as soon as they got to the building." He took a breath and let it out. "It was just too late. It has nothing to do with you."

"Tim is right," Rose said. "It's not your fault."

"I know that here," Debra said, lifting her head to look at Rose and at the same time tapping the side of her head with one hand. "But not here." She put her hand over her heart.

Rose picked up the teapot. "That will take time."

Socrates had come from somewhere and had been winding around my legs. Suddenly he launched himself onto my lap.

"I'm sorry, Sarah," Debra said, reaching to take the cat.

"It's okay," I said. "He's fine here."

As if to add credence to my words Socrates leaned against my chest and blinked his copper eyes at Debra.

"Thank you," she said. "He knows something's wrong."

Rose finished pouring for everyone. I added milk and a little sugar to my cup.

Socrates lifted his head to see what I was drinking but didn't seem interested once he knew what it was.

Debra put one of the tiny muffins on a napkin,

broke it in half and spread a little of the cheese on one piece. "There's another reason I want to stay here," she said. She glanced at me and then at Rose. She didn't look in Tim's direction at all.

"What is it?" I asked. I had a feeling I knew what her answer would be.

"Socrates and I are doing the show."

"You're not serious," Tim said.

Debra did look at him then. "Yes," she said. "Christine and I always had a good time together at the shows and I think she'd want me to."

I remembered Christine telling me, that first time we had coffee, how much fun she had being at the cat shows and how much she liked Socrates, who she thought was a pretty good judge of character.

"You don't have a place to stay anymore," Tim said, "and most of Socrates's things were damaged in the fire." He tented his hand over the top of the cup of tea in front of him. "I knew Christine, too, you know, and she would understand about you skipping this show."

I saw a flash of uncertainty on Debra's face.

"Stay with me," Rose said.

Debra stared at her. "Are you serious?"

Rose leaned sideways in her chair and looked at Socrates nestled on my lap. "Would you like to come stay with me for a while?" she asked.

He seemed to think about her words. His whiskers twitched and then he meowed softly.

Rose shifted her attention to Debra. "Socrates is in. All you have to do is say yes. We'll help you get whatever you need to be set up for the show."

I nodded. "Socrates can come hang out with Elvis

and you can take some time to figure out what you want to do next."

Debra shifted her attention to Tim. "I know you think I should go back to Portland with you, but this is where I want to be until we know for sure what happened to Christine. You understand, don't you?"

He took a deep breath and exhaled slowly. "If this is what you want to do, I'll help any way I can."

"Splendid," Rose said. "We'll pick you up on the way home."

Her eyes flicked to me to confirm and I gave the tiniest of nods.

Tim was already shaking his head. "That's not necessary. I can drop Debra off."

Rose waved away his words. "You lost a friend, too, Tim. It's no trouble."

"I don't know how to thank you," Debra said.

Rose smiled. "I'm just glad I can do something to help. And it will be good to spend more time together. I'm only sorry it's happening this way."

We finished our tea and said good-bye to Debra and Tim.

"See you soon," I whispered to Socrates.

Maud came out of the kitchen to say good-bye and once again promised she'd stop by the store the first chance she got.

Once we were outside in the SUV, I turned to Rose. "I saw what you did," I said.

"Really?" she asked, all sweet little old lady innocence. "What did I do?"

"You invited Debra to stay with you so we can keep an eye on her."

She shrugged one shoulder as she fastened her seat belt. "Maybe, or maybe I was just trying to help an old friend." The gleam in her gray eyes told me she was just toying with me. "I didn't ask if it was all right with you if Debra stays for a few days."

"Of course it is," I said. "It's your apartment. And if someone is trying to get to her or Socrates, she'll be a lot safer with us." I paused for a moment.

"What is it?" Rose asked.

"Are you going to tell Debra you have two cases that she's connected to?" I didn't say that I couldn't get rid of the niggling feeling that those two cases could actually be one.

"*We* have two cases and no, I'm not. Not yet. We don't know anything yet."

I stuck the key in the ignition and then looked at her again. "She's going to be living in your apartment. Do you really think you can keep all that a secret?"

"I just won't talk about the case when I'm home. Don't worry. It'll be fine."

I wasn't sure her plan was going to work. And it bothered me a little, not being straight with Debra. But I knew how hard it was to change Rose's mind once she'd made it up. And none of us thought Debra was a suspect in either case.

She pulled out her cell phone. "I'm just going to check in with Alfred before we head back, just in case he needs anything."

I waited while she called Mr. P. From her side of the conversation, it sounded like things were going well at the pet expo.

"How about a little detour on the way back to the shop?" I asked.

"Alfred did say he left a couple of passes for us," Rose said.

I smiled. "He knows us well."

The parking lot at the arena was easily two-thirds full.

"I didn't think it would be this busy on a Wednesday afternoon," I said as we got out of the car.

"It's not that big of a surprise when you know about sixty-eight percent of American households have a pet," Rose said. Maybe it was because she'd been a teacher or maybe it was one of the things that had made her a good teacher, but she loved statistics and obscure facts. She could win any trivia game because she knew such a wide range of things and because people tended to underestimate her, big-time.

"I'm guessing more dogs than cats. Man's best friend and all that."

We headed across the parking lot. "Actually no," she said. "There are slightly more cats than dogs."

"So maybe cat people really do rule," I said with a grin.

Mr. P. was just inside the entrance talking to Memphis. They both smiled when they spotted us. Once again Memphis was dressed all in black. He was holding two lanyards in his hand. "These are your passes," he said. "You can use them to get into the cat show and the pet expo."

"Thank you," I said, taking the one he held out to me. I hung the cord, black with tiny white paw prints, around my neck. Rose did the same with hers.

"I'm going to go take another look at that camera," Memphis said. He smiled at Rose and me. "Have fun. You know, I saw a heated cat bed with massage at one of the booths at the pet expo that I'm pretty sure Elvis would like. Just saying." With a grin he turned and headed down the left concourse of the building.

I looked around. People were coming and going, many of them carrying brown paper shopping bags. "Any problems so far?" I asked.

Mr. P. shook his head. "A small issue with the placement of a camera, but Memphis has an idea for a way to fix that. How is Debra?"

"She wants to show Socrates," I said.

"I told her we'd help her get what she needs," Rose added. There was a question in her gray eyes.

"Of course we will," Mr. P. said. "I'll ask Avery to help."

"I'll help as well," I said. "Just tell me what you need."

He hiked his pants up a little higher even though they were already under his armpits. "I don't know if you noticed, but Socrates had a litter box with a domed cover. I remember Debra saying it was the only kind of covered box he'd use. Apparently he doesn't like small spaces."

I was already nodding. The covered litter box had reminded me of a structure I'd once seen for drying seaweed. "I did notice that. Would you like me to find one?"

"Please," he said. "That would be a big help."

"And Debra and Socrates will be staying with me," Rose said.

Mr. P. nodded. "Good." I realized that he had known

Rose was planning on inviting Debra to stay. As usual the two of them were several steps ahead of me.

"We're going to take a peek in the pet expo before we head back," Rose said.

"And Memphis is waiting for me," Mr. P. said. "I must get my jacket."

"Call if you need me to pick you up," I said.

He nodded. "Thank you, my dear. I will."

He headed in the same direction Memphis had taken. Rose and I walked over to the main-floor entrance and showed our badges to a young woman who checked each one carefully before she smiled and handed us a map of the space.

The first thing that struck me was just how many people there were inside the gym space. There were more than I'd expected to see based on the number of cars outside in the parking lot.

"Good heavens, this is a busy place." Rose craned her neck to look around.

"What if we just follow the crowd and walk around for a few minutes?" I said.

"That's an excellent idea," she said.

The booths were arranged in two long loops, one inside the other with a wide aisle separating them. Vendors were offering everything from pet food to beds to boots for cats and dogs. There was a large selection of pet carriers, leashes and harnesses. One booth featured bike trailers to transport dogs and cats.

I nudged Rose. "Can you picture Elvis coming to work with me in that?"

She studied the mesh-and-nylon wheeled carrier for a moment. "I'm not certain he'd like it," she said, "but I think I'd fit inside." There was a mischievous twinkle in her eye.

I got a mental image of Rose sitting inside the bike trailer wearing a helmet with her knees up around her ears. I grinned at her. "True," I said. "You are the little package good things come in, but where would I put Mr. P?"

She pointed at a bright blue bicycle with a metal-and-canvas carrier attached to the handlebars. "Just think of how good that fresh air would be for all of us." Her lips twitched.

"I'll get my fresh air running," I said, "thank you very much."

We kept on walking. I was amazed at how much there was to see: pet celebrities; trainers; automated feeding systems; plans and examples of houses for dogs, cats, hamsters and other animals; and workshops on everything from grooming to making pet food. Tilley the fire dog and a group of firefighters from the area were talking about fire safety. Lily the library cat—a hand puppet, not a real cat—was there promoting reading to kids.

Rose waved at a woman ahead of us. The woman waved back. She was wearing a set of fuzzy black cat ears and a pair of retro cat's-eye glasses with sparkling rhinestones at the corners. "That's Junie," Rose said. I must have looked confused—which I was—because she added, "Millicent's mother."

I nodded. Junie, aka Millicent's mother, was the person who had told Rose about Suzanne and Paul Lilley wanting to start their own cat registry. I wondered whether Mr. P. had had any luck digging into their background. I'd never known one of his gut feelings to be wrong.

Rose grabbed my arm and threaded her way through the crowd, pretty much pulling me along with her as she made her way over to Junie, almost like I was a wagon she was pulling behind her.

"Junie, this is my friend Sarah," Rose said when we finally reached the woman. Junie was short and round with bright blue eyes that held a mischievous twinkle.

She smiled. "It's nice to meet you. You own Elvis, don't you? He's a beautiful boy."

"Thank you," I said, "and the jury's still out on who owns whom."

The smile got wider. "Tell me about it," she said. She turned to Rose. "Did you try the crackers yet?"

Rose shook her head. "I need Alfred to bring me a fan first."

Junie gave a knowing nod.

"Am I missing something?" I asked. "You're talking about the sardine crackers, aren't you?"

"Yes," Rose said. "They're a little . . . aromatic."

"She means they stink," Junie said flatly. "When you make them you need to open all the windows and run a fan. Trust me on that. Cats love 'em, though."

Junie gave Rose a couple more cracker-making tips and then we parted company. I realized I *still* didn't know what species Millicent was. As we walked around I saw several people using their phones to record what was going on. Ahead of us one man was walking backward, recording video and somehow managing not to run into anyone. He looked familiar; average height and build, cropped gray hair and beard. I realized the man was one of the producers who had been involved in filming the pilot for a treasure-hunt reality show in North Harbor during the summer. Our street had been clogged from early in the morning until late at night and my patience had quickly become frazzled.

I'd met the producer because one morning Rose and I had arrived to find half of our parking lot filled with the crew's vehicles and the entrance blocked— without permission. Rose had dealt with the immediate problem of the truck in the driveway as only a former middle school teacher could and I'd gone in search of someone in charge. Half an hour later the crew's vehicles were still in our parking area, but I had a check in my hand large enough to take the edge off my annoyance. I wondered what the man was doing back in town.

We made it back to the main entrance. "We should get back to the shop," Rose said.

I nodded my agreement. There was more to see, but it would have to wait for another time.

As we walked across the parking lot I saw Rose look over to the adjoining building where the cat show would be held.

Cleveland was standing by the main doors having a heated discussion with a woman. Actually only her part of the discussion seemed heated; Cleveland looked like his usual, laid-back self.

I looked at Rose and inclined my head in the direction of Cleveland and the woman. She nodded and we changed course. As we approached I could see that the woman was holding a cat in her arms. It was a big cat; long, not chubby, with markings like a leopard or a jaguar. I knew from some of the prowling around online that I'd done that it was a Bengal.

The woman, who I took to be the cat's owner, was in her earlier forties with dark blonde curls just brushing her shoulders and pale-framed glasses. She wore a black hooded raincoat and black rain boots with cartoon cats all over them and she was gesturing with a fair amount of agitation.

Cleveland was listening patiently to her, his blue eyes fixed on her face, hands clasped in front of him.

"I just need to walk around the space where the show is going to be held before things are set up so that Basil can adjust to the room," the woman was saying. I assumed that Basil was the cat. "Basil is a very sensitive soul," she continued with complete seriousness. Basil, meanwhile, was staring at a nearby BMW.

Cleveland looked at me and one eyebrow went up. I wondered how long he and the woman had been standing there having the conversation.

"I didn't mean to eavesdrop," Rose said to the woman, "but there will be lots of time at setup tomorrow for Basil to adjust to his new surroundings."

The cat turned his head. It seemed Rose was more interesting than a BMW.

She held out a hand to him. "He's beautiful."

He sniffed curiously and reached a paw toward Rose. The woman immediately took two steps back and glared at her. "Please don't touch him," she said. "I have no idea where you've been."

"Merow!" the cat said. He didn't seem to care where Rose had been.

The woman focused her attention on Cleveland again. "Well?" she said.

"I'm sorry, Ms. Watson," he said. "I can only let people on the floor who have permission from Mr. or Mrs. Hartman and I'm sorry, you're not on my list. However, if you'd like to call either one of them I'd be happy to let you use my phone."

Her jaw clenched and her shoulders tightened. "You're just wasting my time," she said, her voice laced with anger. "If Basil doesn't do well in the show it will be your fault. And I promise you, I will make you pay!"

The woman turned and stalked away without another word, the cat watching us over her shoulder.

Cleveland shook his head. "That was fun," he said. He really was unflappable. I'd once seen him pry the top off a damaged tea chest to see what was inside and come face-to-face with a very pissed-off raccoon. He'd reacted about the same way that time as he had now. And come to think of it, the raccoon had been in about the same mood as the woman.

"You handled things very well," Rose said.

"Alfred warned me that she'd try to get into the building. She tried to get into the Searsport show early, too."

"Do you think she could be behind the vandalism at the other shows?" I asked.

He shrugged. "Anything's possible, I guess. But she doesn't strike me as the kind of person who would hurt an animal. She seems, I don't know . . . kind of eccentric."

I struggled not to smile. People often said the same thing about Cleveland.

He gestured at the building behind us. "Alfred and Memphis are inside taking a last look at the security cameras if you want to go in and talk to him."

Rose smiled. "No, that's fine. We'll see him back at the office."

"Do you know who that woman was?" I asked Rose as we walked back to the car.

"Her name is Kimber Watson," she said. "And the cat, as you probably guessed, is Basil."

"He's a Bengal?"

She nodded. "And he's been Socrates's main competition for the last several years."

I unlocked the SUV's doors and walked around to the driver's side. "Kimber Watson is on your list of suspects, isn't she?" I asked as I slid behind the wheel.

"Let's just say she's a maybe." Rose fastened her seat belt and folded her hands in her lap.

I didn't like the term 'crazy cat lady,' but Kimber Watson did seem like a bit of a fanatic when it came to her cat. On the other hand, I let Elvis sit on a stool at the counter for breakfast so who was I to judge?

"What did Mr. P. find out about her?" I asked.

"She's married with no children," Rose said. "No one has ever seen her husband so there's a rumor that he doesn't actually exist."

"Do you think it's true?"

"I think it's just silly gossip. Kimber is a quiet, solitary person. She's very attached to Basil. She's not very outgoing and she hasn't been very welcoming to new people for the most part."

I was about to say something and then I stopped myself. I'd forgotten that Rose missed very little.

"You were going to say something," she said. "What was it?"

I chewed my lip for a moment. "You said Kimber was on your suspect list as a maybe."

I saw her nod out of the corner of my eye.

"Why just a maybe? She seems a little obsessive when it comes to her cat and the shows. And you just said she hasn't been very welcoming to new people. Those sound to me like two reasons she may be behind what's going on."

Rose took a moment before she answered. "At first glance, I agree with you," she said.

"I sense a 'but' coming." I glanced over at her and she smiled.

"Yes, there is a 'but' coming. More than one. First of all, I agree with what Cleveland said. You saw her when she thought I was going to touch Basil. Kimber was very protective. I don't think she'd do anything that might hurt another animal."

"Okay," I said, slowly, "what's the second 'but'?"

"I think she's shy. She doesn't seem to have a lot of friends. That doesn't mean she's been trying to derail the shows. Maybe it just means she's a bit lonely."

I thought about the woman I'd just met. She had been very protective of her cat. And she'd threatened Cleveland. Rose tended to see the best in people most of the time. Maybe she was right about Kimber Watson.

But maybe she wasn't.

Chapter 11

Rose and I picked up Debra and Socrates at the end of the day. I was a little worried that Elvis might have a problem with another cat being around. Rose had kept him on the front seat with her and I'd heard her explaining to him that Debra and Socrates were going to be staying for a few days.

"I'm sure the cats will get along just fine," she'd said as we headed for the inn. "They're already friends from the show."

When Debra climbed into the SUV with Socrates in his carrier, Elvis peered over the seat and meowed. Socrates meowed back. Neither cat seemed bothered by the other. Maybe Rose was right. Maybe they did consider themselves friends. Maybe I was overthinking everything.

"I like your house," Debra said as we pulled into the driveway.

"Thank you," I said.

"Rose, are you sure I'm not imposing?" she asked.

Rose was shaking her head before Debra had finished asking the question. "Of course you're not," she said. "I'm happy to have you and I'm glad you decided to stay for the show." She held up one hand. "And before I forget, Alfred has everything you need for Socrates."

Debra blinked hard several times. "I don't know how to thank you."

"We just want to help," I said. "I'm glad we can. Even just a little."

We helped Debra carry in what few things she'd brought with her.

"Can you join us for supper?" Rose asked me.

"Merow!" Elvis said, starting for her apartment door.

"Elvis!" I called after him. He stopped and looked back over his shoulder at me, eyes narrowed in annoyance.

I smiled at Rose. "Thank you for the invitation, but Mac is bringing pizza."

I had no idea how many words the cat actually understood—sometimes I suspected it was a lot more than I knew—but he definitely knew the word "pizza." He did an about-face and came back to our apartment door, giving a soft murp in Rose's direction as he passed her.

Rose smiled. "Another time, then," she said. I wasn't sure if she was talking to the cat or me.

I told Rose we'd head to the shop at the usual time in the morning and we said good night. Then I unlocked the apartment door. Elvis went inside ahead of me the way he always did, but then he stopped and turned to face the door again. I almost fell over him.

"Move," I said.

His response was to lean sideways so he could see around me.

"Move out of the way," I said in a louder voice as though hearing me had been the problem—which it hadn't.

All he did was flick his tail at me.

I knew he was waiting for Mac and the pizza.

I kicked off my shoes and made my way around him. "Mac isn't going to be here for probably half an hour," I said.

He made a sound a lot like a sigh, but he didn't move.

Mac arrived twenty-nine minutes later with the pizza and my favorite salad from The Black Bear. "I told Sam it was for you so there's extra cucumber and those roasted pumpkin seeds you like."

I clasped my hands together and grinned at him like I was a little kid. Elvis launched himself onto one of the stools at the counter, licked his whiskers and looked pointedly at Mac.

I shook my head. "You can't have pizza," I said. "It's people food, not cat food."

Elvis licked his whiskers again and kept his green eyes on Mac as though I wasn't even in the room.

"It's not good for him," I said to Mac.

He nodded. "I know." He fished something out of his pocket. "How about this instead?"

It was a can of sardines.

It got an enthusiastic meow from Elvis.

Mac went into the kitchen to open the can. Elvis

jumped down to follow him. I took the stool the cat had just vacated.

"Are you trying to get my cat to like you with tiny, smelly fish?" I asked as Mac leaned down to put two sardines into Elvis's dish.

"Of course not," he said as he straightened up. "He already likes me. I'm trying to get his owner to like me with tiny, smelly fish."

I leaned my elbows on the counter and grinned at him. "For future reference, chocolate works a lot better than little fish."

A smile spread across Mac's face as he moved closer to me. "Hence, my backup plan." He reached into his other pocket and pulled out a small paper bag from Glenn's shop.

"Chocolate chip?" I asked. I was pretty sure I could smell vanilla and chocolate, which meant the bag held at least one of Glenn's chocolate chip cookies.

He handed me the bag. "Yes."

I swept one hand through the air. "So basically you're trying to buy my affections with all this?"

He nodded solemnly.

I reached across the counter, caught the front of his jacket and pulled him in for a kiss. "Lucky for you, that works," I said.

We had our pizza and the chopped salad with extra cucumbers and roasted pumpkin seeds and then we curled up on the couch for another Star Trek movie. I tried to teach Mac how to do the Vulcan salutation, laughing so hard I gave myself hiccups because it was impossible for him to keep his ring and middle fingers apart. It felt good to be a little silly, to stop thinking—for a brief time—about how the world could sometimes be a very dark place.

I woke up in the morning before my alarm went off. I padded over to the window and looked outside. It was partly cloudy, but it didn't look like imminent rain or snow. Elvis lifted his head and yawned. "I'm going running," I said. "Are you coming?"

He yawned a second time and rolled over onto his back. I knew a no when I saw it.

I got dressed, found my favorite red beanie and fingerless gloves and laced up my shoes. It was cold outside, but there was no wind and I decided I could run my longer route. Running was when I did some of my best thinking and as my feet hit the pavement I went over the list of possible suspects in the cat show case. While Suzanne and Paul Lilley may have had a reason to disrupt the shows, I agreed with Mr. P. that there was something off about their disguises and behavior. I thought about Kimber Watson. Was she capable of vandalizing a sprinkler system? Could she have damaged the crates? Rose seemed to think the woman wouldn't do anything to hurt a cat, but she did seem to have a very competitive streak. Then there was Jeffery Walker, who I hadn't met yet, and whose cat, Nikita, was also in the running for the top spot. Christine had said that many of the other competitors saw him as an upstart because the white Persian had been so successful so quickly.

And what about Christine's death? Did it have anything to do with what had been happening at the shows? As I turned for home, I knew I didn't have any more answers than I'd had when I left.

Elvis and I had breakfast—cat food for him and scrambled eggs with spinach for me—and then we both got ready for work. Since getting ready for the cat just meant cleaning his fur, he was sitting by the door when I came out of the bedroom.

He meowed impatiently.

"Give me a minute," I said. "I made a very good sandwich for lunch and I'm not leaving it behind."

Elvis narrowed his green eyes at me.

"Chicken and peppers," I said in answer to what I thought was his unspoken question. "Play your cards right and I'll give you a bite."

"Chicken" was another word that was definitely in his vocabulary. He immediately cocked his head to one side.

"Cute won't get you everything you want in life, you know," I said.

"Mrrr," he said. From his perspective it was working just fine.

Rose came out of her apartment just as I was locking my door. "Good morning," she said. She was carrying her green and navy tote bag in one hand and a wooden hanger with two fleece blankets draped over it in the other.

"Good morning," I said. "Let me take those blankets."

She handed me the hanger. "Thank you. I would have put them in my bag, but I ran out of space."

I recognized the purple blankets. We'd used them at the Searsport show. "I could have washed these, Rose," I said.

"I know you could, sweetie," she said, "but it's not like I had to go down to the river and beat them on a rock. And I hung them on Charlotte's clothesline to dry, so they smell nice and fresh." She smiled at Elvis, who smiled back at her.

I looked down at him as I opened the front door. "Is there a cat anywhere in this state that is more spoiled than you?"

He wrinkled his nose at me and headed for the SUV.

I held the door for Rose. "Elvis is not spoiled," she said as she passed me.

"Says the chief spoiler."

"He's not spoiled," she repeated. Her chin came up a little in that defiant stance she used when she was about to argue something with me. "He's cherished."

"Cherished?"

"Yes. A transitive verb meaning to hold dear something or someone." Rose poked me with her elbow. "Just like you are."

I shook my head. "Why do I even try to win an argument with you?" I asked. I pointed my keys at the car and unlocked the doors.

Her guileless gray eyes studied my face. "I've been wondering that myself," she said, then she opened the front-passenger door for Elvis. He hopped onto the seat and looked at me for a moment before he moved over so Rose could get in. I didn't think it was my imagination that he looked more than a little smug.

*   *   *

I drove into the parking lot to find Liz's car parked by the back door. As I pulled into my regular space, Avery came out and took a cardboard box from Liz's backseat.

"Why isn't Avery in school?" I said.

Rose reached for the tote bag at her feet. "Parent-teacher meetings."

I made a face. "That's right. I forgot. Mac has a project he wants her to work on."

We got out of the SUV and headed across the lot. I had my messenger bag over one shoulder. I'd left the hanger with the blankets in the backseat since we'd be taking them over to the arena right after lunch. Rose was carrying her tote bag with one hand and Elvis with the other. I reached for the bag. "He can walk, you know," I said.

"Well of course he can," she said. "I don't want him to get his feet dirty. The judges will notice something like that."

"We should get Jess to make socks for him." Jess was a very talented seamstress.

Rose stopped walking for a moment. "That's an excellent idea," she said. "Are you going to the jam tonight?"

"I was planning on it."

She beamed at me. "Wonderful. You can ask her about socks and maybe some kind of cape with a hood, to keep Elvis's fur clean as well." She started for the door again. I had no idea if she was serious or pulling my leg, but knowing Jess, she'd be all in.

We found Avery, Liz and Mr. P. in the workroom. There was a pile of boxes next to the workbench.

"Good morning," Mr. P. said, smiling at us.

"Good morning," I said, smiling back at him. "What's all this?" I flicked a finger at the boxes.

"It's everything Debra will need for Socrates," he said. "Avery found all the items on my list." He turned his smile on the teen and she ducked her head even as she smiled herself.

"Thank you, Avery," I said. "I know Debra will appreciate all your hard work." I caught Mr. P.'s eye. "The litter box with the cover is up in my office."

"Thank you, Sarah," he said.

Avery looked at her grandmother. "Nonna helped, too," she said. "She drove me to two places last night and another this morning."

Rose smiled at her old friend. "That was so nice."

I leaned sideways and kissed Liz's cheek. "Yes, it was."

She swatted me away with one hand. "So is that everything that was in the car?" she said to Avery.

The teenager nodded.

"Is there anything I should know before I go to that teachers' meeting?" Liz asked. "You haven't been planning to overthrow the faculty?" She was wearing a black suit with a cream-colored blouse and high-heeled black pumps that I wouldn't have been able to stand up in let alone walk anywhere. I knew Liz well enough to know that the conservative and expensive suit had been chosen to let anyone she encountered at Avery's very expensive school know that she was not someone to ignore.

Avery wrinkled her nose and shook her head. "No. My French teacher thinks I have a bad attitude, but I think he has a bad accent so that pretty much evens out." Elvis was nosing around the boxes and she leaned down to pick him up. "Oh, and you might not be happy with my biology grade." Elvis nuzzled her chin and she kissed the top of his head. "Or depending on what you were expecting, maybe you will be."

"Good to know," Liz said. "Anything else?"

Avery thought for a moment, her mouth twisting to one side. "Mr. Harrison, my gym teacher, said I run like a girl and I said well sure I do because I am a girl and then he made me run five more laps because he said I was insolent, which, by the way, I don't think I was."

"Also good to know," Liz said. I saw a muscle tighten in her jaw. She nudged me with her shoulder. "Walk me out."

"I'd love to," I said.

"I'm going to put the kettle on," Rose said.

"I'll come with you," Mr. P. said. He held out a hand and I gave him Rose's bag. They started for the door into the shop.

"Mac made coffee," Avery said. "He's on the phone with those guys who own the bed-and-breakfast."

The guys she was referring to were the owners of Herrier House, a bed-and-breakfast in Camden. They had discovered Second Chance *by* chance when the two of them had pulled off the highway to get coffee on the way to a funeral and had turned into loyal customers.

"So do you want me to get you a cup of coffee?" Avery asked. She pushed her hair out of her eyes. "I don't mind."

I nodded. "I'd like that. Thank you."

"No problem," she said, heading after Rose and Alfred and still carrying Elvis.

I linked my arms through Liz's. "I asked you to walk me out, not help me out," she said. "I'm not decrepit, you know."

"I know," I said, leaning my head against her shoulder for a moment. "This is a gesture of affection."

She shook her head but didn't say anything.

"So what's up?" I asked once we were outside in the parking lot.

Liz pulled her arm free of mine and turned to face me. "Elspeth called me this morning. She said something had been bugging her ever since I'd asked her about Chloe Hartman. She had the feeling someone had mentioned the Hartmans so she asked around."

"And?" I prompted.

"And it seems they aren't particularly good at paying their bills on time."

"And you don't want to see the Angels get short-changed."

Liz shook her head. "No, I do not. I also don't want Rose to think I'm getting on my high horse because I wasn't a fan of taking on this case."

"So you're throwing me under the bus instead?" I crossed my arms over my midsection and narrowed my eyes at her.

"I prefer to think of it as I'm asking you to do a favor for me," Liz said.

"Oh, a favor," I said, drawing out the final word.

She moved toward me until there was about a finger's width of space between us. "Ask your friends in the neighborhood about me," she said in a low voice, quoting Vito Corleone from *The Godfather*, one of her favorite movies. "They'll tell you I know how to return a favor." Then she turned, walked around to the driver's side of her car and climbed in.

I watched her drive away and felt a small twinge of sympathy for Avery's gym teacher.

Avery was just coming down the stairs with my coffee when I stepped into the store. "Thank you," I said, taking the mug from her.

She was also holding a red polar fleece jacket. "Mac wants me to bring all the chairs from the workshop inside," she said. "Do you want me to do anything before I do that?"

I shook my head. "No, go ahead. And thank you again for helping Mr. P. get everything for Debra and Socrates."

She smiled. "It was fun. I made a spreadsheet of what we needed to get and then I figured out the most efficient route. And Nonna said we had to drive all over kingdom come, but I know she didn't really mind because she got up this morning to take me to get the special food the cat eats even though I was planning on walking."

That was Liz. No matter how much she might bluster about the hours at Avery's private school or the healthy smoothies she was always trying to get Liz to drink, Liz loved her granddaughter with the fierceness of a grizzly bear. Living with her grandmother had been very good for Avery. She was still defiant on occasion and she could be argumentative at times—

the apple didn't fall far from the tree, I liked to remind Liz—but she wasn't hiding from the world anymore. She smiled, she laughed and sometimes she hugged people. She was confident. She was happy.

Avery shifted from one foot to the other, twisting the collection of bracelets she was wearing on her arm around and around. "You're going to get set up at lunchtime for the show, right?"

I nodded. The plan was to drop off Rose, Elvis and Mr. P. with all of the gear and then I'd pick up Debra and Socrates and ferry them to the arena as well.

"I was wondering . . . could I come with you, just for a while until you're ready to come back to the store? I can help Mr. P. get everything set up and stuff."

I could hear the enthusiasm in her voice and the hopeful smile on her face. "How would you feel about spending the afternoon at the show?" I asked.

"Seriously?" Her eyes lit up, but almost as quickly the excitement faded. "But I have to work this afternoon. I was going to wash more teacups because we're out of teacup gardens and those chairs that Mac wants me to bring in are going to have to be cleaned and—"

I held up one hand. "The cups can wait one more day."

"But what if we get more bus tours? Those people love the teacup gardens."

I smiled at her. "First of all, there are no bus tours coming today that I've heard of. And number two, if one shows up this afternoon there are a lot of other things they can buy."

She opened her mouth to say something, but I

didn't give her the chance. "Charlotte will be here and so will I. We can both vacuum and wipe down chairs. The question is, do you want to spend the afternoon setting up for the cat show?"

Avery nodded.

"It's settled then," I said. "Go check in with Mac."

She hesitated for a second, then flung her arms around me in a fast, tight hug. "You're the best, Sarah," she said.

I watched her cross the room in large strides before disappearing through the door to the workroom and it struck me once again that coming to live with Liz hadn't just been good for Avery. It had also been good for the rest of us, too.

Charlotte arrived at eleven. By that time, Avery had brought in eight chairs—all different styles. She'd also found time to wash half a dozen teacups and plant them with tiny zebra plants from the collection that lived on one of the wide windowsills in Mac's apartment.

We loaded all of the supplies for both cats in the SUV. Then I drove Rose, Elvis, Avery and Mr. P. over to the arena. The parking lot was busy, but I managed to find a spot at the end of a row. I backed in and Elvis craned his neck to look out the rear window, backseat driving as usual.

Mr. P. had spoken to Memphis and there was a participant badge waiting for Avery. "Oh wow!" she exclaimed as she stepped into the show space. Since the North Harbor show was bigger than the one in Searsport, it was being held in a larger space and there were a lot more people. This time the staging areas for the cats were set up in two sections with a wide aisle down the middle. The judging stands were against the back wall of the space with the same setup as the previous show. Even though the pet expo was in the adjoining building, there were some smaller vendors set up in the show space, too. At the far left end I spotted an area set up like a small café. I remembered getting coffee with Christine at the previous cat show and had to take a couple of deep breaths.

"Here we are," Mr. P. said, putting a hand on an empty section of table at the end of a row to the right of the main aisle.

The space just to the left of us was empty as well. Rose followed my gaze and guessed what I was thinking. "Yes, Debra is beside us again," she said. "Alfred spoke to Jacqueline and she arranged it."

Jacqueline. It took me a moment and then I remembered that Jacqueline was Jacqueline Beyer, the Hartmans' social media director.

Rose set her tote bag up on the table. "I thought Debra might feel better to have a friend beside her and I feel better knowing we can keep an eye on her just in case."

Mr. P. got Elvis settled in his crate and Rose and Avery began opening the boxes. I checked my watch. "I'm going to head out to get Debra and Socrates," I said. "Is there anything else we need?"

Mr. P. slid a practiced eye over everything we'd brought. Then he smiled at me. "We seem to have what we need," he said.

I zipped up my jacket. "Okay. I won't be long."

*   *   *

Debra was waiting on the front steps, a carrier bag very similar to the one I used with Elvis slung over one shoulder and a tote bag that I recognized as one of Rose's at her feet. She climbed into the driver's side of the car and smiled. "Before you ask, no, you're not late," she said, settling the cat carrier at her feet. "I was just getting antsy, which Socrates always picks up on, so I decided to come outside to wait." Both her smile and the cheery tone of her voice seemed a little forced.

"Rose and Alfred are already at the arena getting everything set up," I said as I backed out of the driveway. "Socrates is right next to Elvis again and everything he needs is already over there."

"All of you have been so generous," Debra said.

"A friend of Rose is a friend of the rest of us," I said, giving her a quick, sideways glance. "I should warn you that's not always a good thing."

She smiled again, a little less forced than the previous time. "Can I ask you how you make it work? Living with Rose and your grandmother? If I'm being nosy, just tell me."

"You're not being nosy," I said. "It's not the first time someone has asked me that question."

"So what's your secret?"

I laughed. "Well, it helps that we each have our own space. And we have our own lives."

"I thought someone had told me that Rose was living in a seniors' apartment complex," Debra said. "Legacy something?"

I nodded. "Legacy Place. She was. Let's just say the

building wasn't a good fit for her. Most of the time she referred to it as Shady Pines."

She laughed. "That sounds like Rose."

We spent the rest of the drive with Debra telling me more about the presentation Rose had done for their instructional methods class. "You should have seen the instructor's face when she started out by playing 'Walk This Way.'"

We were still laughing when I drove in to the parking lot at the arena complex. A half-ton truck was just pulling out so I managed to snag a spot close to the main doors.

Debra looked around. "There are a lot of cars here."

"More than half of them are people at the pet expo," I said. "It'll be even busier tomorrow once the show starts."

She nodded, lips pressed together. I waited, letting the silence hang between us.

"Sarah, what am I doing here?" she finally said.

I exhaled slowly. "I didn't know Christine very well, but there was something about her, something that made me hope that we'd end up as friends."

"She was like that," Debra said quietly.

"But you already were her friend," I continued, "and I can't imagine how you feel. From the short time I knew Christine I don't think she'd want you to get swallowed up by your grief. I think she'd want you to keep going. If this is your way of keeping going, then let's head inside. If it isn't, or if it's just too soon, then I'll take you and Socrates anywhere else you want to go—at least until we run out of gas."

The crack about the gas got me a tiny smile. Debra stared at the building for a long moment. Then she squared her shoulders and reached for the strap of the carrier bag. "Let's do this," she said.

Inside the building we found Rose brushing Elvis's fur and Avery deep in conversation with a woman holding a Sphynx cat in her arms. The hairless cat was wearing a pink knitted sweater and seemed to like Avery. Mr. P. was nowhere to be seen.

Rose smiled at her friend. "We have everything you need," she said. "And you can put Avery and me to work getting set up."

Debra set Socrates on the counter next to Elvis's crate. Socrates peered through the mesh top at Elvis. "Mrrr," he said.

Elvis meowed back in response.

Avery ended her conversation with the Sphynx cat and its owner and joined Rose, who introduced her to Debra. "Your cat's beautiful," Avery said. "Rose showed me pictures of him."

"Thank you," Debra said. "I like the privacy screen you made for Elvis's litter box."

Avery smiled. "Thanks. He likes his privacy when he does his thing."

Rose started to cough. I wasn't sure if she had a dry throat or it was because of Avery's comment.

I patted her on the back. "Oh goodness," she said. "Something went down the wrong way." Her gaze shifted to Avery for a moment. Okay, so it wasn't a dry throat.

"Is there anything else you need from me?" I asked.

"Nah, we got this," Avery answered.

A hint of a smile played across Rose's face. "As Avery said, everything is under control."

I zipped up my jacket and felt for my keys. "Okay, I'll be back to pick you up. If anything changes, let me know."

Debra caught my eye. "Thank you, Sarah, for everything," she said.

"You're very welcome," I said. I shifted my attention to Avery.

"I know. Stay out of trouble," she said.

I smiled. "I was going to say have fun."

She pushed back her sleeves and slid her bracelets up her arm. "I'm already having fun." She wrinkled her nose thoughtfully. "What do you think Nonna would say about getting one of those hairless cats?"

I could think of several potential responses Liz would have to a hairless cat—to any kind of cat at all. She was a dog person through and through.

Rose laid a hand on the teen's arm. "There are a lot of different breeds here. Why don't you wait until you've seen a few more before you tackle your grandmother?"

Avery nodded. "Yeah, I should probably do that. But you know she'd freak, right?"

"Yes, we know," I said.

She smiled and went to help Debra with a box.

"What was Liz like at that age?" I said to Rose.

"A lot like Avery," Rose said. "Opinionated. Stubborn. And soft-hearted underneath that prickly outside."

"So pretty much the way she is now?"

Rose laughed. "Yes." She brushed some cat hair off the front of her sweater. "So are you going to tell me to stay out of trouble?" she asked, a teasing edge to her voice.

I shook my head. "I am not," I said solemnly. "I know an exercise in futility when I see it." I leaned down and kissed her cheek. "I'll see you later." I poked a finger at the side of Elvis's tent. "You, too."

He murped at me and rolled over onto his back. It seemed the life of a show cat was very tiring.

Chapter 12

I was cleaning chairs in the workroom about forty-five minutes later when Nick came in the back door. "Hey, what are you doing here?" I asked, looking up at him.

"Mom said that Debra Martinez is staying with Rose. I was wondering if she'd said anything more about the night of the fire."

"Not to me," I said. "And Rose didn't mention anything." I got to my feet, dropping the cloth I'd been using back into my bucket. The reproduction of an Eames fiberglass shell chair wasn't what Maud Fitch would be looking for, but it was interesting enough to put out in the shop.

Nick looked around. "Is she here?" he asked.

I shook my head. "No. She's getting set up for the cat show over at the arena complex. If Debra said anything to her, Rose would tell you."

His snort told me what a bad liar I was.

"Probably," I added. "Eventually." I wiped my

damp hands on my jeans. "What about you? Have you come up with anything that proves the fire wasn't an accident?" I wasn't sure whether he'd answer my question.

"Tom Manning, the arson investigator, has already talked to several neighbors who knew Christine and they all say she would never have taken the battery out of the smoke detector."

"Do you think someone deliberately disabled it?"

He shrugged. "Maybe. It's also possible the battery was running down and making that annoying beeping sound and she just took it out because she was trying to study and planned to replace it later."

"First of all, it doesn't take that long to replace a battery. And second, the old battery would have been in the trash or with her recycling, or on the closest table. It had to be somewhere in that apartment. Did you look?"

There was an awkward pause. "This is not my first investigation, Sarah," Nick said. "It's not Tom Manning's, either."

"I'm sorry," I said. "I didn't mean it the way it sounded. It's just that this case feels personal. I had lunch down at Glenn's with Christine and a few hours later she was dead."

Nick's expression softened. "I know. Just try to remember it's my job to collect evidence, *all* the evidence, no matter where it leads."

My stomach flip-flopped. "Does this mean you have some sort of proof one way or the other?"

The silence stretched between us. "I shouldn't be telling you this," Nick said.

I stayed silent.

He blew out a breath. "Look, I know this isn't what you want to hear, and it's still really early in the investigation."

I knew there was a "but" coming.

"But it's looking more and more like the fire was an accident."

I was shaking my head before he'd gotten all the words out. "C'mon, Nick. That doesn't fit with the battery being out of the smoke detector. It doesn't fit with all the other coincidences. Too many coincidences. I'm not saying someone set out to kill Christine, but I do think the fire was set deliberately."

"Coincidences happen," he said. "I'm sorry. Sometimes people die because of stupid accidents. Just because you were right about the smoke detector battery doesn't mean Christine Eldridge was murdered."

"Where did the fire start?" I asked, ignoring what he'd just said.

"The sofa, just as I suspected. You know that little lamp Mom has in her spare room? The bottom is just a cube and it has a fabric shade."

"Gram gave it to her."

"Christine had the same lamp. It looks as though it fell over onto the couch. There was an old incandescent bulb in the lamp that would have gotten very hot. Someone had probably been sitting there reading because there were a few potato chips on the sofa. At first glance, the firefighters thought they were pieces of cardboard. They would have ignited very quickly."

I didn't know what to say. Was I wrong? Was I just trying to find something suspicious about Christine's death because I didn't want it to be just a "stupid accident"?

"Christine died of smoke inhalation," Nick continued. "The sofa and foam cushions were old. The smoke was dense and it spread throughout the apartment very quickly." He cleared his throat. "She didn't . . . suffer. She was likely overcome before she realized what was wrong."

"I hope that's true," I said. There didn't seem to be much more to say. Nick seemed certain that Christine's death was an accident and I wasn't sure what to think.

"I have to get back to the office," he said. "I'm going to try to make the jam tonight. You'll be there, right?"

I nodded, accepting the change of subject because I really didn't have anything more to say.

"Is Mac going, too?"

"Yes, finally," I said. I saw a hint of a smile play across Nick's face.

"Good," he said. "I need more testosterone at the table. You and Jess always stick together."

"Jess and I are like peanut butter and jelly—good apart but even better together."

Nick laughed. "And sometimes when the two of you are together, things can get very sticky."

I smiled at his bad joke.

"I've really gotta go," he said. "See you tonight."

I watched him head out the back door and thought about how much his attitude had changed toward the Angels since he'd first found out what his mother and her friends were doing. Back then, Nick spent more time trying to shut the agency down than he did listening to their ideas—or mine. He actually *had* listened this time even though he thought I was wrong. And he hadn't said a word about the Angels looking into Christine's death even though he believed it had been an accident.

I knew it made me sound like Rose, but in my gut I knew Nick was wrong. So as far as I was concerned, the case was going forward until I had incontrovertible proof that gut feeling was wrong.

It was a quiet afternoon and Mac booted me out a few minutes early to head over to the arena. "I'll see you at the pub," he said. The number of times we'd been derailed was becoming laughable. A water main break downtown the previous Thursday had meant the jam was cancelled altogether.

I smiled at him. "Jess and I will save you a table."

When I got to the arena, I found Avery holding Elvis, pointing out the banners all over the space with different sayings about cats on them. I remembered Rose telling me the banners were the idea of Jacqueline Beyer. Debra was brushing Socrates's fur and Rose was just ending a call on her cell phone.

"Hello, sweet girl," she said. "You're right on time."

"I was afraid I wouldn't be," I said. "I had to circle the lot twice to find a parking spot."

Rose had on one of the aprons she wore in the shop and she plucked a bit of cat hair off the front. "The pet expo has been busy since they opened the doors yesterday. Record attendance, according to Chloe Hartman."

"Any problems here?"

She shook her head. "Aside from two cats getting away from their owners, no."

"Any sign of the Lilleys?" I asked.

Again Rose shook her head. "I haven't seen hide nor hair of them and, according to Alfred, neither has anyone else."

"Where is Mr. P.?" I asked.

"He's having a meeting with Chloe," she said.

I remembered what Liz had told me about the Hartmans' financial dealings. I shifted uneasily from one foot to the other. "About the Hartmans," I began. "It's none of my business how you run *your* business, but I have heard a rumor that they aren't always good about paying their bills on time."

Rose smiled. "Let me guess. A little bird with blonde hair and high heels told you that."

I made a face. "Yes."

"Honestly," she said in exasperation. "Sometimes I swear Liz still thinks I'm six years old trading my lunch for marbles."

"You traded your lunch for marbles?" I said.

"You say that like I traded it for a handful of magic beans."

I held up one hand. "I'm sorry. I didn't mean it that way." The conversation was getting derailed. "How did you know about the Hartmans?"

She stood a little straighter. "Channing," she said. I'd seen that same self-satisfied look on Elvis when he'd conned me out of a treat.

"Channing Caulfield? Liz's Channing?"

"The jury is still out on whether or not he's Liz's Channing, but yes."

The conversation may have been back on track, but I was lost. "Why did he tell you? How did he know the Hartmans had hired you?"

"Channing told me because I asked him," Rose said. "And he knew the Hartmans hired us because I told him." She patted my arm. "It's okay. I know you're tired."

I rubbed the space between my eyebrows with two fingers. "When did you see Channing?"

Rose looked over at Avery. "We're leaving in a few minutes," she said.

Avery nodded and pulled the carrier bag out from under the table by catching the strap with her foot.

Rose refocused her attention on me. "I didn't see Channing. I called him."

We still didn't seem to be getting anywhere. "Because?" I prompted.

"Why don't you and Elvis come and have supper with me?" she said. "Debra is having dinner with Tim and you can just relax."

I took a breath and let it out, trying to rein in my frustration. "It's Thursday. I'm going to the jam. But thank you."

"All right," she said. "But don't stay out too late." She shook her head. "And as for Channing, I called him because it's easier than getting him to come to our office."

Finally something clicked into place and the conversation suddenly made sense. "So do you always check out clients with him?"

"Most of the time. Channing is very knowledgeable."

"So everything's fine?"

She smiled again and for a moment I thought she might pat my cheek. "Of course it is. Don't worry about a thing."

I was saved from answering by Mr. P., who rejoined us. He checked his watch. "I didn't realize it was this late," he said.

"If you're not ready to leave, I can come back for you," I said.

He smiled. "Thank you. I do have a couple of things I still need to take care of, but Memphis has already offered to drop me off."

Rose and Avery seemed to be debating over the contents of a box that Avery had set next to Elvis's crate.

"Have you found anything yet to support your hunch about the Lilleys?" I asked, lowering my voice a little.

He shook his head. "Nothing yet, but I'm not giving up. Do you remember Jacqueline Beyer? You met her in Searsport."

I nodded. "I remember."

"She knows a lot of people in the cat show world. I'm going to see if she knows anything."

"Let me know if I can help," I said.

Rose and Avery were still looking in the cardboard box. "Nick came by the shop," I said.

Mr. P. nudged his glasses up his nose. "Am I correct that you didn't like what you learned from him?"

I explained what Nick had said about how the fire

started. "I don't see how the fire could be an accident if the battery had been taken out of the smoke detector. It wasn't the kind of thing Christine would have done. Nick says the battery may have needed to be replaced and she was planning on doing it later."

"It's Nicolas's job to look at things that way," Mr. P. said. "It's not ours."

Just then a familiar-looking man approached Debra. He was heavyset, about average height with dark hair and a dark beard that were a little at odds with the lines on his face. He wore a gray tweed jacket with a white shirt and a blue and gray tie and seemed to be in his late sixties.

"Hello, Jeffery," Debra said.

It was Jeffery Walker, I realized. The man I had seen arguing with Christine at the Searsport show. The man who owned Nikita, the cat who was Socrates's main competition, along with Basil, the beautiful Bengal who belonged to Kimber Watson.

"Debra," he said. "I heard about Christine. I wanted to express my sympathies."

He had a beautiful voice, deep and smooth. "She was very kind and welcoming to me. I'll miss her."

Debra swallowed. "Thank you," she said.

He nodded and went back down the aisle.

"Are you all right?" Mr. P. asked.

She managed a small smile. "I am. Thank you," she said. "I'm going to have to get used to people coming to tell me how sorry they are. A lot of people liked Christine."

"She was very easy to like," Mr. P. said. He gestured to the carrier bag on the table behind Debra.

"Do you mind if I take a look at your carrier? I like the mesh panels at either end."

"So does Socrates," she said. "He's very inquisitive." She undid the zipper on the top of the bag so Mr. P. could look inside.

I walked over to Rose and Avery. The latter was putting Elvis's dishes into Rose's tote bag and talking to the cat.

"What did Jeffery Walker want?" Rose asked.

"He came to tell Debra how sorry he was to hear about Christine. He seemed nice."

"You mean he doesn't seem like someone who would damage crates or set a fire."

I jiggled my keys in my jacket pocket. "I know Mr. P. has to have checked him out. What do you know?"

"Jeffery is a retired science teacher who got involved in the cat show circuit after the death of his wife," Rose said. "He's pleasant, well-read and easy to get along with, but he does have a competitive streak. More than one person has heard him call second place 'first loser.'"

"Do you think the fact that he was a science teacher may be important?"

"Maybe," she said. "He taught chemistry and he was also the adviser for the student radio station."

I raised an eyebrow. "Which means there's a good chance he'd know how to tamper with a sound system."

"That's what I thought," Rose said. "So far, there's nothing to suggest he's behind the vandalism at the other shows, but there isn't anything that says he wasn't, either. I know a couple of people who taught at the same school. I have some feelers out."

The information superhighway had nothing on the Angels and their connections. They knew just about everyone in our half of the state, and if they didn't, they knew someone who did. As Jess liked to put it, they knew who was doing what and with whom.

As if she'd somehow known that I'd thought of Jess, Rose nudged my arm. "We need to get going if you're going to get down to Sam's on time." She looked at Avery. "Time to get the lead out, child," she said.

I made it to the pub with time to spare. As usual, Jess was holding a table. "What took you so long?" she asked.

"Sorry," I said, sliding onto a chair beside her and wondering if I had time to order before the music started. "I had to pick up Rose and Elvis and Avery."

She shifted in her seat so she was facing me, one arm leaning on the back of the chair. "So today was just a setup day, am I right?"

I nodded. "Yes. Competition starts tomorrow."

Jess grinned. "Go Elvis!"

"Do I have time to get food?" I asked.

"Absolutely." She held up a finger, literally one finger, and all at once a waiter headed in our direction.

"I will never understand how you do that."

"It's one of my superpowers," Jess said. "Aren't you glad I use them for the forces of good and not for the forces of evil?"

"Very glad," I said as the waiter reached us. I ordered a spicy chicken burger with extra cheese and the biggest size of onion rings because I knew that Jess—and Nick, if he showed up—would decimate them.

"So where's tall, dark and handsome?" Jess asked.

"Mac should be here anytime now." My phone buzzed in my pocket. I fished it out. It was Mac. "Hi. Where are you?" I said.

"I'm sorry, Sarah," he began.

"No," I groaned, slumping against the back of my chair. "What happened?"

"I'm on the way to Owl's Head."

"Tell me you have a really good reason."

"I do," he said. "Memphis had car trouble and he couldn't reach Cleveland so I'm going to rescue him and Alfred."

"What are they doing in Owl's Head?"

"Technically, based on the directions Memphis gave me, they're just outside of Owl's Head and it seems to have something to do with the case. Alfred didn't say what." I could hear his footsteps, which told me he was probably walking to his truck. "I doubt I'll be back in time to make it to the pub. I really am sorry."

I rested one arm on the top of my head. "I know you are," I said. "I'm starting to think this whole idea is cursed."

"It's not. I swear," Mac said. "Next week. It doesn't matter whose car breaks down or whose girlfriend threw all his clothes out on the highway. I will turn off my phone and I'll be there."

"Whose girlfriend threw their clothes all over highway?"

Mac laughed. "A story for another time. I need to get going. Have fun with Jess and Nick."

"I will," I said. "Drive safe."

I ended the call and blew out a breath, lifting my hair away from the side of my face.

"I take it Mac's not coming," Jess said.

I shook my head. "No. He had to go rescue Mr. P."

"I heard you say something about Owl's Head. What's in Owl's Head?"

I dug my fingers into the knot that had formed at the base of my skull. "Aside from Mr. P. and Cleveland's brother Memphis, I don't have a clue." I looked around. "I'm hungry. Where's my food and where's Nick? He said he was going to be here."

"Your food's coming." Jess pointed at the waiter headed our way from the kitchen. "And Nick just came in the door."

The chicken burger, onion rings and Nick all arrived at the same time. Jess gave the waiter a smile that temporarily short-circuited his brain cells. "Beer?" she asked Nick.

"Please," he said, shrugging off his jacket.

"Two of whatever you have local on tap and a small root beer when you have a minute, please," she said to the waiter.

"What if I didn't want root beer?" I said. I was already on my second onion ring.

"But you did," Jess said, snagging one for herself.

Nick dropped in the chair next to mine. "Where's Mac?" he asked.

"Rescuing Mr. P." I took a bite of my spicy chicken burger. It was very spicy.

Nick grabbed two onion rings. "Rescuing him from what?"

"Not from what, from where," I said. "Owl's Head."

"Do I want to know what Alfred is doing in Owl's Head? Does it have something to do with their case?"

"I don't know whether you want to know, but I don't have the answer to either of those questions so . . ." I held up both hands and shrugged.

The waiter was already on his way back with our drinks and just then I saw Sam headed for the small stage, holding his guitar.

"Okay, no more talk about cases or people stuck in Owl's Head—which I happen to think is a very nice place," Jess said. "It's time for food, music and beer!"

Nick and I managed to go the whole evening without violating Jess's rule. We talked about music. We talked about my brother, Liam, who was out of town. We talked about one of Nick's paramedic buddies who had taken in a baby skunk he'd found by the side of the road because everyone knows baby skunks can't spray until they're at least six months old.

"Number one: wrong," Nick said. "And number two, this is a guy who thinks he can guess how old a woman is and who generally gets it wrong by at least five years too many. Why on earth did he think he could figure out how old a skunk was?"

It was good to laugh, to not think about either case, to not be at odds with Nick; but in the back of my mind I kept wondering what was so important that Mr. P. and Memphis had driven down to Owl's Head on a Thursday night.

I didn't have to wait that long to find out. I dropped off Nick and Jess at their respective apartments and I was in my kitchen looking in the refrigerator trying to figure out what to take for lunch tomorrow when there was a knock at the door. Elvis was at the top of his cat tree. He lifted his head and looked pointedly at me.

"Yes, I heard that," I said.

I opened the door to find Mr. P. and Mac standing there. "I'm sorry to bother you this late," Mr. P. said, "but I have some information to share and I don't want to talk in front of Debra."

"Come in," I said. "What's going on?"

They stood in the middle of the living room. Elvis sat up as though he wanted to know as well. I glanced at Mac, who raised a shoulder to show he didn't know.

Mr. P. pushed his glasses up his nose. His expression was grave. "I'm sorry, Sarah," he said. "There isn't any easy way to say this. You were right. Christine was murdered."

Chapter 13

"What makes you say that?" I asked. Even though it was what I'd believed all along and even though Mr. P. hadn't doubted that belief I was a bit surprised by his certainty.

"It was what Nicolas told you about how the fire started," he said.

"The lamp falling over onto the sofa."

He nodded. "Yes, and the fact that it allegedly ignited a couple of spilled potato chips."

"So you don't think that's how the fire started?" Mac asked.

The old man took off his glasses, adjusted the nose-piece slightly and set them on his face again. "I actually do think that's how the fire started. I just don't believe it was an accident."

"Why?" I said.

"First of all, you said Nicolas told you the lamp was just like the one Charlotte has in her spare bedroom."

I nodded. "It's the one Gram gave her."

"Rose and I were with Isabelle when she bought

that lamp. It has a weighted bottom. It doesn't tip over easily."

"No offense, Alfred, but you have to have more than that," Mac said.

Mr. P. regarded him with a quiet smile. "I do."

I gestured at the sofa. "We don't have to stand in the middle of the room. Please, sit down."

Mr. P. took a seat on the couch. I sat down beside him and Mac pulled out one of the stools at the counter. Elvis jumped down from his tower. It seemed he didn't want to be left out. He launched himself onto my lap and turned so he was facing Mr. P.

The old man smiled and reached over to scratch behind the cat's left ear. Elvis began to purr. Mr. P. turned his attention to me. "You said that Nick told you when the lamp fell over, the heat from the bulb caused some potato chips that had been spilled on the sofa to ignite."

"That's right," I said.

"You know that I volunteer at a Legal Aid clinic."

I smiled. "Yes. That was one of the things that helped you get your private investigator's license."

He nodded. "Indeed. I knew there was something about potato chips and fires but it took me a little time to remember."

"Remember what?" Mac asked, dark eyes narrowed in curiosity.

"A client from several years ago, a young woman. We started talking and she told me about some of the ways people sometimes start fires."

"You mean arson?" I said.

Alfred shifted in his seat and brought his attention

back to me. "Yes, I do," he said. "I remembered her telling me about a fire that looked like it was caused by a short in a wall outlet but had in fact been set using potato chips. I wanted to know more. So I called her. I've helped her with a couple of things over the past couple of years," he added by way of explanation.

"And she lives in Owl's Head," Mac said.

Mr. P. glanced at him again. "Yes, she does. She has had some issues and she is a bit paranoid about conversations of any length over the phone in case the government is recording them. But she said I could come talk to her."

He held up a hand. "I know you may be thinking that she isn't a good source of information, but I can assure you that's not the case. She is extremely intelligent and very well-read."

Elvis shifted so he was leaning against me and I took over stroking his thick fur. "I trust your judgment," I said.

"Ella confirmed what I had remembered: that potato chips can be useful for starting a fire if one's intentions are less than honorable." His tone was matter-of-fact. "But what was even more interesting was that she told me about six months ago there was a fire in Portland that got a lot of coverage in the local papers. A fire that at first was believed to be accidental." There was a gleam in his eye. "A lamp fell over and the heat from the old incandescent lightbulb ignited some potato chips . . . spilled on a sofa."

I shook my head. "Another coincidence."

"So it seems."

"Alfred, did they catch the arsonist?" Mac asked. He was perched on the edge of the stool, one foot on the floor.

Mr. P. nodded again. "Yes, they did. There's no connection with what happened here."

"Except for the method," I said.

"According to Ella, the coverage in the newspapers was a blueprint for anyone looking to set a fire."

"Both Kimber Watson and Jeffery Walker live in Portland," I said. I remembered seeing that in the bios of the front-runners.

"So do Suzanne and Paul Lilley," Mr. P. said.

"Is it possible there *is* a connection between Christine's death and the vandalism at the other cat shows?"

Mr. P. didn't answer right away. "Maybe," he finally said. "I don't want to say yes, but I don't want to say no, either. I think for now we keep working on both cases, but we keep our eyes open for any potential links between the two."

That worked for me. Now that we knew Christine's death wasn't an accident, we could work on finding the person who'd killed her. I felt vindicated. "I was right. From the very beginning I was right."

Mr. P. reached over and patted my hand. "Yes, you were."

"We're going to catch the person who killed Christine," I said. I didn't phrase the words as a question because as far as I was concerned, there was no question to be asked.

"We most definitely are," he said. "I will share what I've learned with Nicolas in the morning—keeping Ella's name out of things, of course."

"We need to talk to Michelle as well. Maybe we should do that first. I'll call her in the morning."

"An excellent idea, my dear." He got to his feet. "I'll be here in the morning to drive in to the shop with you. We can tell Rosie everything then."

"I don't mind picking you up," I said. I stood up as well, setting Elvis on the sofa.

"Thank you, but the walk over will do me good."

I nodded. "All right, but call if it's cold or you change your mind."

He smiled. "I will." He gave my hand a squeeze. "I'll wait in the hallway," he said to Mac.

Mac wrapped his arms around me and I leaned my head against his chest. "I'm sorry I didn't get back in time to make it to the jam."

"It's okay," I said. "This is a lot more important."

"Do you think what Alfred found out will change Nick's mind?"

"I do. Nick may be pigheaded, but he won't ignore evidence and that's what this is." I tipped my head back to look up at Mac.

He smiled. "Get some sleep," he said. He kissed me and I could have happily stayed like that, but there was a little old man in the hallway waiting for a ride home.

We said good night and Mac left. I picked up Elvis. "Well, furball," I said, "it looks like we're finally getting somewhere."

"Mrrr," he said. Then he licked my chin. I took that as agreement.

Mr. P. arrived just as I was locking my door in the morning. "Good morning, Sarah, Elvis," he said. He wore a gray hat and a gray-and-red-striped scarf was wound around his neck several times. I knew Rose had knitted both for him.

Rose came out of her apartment then, smiling when she saw Mr. P. standing there. "Alfred, what a lovely surprise," she said. "I thought you were going straight to the arena with Cleveland."

"There's been a change of plans," he said. He glanced at me and I gave him an encouraging smile.

"Let's get going then," she said, bustling past us.

I unlocked the front passenger door for Rose and the back one for Mr. P. Elvis waited patiently at my feet. When I opened the driver's-side door he looked up expectantly at me.

"I don't think you've forgotten how to jump," I said.

He gave an indignant meow.

"He doesn't want to mess up his fur or his feet," Rose said. "Could you help him, please?"

I bent down to pick up the cat. "Don't get used to this," I whispered. He wrinkled his whiskers at me.

Elvis settled himself on the seat next to Rose. She fastened her seat belt and folded her hands in her lap. I saw her glance at Mr. P. in the back as I did up my own seat belt. She spoke before I could stick the key in the ignition. "Now that everyone is settled, would you two like to tell me what's going on?"

"What do you mean?" I said.

Rose shook her head. "Honestly, the two of you look like Elvis the time he got into my pie—minus the blueberry stains, of course."

I didn't think I looked guilty and I certainly didn't

think Mr. P. did, but Rose had some kind of extrasensory perception when it came to subterfuge. Probably all those years as a middle school teacher.

"Rosie, there is something we need to talk about," Mr. P. said, putting a hand on the back of the front seat and leaning forward. "We have some new information about the fire. I told Sarah last night and I would have told you, but neither of us wanted to upset Debra. Not yet."

Rose reached over and put a hand on top of his. "You did the right thing," she said. She glanced over at me and gave me a smile. "But we can't keep that kind of secret forever."

"Can we keep it until we talk to Michelle?" I asked. "I called her this morning and she's stopping by the shop a little later."

Her smile faded. "This new information is serious then."

"Yes, it is," Mr. P. said.

"I think we can wait at least that long," Rose said. "What on earth did you find out?"

I'd already told Rose about my conversation with Nick the day before. She'd shaken her head and said, "I'm going to need to have a talk with him."

Mr. P. explained how hearing about the lamp and the potato chips had twigged something for him. He told her about the trip to see the young woman in Owl's Head and about the arson story in the Portland-area papers.

"Have you talked to Nicolas yet?" Rose asked me.

I shook my head. "We wanted to see what Michelle thinks first."

She nodded slowly. "I think that's an excellent idea." She gave Mr. P.'s hand a squeeze and turned back around in her seat, giving Elvis a smile as she did. "Let's put the pedal to the metal," she said to me.

I stifled a smile. "Yes, ma'am," I said, turning the key in the ignition.

Charlotte and Mac were in the shop when we arrived. Rose bustled over to Mac. "Thank you for rescuing Alfred last night," she said, smiling up at him.

"It was no trouble," Mac said.

I knew he meant the words. He and Mr. P. had gotten close in the time Mac had been in North Harbor. I also knew that Mac would have done the same for any of the others. For Rose. For Avery. He would have driven to Canada or all the way to Boston without thinking twice. It was just the kind of person he was.

Charlotte was fastening her apron. "I talked to Nick last night," she said to me. "And I want to say I think he's wrong."

I knew she was referring to Nick's opinion about the fire.

"Alfred has some information that's going to change his mind," Rose said. I liked her confidence.

"Good," Charlotte said. "Sometimes Nick just can't see the forest for the trees." She turned her head to look at me. "And no comments about apples and trees."

I held up a hand. "I don't have a thing to say about trees whatsoever. In fact, I'm going up to make the tea."

"I'll bring Charlotte up to date," Rose said.

Mr. P. nodded. "I'm going to find those newspaper articles."

Mac looked around. "And I'm going to . . . do something."

I was leaning against the counter in the staff room, waiting for the kettle to boil a couple of minutes later when Mac appeared in the doorway.

"I thought you were doing . . . something," I teased.

He grinned. "I was." He held out a bag of coffee. "We were out."

"How did that happen?" I said. I'd been lost in thought and hadn't even pulled out the coffeepot.

He gave an elaborate shrug. "I don't know. It couldn't be because someone ran out of coffee at home and took the spare bag that was here."

"Can't be," I said. "We have a policy against that kind of thing."

He set the coffee on the counter next to the teapot and kissed me. "Do we have a policy against that?"

"Absolutely not," I said.

Mac reached past me for the filter and the coffeepot.

"That was good of you to drive down to Owl's Head last night," I said.

"It really wasn't a problem." He got the coffee scoop out of the drawer to my left. "I'm just sorry I didn't make it to the jam."

"Next time." I smiled. "Just so you know, Jess says she's going to rope and tie you like a rodeo steer."

"Why do I think she's perfectly capable of that?" he asked.

I folded my arms over my chest. "Because she is. She dated a bullfighter. Not the kind with the red cape. The kind who distracts the bull at a rodeo. Plus, she's really good at knots."

Mac held up his thumb and finger about half an inch apart. "That scares me just a little bit."

I grinned. "It should."

He leaned against the counter next to me.

"Do you think what Mr. P. learned last night will convince Michelle and Nick *and* the arson investigator that Christine's death wasn't an accident?" I asked.

Mac nodded. "I do. If Alfred's friend knew about that fire in Portland and all the coverage it got, you can bet the investigator here does."

"I've been so focused on trying to convince Nick that fire *wasn't* an accident and now I'm finding I almost wish it had been."

"What do you mean?" he said.

"Someone killed Christine. Someone deliberately set the fire. It didn't happen because of bad wiring or a faulty outlet. It happened because someone planned it. I'm not saying I think it was a deliberate attempt to kill her, but it had the same result." I sighed softly.

"And whoever it was will pay for that," Mac said. "The police—all of us—will catch the person who started that fire."

"You sound pretty confident," I said.

He smiled. "I am. Remember, we're on the side of the Angels."

Michelle showed up about half an hour later. Mac had brought in two more chairs to show Maud Fitch, who had called to say she'd be stopping in that afternoon. I was wiping the dust off them when Michelle came in the back door.

"It's good to see you," I said, giving her a hug.

"You too," she said.

Ever since Liz had proven that Michelle's father hadn't been guilty of the embezzlement that had sent him to prison, Michelle had seemed happier. Even though Rob Andrews had died years earlier, Liz had used her considerable influence and connections to make sure his innocence made the news all over the state. Michelle still wore her father's watch on her left arm, but now when she looked at it she smiled.

"You have some information about the fire on Tuesday night." She was wearing gray pants with a pale blue shirt and a black wool jacket. Her red hair was pulled back into a ponytail.

I nodded. "Rose and Mr. P. are waiting for us in the office," I said.

We walked across the workroom and I knocked on the open door.

Mr. P. looked up from his computer. "Good morning," he said with a smile.

Michelle smiled back at him. "Good morning, Alfred," she said.

Rose was just ending a call on her cell phone. "Hello, Michelle," she said. "I received a note from your mother just a few days ago. It was lovely to hear from her."

"She was so happy to get the photos you sent her."

Rose nodded. "I'm glad."

Revitalization of the harbor front had been going

on for months now. We had hosted an auction on our website of items, mostly toys and photographs, that had been found in several of the buildings that were torn down as part of the new development. Rose had bought a collection of photos, many of them more than thirty years old. She and Avery had had great fun tracking down the people in the pictures and getting the photographs to them. There had been several of Michelle's parents that looked like they had been taken during some sort of summer festival. She had gotten her mother's address from Michelle and sent the photos to her. Rose had smiled all day after the thank-you note arrived.

"Sarah says you have some information about the fire Tuesday night," Michelle said.

Mr. P. nodded. He explained about learning how the fire began without mentioning Nick's name, although Michelle had to guess that was where the information came from. He told her how things twigged for him after he heard about the lamp and the potato chips. And he recounted the trip to Owl's Head.

"I gave my word that I wouldn't give up my source, but I do have the links to the newspaper articles," he said.

"It's all right," Michelle said. "I don't need them."

I'd watched as Mr. P. talked and I realized that Michelle didn't seem surprised by his conclusions.

"Something's changed in the last day," I said.

She nodded. "It's going to be news when we have a press conference at lunchtime so I'll tell the three of you now. Christine Eldridge's death is being investi-

gated as a homicide. Tom Manning, the arson investigator, came to the same conclusions as you did."

Rose and Mr. P. looked as surprised as I felt. "How?"
I asked.

"I'm sorry, Sarah," Michelle said. "That's all I can
tell you."

She shifted her attention to Rose and Mr. P. "I know
there's no point in telling you not to investigate, but
please call me if you find anything and don't take
any . . . risky chances."

"When we know something, so will you," Rose said.
I noticed she didn't say how quickly Michelle would
know.

Michelle glanced at her watch. "I know you and
Sarah had lunch with Christine and her friend the
day of the fire. Did she say anything about any trouble with anyone—a neighbor, someone in her classes,
someone at the earlier cat shows?"

Rose shook her head. "No."

I hesitated.

"Sarah?" Michelle said, green eyes narrowing.

"You know that the Angels have been investigating some incidences of sabotage at a couple of cat
shows."

"I heard."

Rose looked at me. "What is it?"

"Christine did say something that at the time I dismissed, but now I'm not sure. We were talking about
the vandalism that had happened at the earlier cat
shows and she said, 'Maybe it doesn't have anything
to do with the cats. Maybe it's more personal.'"

"Did you ask her what she meant?" Michelle said.

"I did. She said she was just speculating."

"But now you think she wasn't?" Mr. P. said.

"Maybe."

"Alfred, do you have any serious suspects?" Michelle said to Mr. P.

"I'm sorry to say we don't. We're looking closely at several people, but there's nothing that points directly at anyone. And there were no issues at the Searsport show and there haven't been so far at this one." His phone rang then. He picked it up from his desk and checked the screen. I saw a flash of something—concern, maybe—cross his face. "I'm sorry," he said. "I have to take this. Please excuse me." He walked out into the workroom.

Michelle touched her jacket pocket as though checking to make sure she had her own phone. "Can the two of you think of anything else I should know?"

I looked at Rose. She shook her head. "I don't think there is anything else," I said.

She nodded. "I'm on my way to talk to Debra Martinez. Maybe she'll have some ideas."

"Debra is staying with me," Rose said. "She should be there for about another hour before she leaves for the arena." She frowned. "Are you going now?"

"I am," Michelle said.

"Could I go with you?" Rose asked. "Just to be moral support."

Michelle hesitated for a moment. "All right."

Rose smiled. "Thank you. I just need to get my coat." She looked at me. "I'll drive over to the arena with Debra and if anything changes I'll call you."

"I'll bring Mr. P. and Elvis," I said.

Just then Alfred came back in. His expression was somber, his lips pulled in a tight line. "It appears I spoke too soon," he said. "There's been a problem at the arena."

"What happened?" Michelle immediately turned toward him.

"There were two mice found in one of the booths."

"Good heavens! How did that happen?" Rose exclaimed. "Where did they come from? The pest control company did a sweep on Tuesday before anyone was allowed in to set up."

"Cleveland thinks these are domesticated mice," Mr. P. said.

"So pets?" Michelle said.

Mr. P. nodded.

"How does he know that?" I asked.

"I'm not certain," the old man said, "but I believe if anyone would know the difference, it would be Cleveland."

I thought about some of the places Cleveland had gone picking in and had to agree.

"So you think this was vandalism?" Michelle asked.

"I do," Mr. P. said. "According to Cleveland, the damage to the vendor's products looks more like it was done by a person tearing things apart than by a rodent's teeth. And again, I'm deferring to him on this."

Michelle nodded her agreement. "Do you want the police involved?"

"Can it be done quietly?" he asked.

"As long as nothing ties this act of alleged vandalism to Christine Eldridge's death, yes."

"Memphis is going to review all the security footage from last night," Mr. P. said. "I'll have him send you a copy."

Michelle nodded. "Thank you," she said.

Rose gestured to the doorway. "I'll only be a minute," she said.

While Rose went to get her coat and bag, I walked to the back door with Michelle.

"I'll be checking in with Nick later today," she said. She pulled out her phone, checked the screen and put it back in her pocket. "He's probably already talked to Tom Manning. I take it you don't mind if I share what Alfred discovered."

I shook my head. "No, that's not a problem." I didn't say that Rose considered Nick part of the team so if Michelle didn't update him Rose would.

I thought about Charlotte wanting me to find someone for Nick and wondered for a moment if he and Michelle would be a match. As quickly as the thought came, I dismissed it. If things didn't work out they'd still have to work together.

"Could we have dinner sometime soon?" Michelle asked. "I'm thinking about starting to look for a house and I'd like to pick your brain. I know nothing about home ownership."

"I love the idea," I said. "And if you eventually find something you like, I'll loan you Liam to check it out for you." My brother was a building contractor and his advice had been invaluable when I'd been looking at my old Victorian.

"Seriously, do you think he would mind?"

I gave her an incredulous look. "Would Liam mind

being asked to give his opinion on a house—or anything, for that matter?"

Michelle laughed. "Okay, I get your point. But I really would like your opinion as well."

I smiled at her. "You may regret saying that, but you can have it."

Rose came back then, wearing her jacket and carrying her tote bag. It reminded me of Mary Poppins's carpetbag. I was never really sure what Rose was going to pull out of it.

Michelle and Rose headed across the parking lot to Michelle's car. I turned to go back into the shop and Mr. P. was standing in the office door. "I just wanted to say you were correct about the fire from the very beginning," he said. "And you stood your ground. You should be proud of yourself."

"So what happens now?" I said.

He gave me a small smile. "That's simple: We catch the culprit."

Chapter 14

I went upstairs and got another cup of coffee then I came back down to the shop to bring Mac up to date on Michelle's visit. There were no customers and Charlotte was in the workroom ironing a beautiful cream linen tablecloth that she was convinced would sell if we displayed it properly. I was equally certain it wouldn't because it needed to be starched and steam-ironed to look its best and most people didn't have time for that anymore.

"So what happens now?" Mac asked.

"I'm going to take Mr. P. and Elvis over to the show in a little while," I said. "As for the case, we keep digging. I am glad Michelle is involved now, though. The police have resources the Angels don't."

"The Angels have connections the police don't," he said. "Don't discount that."

"Good point," I said, shifting restlessly from one foot to the other.

Mac inclined his head toward the street. "Go," he said.

I frowned at him. "Go where?"

"Get Elvis, get Alfred and go over to the show."

"Are you trying to get rid of me?"

He smiled. "Of course not, but you know you want to find out what's going on over there and so does Alfred. So do it. I'm here. So is Charlotte. And Avery will be along in a little while. We can handle things here. And look at Elvis. He's a bundle of nervous energy."

Elvis was sprawled on his back in the reproduction Eames chair that I had brought in from the garage workshop, his tail hanging over the edge of the seat.

"Okay, I'll go," I said. "But only because Elvis is so antsy."

Mac pressed a hand to his chest. "You just give and give," he said with mock solemnity.

I laughed and went out to the Angels' office to see if Mr. P. felt like leaving.

Alfred was ready to go over to the arena complex. I gathered up Elvis and his things and we were quickly on our way. Because we were early, I found a spot to park in the second row of the lot. Mr. P. took one of the bags Rose had packed and I got the other. Rose and Debra weren't inside yet and I hoped things were going well with Michelle.

"Sarah, I need a small favor," Mr. P. said, setting the bag he was carrying under the table at our station.

"Of course," I said. "What is it?"

"Could you stay here with Elvis until Rosie arrives? I'd like to go over to the other building and talk to Cleveland."

"Of course I can." I lifted Elvis out of the bag. He yawned and looked around.

"You're sure?" he said.

I smiled. "Positive. We might walk around and scope out the competition." As if he'd understood my words, Elvis took a couple of passes at his face with one paw.

Mr. P. left and Elvis and I walked down to the end of our row, looking at the banners that were hung all over the space. "'Dogs have owners. Cats have staff,'" I read aloud.

"Mrrr," Elvis said.

"Yeah, I thought you'd like that one. How about this? 'In ancient times cats were worshipped as gods. They have not forgotten this.' Terry Pratchett. Very wise man."

Elvis bobbed his head as if in agreement.

I spotted another banner, a little farther down. "This one is an old English proverb. 'In a cat's eye, all things belong to cats.'" I scratched the top of his head. "Why do all of these sayings seem to apply perfectly to you?"

All I got for a response was an unblinking, green-eyed stare.

At the end of the aisle we turned and started back to our station. I kept on reading the overhead signs. "I like this one," I said to Elvis. "'Dogs come when they're called. Cats take a message and get back to you.'"

We had just made it back to our section when Kimber Watson almost ran into us. Her head was bent over her phone and her cat was in a black and gold carrier slung over her shoulder. She stopped abruptly and blinked at me.

"Are you all right?" I asked. Elvis eyed her, squinting his green eyes as though he was trying to decide if she was friend or foe.

"I know you," Kimber said, pointing a stubby finger at me. "You were outside the arena with an older woman the other day when security was being so unreasonable."

I nodded. "That's right. Has Basil adjusted to the space?"

"He's been very unsettled. Which wouldn't have happened if I'd just been able to let him feel the energy of the room in advance."

I glanced at the carrier bag. Basil didn't look unsettled. He appeared to be sound asleep.

"I'm sure he'll do well in the competition," I said.

Kimber frowned in annoyance. "Well, of course he will. Basil is a professional." She squinted at Elvis. "This moogy is yours?" she asked.

I had no idea what a moogy was, but the way she said the word didn't make it sound like a compliment. "Yes," I said. "This is Elvis."

She held out her fingers and let him sniff them, then ran her hand over his fur. "He does have a nice coat." She looked around. "Do you know where Debra Martinez is?"

"She isn't here yet, but she should be arriving in just a few minutes. Would you like me to give her a message?"

"I wanted to tell her I was sorry about her friend," Kimber said. "I'll come back." She turned to leave.

"Good luck today," I said.

She looked back over her shoulder at me. "I make my own luck," she said.

I watched her walk away and wondered what exactly that meant.

Rose and Debra showed up with Socrates just as I was getting Elvis settled in his tent.

Debra was more composed than I expected. She looked at Rose. "Sarah knows?" she asked.

Rose nodded. "Yes."

"I'm sorry," I said. "I wish that there hadn't been a fire at all and I wish . . ." I couldn't finish the sentence.

"I want to know who killed Christine and why," Debra said.

I saw the determination in Rose's eyes. I knew what she was going to say before she spoke. "I give you my word," she said to Debra, "we will figure it out."

I was pulling out of the arena parking lot when I realized I never did pack any lunch because Mac and Mr. P. had shown up at my door. I decided to drive over to the sandwich shop.

"Hey, Sarah," Glenn said. "I'm so sorry about your friend. I liked her. She had a great laugh."

"You're right," I said. "She did." I cleared my throat. "What's the sandwich special today?"

"Turkey with cheese and arugula."

"Okay, I'll have that and coffee." I handed over my stainless steel mug. Avery had reminded me more than once that I used too many disposable cups and I was trying to do better.

"How's Elvis doing in the show?" Glenn asked as he poured my coffee.

"Judging starts today," I said.

He smiled. "I'll cross my fingers." He handed me my mug. "Hey, do you remember the people filming the reality show over the summer?"

I made a bit of a face. "Vividly. I think they messed up traffic all over town."

"Well, get ready for that to happen again. The producer is back in town."

"I thought I saw him at the pet expo," I said. "I guess I was right."

"Rumor has it he's teaming up with a couple who know the cat show circuit to do a pilot for a partly scripted reality show about cat show people."

I took a sip of my coffee. "What does 'partly scripted' mean?"

Glenn shrugged. "From what I can tell, it means the reality won't be very real. Apparently this couple, whoever they are, will play quirky cat lovers and try to get a rise out of other people." He made air quotes when he said the word "quirky."

I rested my cup on the counter and folded my hands around it. "I think the whole thing sounds mean."

"I agree," Glenn said. "And let's face it, the treasure hunt idea from the summer didn't exactly bring out the best in people." He glanced over his shoulder. "I'll go check on your sandwich."

He came back with my lunch and I paid and let him top up my coffee, on the house.

"Tell Elvis I'm rooting for him."

I laughed. "I will," I said.

I slid behind the wheel and fastened my seat belt, but I didn't start the SUV. I thought about what Glenn had just told me, especially the part about the structure of the potential show: a couple pretending to be quirky cat lovers trying to get a rise out of other people. The first thing that had occurred to me was the Lilleys in their ridiculous disguises. Was that why they had shown up at the Searsport show? Was that why Cleveland had seen them shooting video in the parking lot? People could go to some pretty ridiculous extremes to get on TV, I'd learned when the treasure show had been filming. Could it be as simple as the Lilleys being involved in this reality show? I didn't know, but I was betting Mr. P. could find out.

I pulled into the Second Chance parking lot just as Avery was coming up the sidewalk. I waited for her and she smiled when she saw my coffee mug.

"If that had a green drink, it would be even better," she said. I saw a smile pull at the corners of her eyes and mouth and realized she was teasing for the most part.

"Coffee beans are green before they're roasted," I said.

She smiled. "You're funny."

"How did the parent-teacher meetings go?" I asked.

Avery made a face. "Nonna agreed with my French teacher that I have a bad attitude and now I have extra practice three times a week. She also agreed with me that he has a crappy accent, but she said that his accent and my attitude have nothing to do with each other." She sent two bracelets spinning around her arm like two tiny hula hoops. "And Mr. Harrison, my gym teacher, has to take a seminar on gender equality in the classroom." She looked up and grinned. "Nonna rocks!"

I grinned back at her. "She absolutely does."

"Could I switch and work tomorrow morning instead of tomorrow afternoon?" Avery asked then, abruptly changing the subject.

"If Charlotte will switch with you, yes," I said.

"I want to go to the cat show to see how Elvis and some of the other cats are doing, and I want Greg to meet Socrates."

Greg was Avery's sort-of boyfriend. He was quiet and serious and both Rose and Charlotte were always trying to feed him, which worked out well because he had the typical teenage boy's bottomless pit of an appetite.

"Elvis will love having a cheering section," I said.

Avery held open the back door. "I decided I'm going to volunteer with the cats at the animal shelter. I talked to a guy from there the other day. He said they could always use more volunteers."

"That's a great idea. You could talk to Jane. She's been volunteering there for years."

"Nonna's Jane?" She frowned. "I didn't know that."

Jane Evans was Liz's assistant and probably the only person on the planet who could get away with telling Liz what to do. "You'll have to clean cages and empty litter boxes," I warned.

"I don't care," she said. "I thought Elvis was the only cat I liked, but it turns out I like pretty much all of them. I like Elvis better than some people."

I felt the same way some days myself.

"And I like Socrates, and there's a Sphynx cat named Fifi, who's such a sweetie. And I like Nikita, but her owner is kind of cheap."

She was talking about Jeffery. I gave her a look.

"Well, he is," she said with a shrug. "His hair-dye job isn't very good."

"That doesn't make him cheap," I said, stopping next to the workbench. Mac—or maybe Charlotte—had left a large box sitting there. "Maybe it just didn't turn out."

"It's not the only thing. Remember before the show when I was getting a bunch of Elvis stuff for Mr. P?"

I nodded. "I remember." I lifted a flap on the top of the box and looked inside. There were several large platters wrapped in newsprint. Maybe something a repeat customer had called looking for?

"I saw Nikita's owner. He was in the store. There's a coffee shop right next door and he picked up a half-empty bag of chips someone had walked away from when he thought no one was looking." She frowned. "And who eats chips for breakfast, anyway?"

"People eat cold pizza for breakfast. And as for Jeffery Walker, maybe he has money problems."

Avery gave a snort of derision. "Sarah, he drives a BMW."

"So maybe he's a freegan, someone who tries to use up food other people don't finish. Try not to be so judgy."

"Fine," she said. "But I still say scoring chips that someone else left behind is just cheap; it's not saving the planet." She disappeared into the shop.

I just stood there. Avery had seen Jeffery Walker with a half-full bag of chips. My first impulse was to think that she was wrong or hadn't seen what she thought she'd seen. Maybe he'd absent-mindedly picked them up because he was thinking about something else. It didn't mean the man had started the fire that killed Christine; although if he had, it would make sense that he hadn't bought a bag of chips—a transaction someone might remember.

On the other hand, Christine had believed Jeffery was cheating and they had argued. I remembered what Rose said about the potential for big money for this year's winners. I knew that money made people do stupid, stupid things.

It was a quiet afternoon broken up by Maud Fitch coming in to buy four chairs and by two cars of friends on their way to a wedding in Nova Scotia. After much discussion, they had bought a beautiful quilt for the bride and groom, laughing about it going on the honeymoon bed. It made me smile to listen to them, especially since one of the women had explained that the happy couple were in their seventies.

"I'm a sucker for a happily-ever-after ending," Charlotte said, putting one arm around my shoulders.

"Me, too," I said, leaning against her.

I was getting ready to head over to the arena when Mac came in from the workshop. He'd been working on the teak benches all afternoon, repairing and regluing the joints. "How about dinner a little later?" he asked.

"Does it involve me cooking?" I said. "I will. I just want you to be aware that my success rate is still at about the seventy-five percent mark." Considering that not that long ago I'd been pretty much incapable of cooking anything—at least without starting a fire of some sort—that was a pretty big accomplishment.

And it was only because of Rose's and Charlotte's persistence. Still, if I was cooking for someone, I generally felt better if they knew there was a possibility that we could end up with take-out pizza.

"It does not involve you cooking," Mac said with a smile. "We can go down to The Black Bear for dinner or we can stay in and I'll make burgers and my famous sweet potato fries."

"Stay in," I immediately said. I loved fries of any kind almost as much as I loved coffee and chocolate. "You can cook in my kitchen if you like. It's bigger."

He smiled. "Sounds good."

Before I left I gave him my spare key. "We shouldn't be too long, but it is Rose and Mr. P. so I'm not making any promises."

When I got to the show, I found Elvis smelled like sardines. There was no sign of Debra and Socrates. Mr. P. was on his cell phone. "I take it we have reason to celebrate," I said to Rose.

Rose smiled. "Yes, we do. Both our boys are sitting very comfortably in second place waiting to make their runs at the top spot. The judge called Elvis roguishly handsome."

"The judge is right," I said.

The rogue in question licked his whiskers.

"Do I have a minute to go talk to Junie?" Rose asked. "She's up on everything that's going on and there are a couple of things I want to ask her about."

"Go ahead," I said.

Rose handed the cat over to me and brushed a bit of cat hair from her sleeve. "I won't be long," she said.

"I'm proud of you," I told Elvis. He nuzzled my

chin, which might have meant *Thank you*, and might have meant *Are there any more sardines?* "Mac is making our supper," I added. He looked pretty pleased to me.

Mr. P. ended his call. "Hello, Sarah," he said. "How was your afternoon?"

I smiled. "It was good." I told him about the long-time friends on their way to the wedding that had been a very long time in the making.

"You're never too old to find true love," he said with a smile of his own.

I thought about him and Rose, about Gram and John. About Mac and I.

"I like that thought," I said. Elvis head butted my hand and I scratched under his chin, which started him purring. "There are a couple of things I need to talk to you about."

"I need to talk to you as well." He looked at something over my shoulder. I turned just as Memphis joined us carrying an iPad.

He smiled. "Hey, Sarah."

"Hi, Memphis," I said.

"Since Memphis is here, do you mind if I go first?" Mr. P. asked.

"Merow," Elvis answered.

I smiled at Mr. P. "No, we don't."

He nodded at Memphis, who swiped at the screen of his iPad a couple of times and then turned it so I could see. "This is security footage from early this morning," he said.

The images were black-and-white but sharp and clear. I had no trouble recognizing Jeffery Walker as the person trying to get into the building.

"So you think Jeffery is responsible for the mice Cleveland found at the pet expo?" I asked.

"Man is carrying a shopping bag that has something in it," Memphis pointed out.

"Does he actually get in?"

Mr. P. shook his head. "Not via this door. But there are two others and we've been having problems with the camera at one of them."

"Before we go any further I need to share something," I said. I told them what Avery had told me, how she'd seen Jeffery snag a bag of chips from a table.

Some of the color drained from Mr. P.'s face. Memphis looked at him, one eyebrow arching up.

"She wouldn't make something like this up. I admit I have a hard time coming up with a reason that Jeffery would have wanted to start a fire at Christine's apartment, but they did have an argument and there are a lot more money and endorsements up for grabs this year, as I understand things. I know Christine believed Jeffery was cheating."

"We need to talk to the man," Mr. P. said.

"Fine, but not without me," Memphis countered.

Mr. P. nodded. "All right."

"Where is Nikita's staging area?" I asked.

He pointed to the end of the middle row on the other side of the aisle. "Over there."

"Let's do it," Memphis said.

Tim showed up just as we were leaving.

"Debra will be right back," Mr. P. said.

"Okay, thanks," Tim said. "I'll wait." He looked at me. "I got some good photos of Elvis today. If you're around tomorrow and you have time, you can take a look at them." He gave me a tentative smile. "There's a great one of him with his head to one side and a paw in the air like he's about to high-five the judge."

"I'd like to see them," I said. He seemed less stand-offish than he had before. I wondered if that was because of Christine's death. They'd known each other a long time.

He nodded, leaning against the table next to Socrates's empty tent. "I'll be around all weekend. Just let me know when you have some time."

"Is it all right if I bring Elvis?" I asked Mr. P. I didn't want to wait for Rose and miss the conversation with Jeffery.

"It's fine with me," the old man said.

He glanced at Memphis, who shrugged a shoulder. "Hey, it's all right with me. It's not like there's not cats all over this building."

We started in the direction Mr. P. had indicated.

"Rose said Socrates is in second place," I said. "Who has first place at the moment?" Elvis was hang-ing over the side of my arm, looking at every staging area we passed.

"Nikita," Mr. P. said. "Debra thinks Socrates misses Christine. He was lacking a bit of his usual spark to-day." He hiked his pants up a little higher. Not that they needed it.

"That can happen," Memphis said. "Cats can be very attuned to the emotions around them."

"Are you a cat person?" I asked.

He smiled. "Damn straight. I have four. I'm think-ing about entering them in the show next year." He nudged Mr. P. with an elbow. "What do you say, Alfred? I'd need a second pair of hands."

"I'd be honored," Mr. P. said. "Assuming Sarah and Elvis don't need me."

"We'll let you know," I said. "I have a question, though: Do you know what a moogy is?"

"It's a cat that's considered to be ordinary," Memphis said. "Why are you asking?"

I thought about Kimber. Elvis was far from ordinary. "I just heard the term and wondered what it meant."

"It's really just a word some people use to distinguish between regular cats and ones whose bloodlines can be traced back for generations," Memphis said. He glanced at Mr. P. again. "Alfred, I think I should take the lead here."

Mr. P. nodded. "All right."

We found Jeffery getting Nikita settled in a large black carrier bag. "Hello," he said with a smile that included Elvis. "Is there something I can help you with?"

Mr. P. introduced Memphis as his friend and part of the security team for the cat show and the pet expo.

Memphis was wearing a lanyard with his ID badge tucked inside the chest pocket of the long-sleeved, body-hugging black T-shirt he was wearing. He pulled the badge out and showed it to Jeffery, who looked a little puzzled. "Mr. Walker, I'd like to show you some security footage from this morning," he said.

"All right," Jeffery said. If he had any idea what he was about to see, it didn't show.

Memphis tapped the screen of the iPad a couple of

times and swiped a couple more. Then he turned the tablet around so the other man could watch the video.

Jeffery was very smooth. "That's me," he said.

Memphis nodded. "Yes, sir. I'm aware of that."

"You're probably wondering what I was doing."

"It looked to me that what you're doing is trying to break into the building," Memphis said. He was just as cool.

Jeffery nodded. "I can see why you think that. What actually happened is that I left my wallet behind at one of the vendors last night and I was just trying to see if there was anyone left inside who could let me in so I could get it."

Memphis studied him for a long moment without speaking. It was long enough that anyone else would have spoken just to break the silence. "At quarter to five in the morning," Memphis said. "If you're going to lie, sir, come up with a better one than that."

Elvis leaned sideways and nudged Jeffery's arm. He began to absently stroke the cat's fur.

"What were you really doing?" Mr. P. asked.

"I don't see that it's really any of your business," Jeffery said.

Memphis shrugged. "I have no problem calling the police to handle this. It will be one less thing on my plate."

When Jeffery didn't respond, Memphis gave him a polite smile. "Thank you for your time," he said. He turned to walk away. I'd seen Liz use the same trick. It worked just as well for Memphis and without the benefit of high heels.

"Wait," Jeffery said. His composure was slipping a little.

Memphis turned around and looked expectantly at the other man.

"Fine. I was trying to get into the building. But I wasn't trying to do any damage. I just needed to get some things I'd left behind. That's all."

That lie wasn't any better than the previous one he'd told.

"What was in the shopping bag?" Memphis asked.

"Nothing important."

His skill at not telling the truth was rapidly going downhill.

"Where did you get the mice?" Mr. P. asked in the same tone of voice he might have used to ask where the man had bought his shoes.

Jeffery looked genuinely surprised. "Mice?" he said. "I don't know what you're talking about."

"I'm talking about the two that you put in a booth at the expo."

Jeffery shook his head, a frown carving lines into his forehead. "I didn't put any rodents in a booth. Where would I even get one? And why would I do something like that?"

He was still petting Elvis without really paying any attention. And Elvis was still happily settled in my arms.

I looked over at Mr. P., who had noticed the same thing. Jeffery was telling the truth. As strange as it seemed, the cat had an uncanny knack for figuring out when a person was lying. When someone was stroking his fur, if they weren't being completely honest about whatever they happened to be talking about, Elvis somehow knew, that knowledge evident in the disdainful expression on his furry face.

Jess's theory was that Elvis was the feline version of a polygraph machine. Somehow he was responding to changes in a person's heartbeat, breathing and perspiration. Mac had pointed out that since part of a dog's brain was devoted to deciphering emotions in human's voices, why couldn't Elvis differentiate between lies and the truth? Both explanations made sense to me. The problem was that the feline lie detector acted as one only when it suited him.

"What was in the bag, sir?" Memphis asked again. Even though he wasn't as big a man as Cleveland, he could still be imposing.

Jeffery weighed his words for a moment. "Catnip spray," he finally said.

He was telling the truth, at least as far as Elvis was concerned. "Nikita suffers from anxiety and it helps her. I wanted to spray it around the judging area before anyone else was around just to help her relax."

"The use of catnip spray isn't permitted at the show. At any of the shows," Mr. P. said.

"People can use antianxiety medications," Jeffery said, an edge of indignation in his tone. "Why not cats? It's all-natural."

"Where were you Tuesday night?" I asked.

"I was home in Portland," he said.

"Where were you about eight thirty?"

"I was picking up more of the spray from the herbalist who makes it. Nikita uses her proprietary blend."

He suddenly seemed to realize why I was asking. "Wait a minute," he said. "You can't think that I had anything to do with Christine Eldridge's death?"

He'd stopped stroking the cat's fur and Elvis was moving restlessly in my arms. I shifted him to my other shoulder. "You two argued."

Jeffery's dark eyes flashed. "Yes, we argued. It was meaningless. Christine threatened to tell the Hartmans about the catnip spray, but I wasn't worried."

"Why?" Mr. P. asked. Memphis seemed intrigued by the conversation, content for the moment to just stand and listen.

"Because I'm reasonably certain they know and they don't care. The rivalry among Nikita, Socrates and Basil is bringing in more people to the shows, which means more money for them." His expression changed, softened a little. "I would never have hurt Christine. Most of the people who take part in these shows have known each other for years and it's not always easy to make friends, but Christine was kind to me. Winning is what matters to me, but not at the cost of someone's life."

Elvis leaned forward once more, vying for Jeffery's attention, and once again Jeffery smiled at the cat and reached over to scratch behind his ear. Elvis made a little exhalation of happiness.

There was one more thing I had to ask. "Do you like potato chips?"

He frowned at me and then suddenly he sighed and shook his head, closing his eyes for a brief moment. "This show is just one giant hive of gossip," he said. "I mentioned one time in front of two people—

just two—that I had to give up potato chips because of my high blood pressure and it was a bit of a challenge and now everyone is the food police. Yes, I swiped three chips from a bag Debra had today—awful ketchup flavor, by the way—and I will bring her a new bag tomorrow."

"Ever picked up a discarded bag? Say, off a table or the top of a trash can."

Color flooded Jeffery's face. "Do I have to share every stupid thing I've ever done?"

I'd gone too far. I shook my head. "I'm sorry," I said. "You don't."

My instincts said he was telling the truth and Elvis had confirmed it.

Memphis held out his hand. "Thank you, Mr. Walker," he said. "As far as I'm concerned, this is settled."

Jeffery nodded. "Thank you."

"Good luck tomorrow," I said.

"You as well." I think he was talking more to Elvis than to me.

We headed back to our staging area. "I believe him," Mr. P. said. "About the catnip spray, about the fire, about everything."

"So do I," Memphis said. "I'll check his alibi, but I'm confident I won't find anything."

"Do you think the catnip spray really does give Nikita any kind of advantage?" I asked.

"Cat already looked pretty mellow to me," Memphis said.

"I can't believe how competitive the man is."

Memphis smiled. He tipped his head in Elvis's direction. "Right. And you don't want the King of Rock and Roll here to take the top spot tomorrow?"

"Not enough to cheat," I said.

"Good for you," he said. "But for a lot of people, the line that they won't cross isn't exactly carved in stone. After all, no one remembers the losers."

Chapter 15

"I need to get over to the other building," Memphis said to Mr. P. when we reached the center aisle between the rows of tables. "I'll call you later." He reached over and gave Elvis a scratch under his chin. "Good to see you, Sarah," he said to me.

Once Memphis was gone Mr. P. looked at me. "You saw Elvis," he said.

I nodded. "I did."

"There doesn't seem to be any doubt Jeffery was telling the truth."

"For what it's worth, I would have believed him without confirmation from Elvis," I said. "It all makes sense and you or Memphis can check his alibi. It would have been stupid to give you a story you could easily show was a lie."

Mr. P. adjusted his glasses. "I will check to make sure none of what he told us was a fabrication. But like you, I don't think he had anything to do with the sabotage or with Christine's death."

"I'm sorry I hijacked the conversation," I said.

Something had caught Elvis's attention again and he was hanging halfway over my arm. "I don't know what came over me. I needed to know if Jeffery had set that fire. I needed to see what his reaction was."

"There's no need to apologize," Mr. P. said. "I understand how you feel. And the good news is we can move on to other suspects."

As we approached our staging space I could see that Debra and Socrates had returned. Tim had stayed to wait for them and he and Debra were arguing. Tim was talking, hands waving through the air. Debra's arms were crossed over her chest, shoulders hunched. I couldn't make out what they were saying, but I could hear how anger was sharpening both of their voices. They stopped talking when they caught sight of us. Color flooded Debra's face and Tim looked away, his mouth pulled into a thin, tight line. I noticed that Socrates had moved to the back of his cage, his copper eyes firmly fixed on Debra.

"I'm sorry," she said. "Tim and I were having a disagreement and I got a little loud."

"It's all right," I said. "We didn't mean to intrude."

Tim turned to face us. "You're not intruding. I was pushing. It's my fault." His gaze shifted to Debra. "I'm sorry. I'm just worried about you."

"I know you are," she said, her body rigid. She took a breath, let it out slowly and then looked at Mr. P. and me. "Tim has been trying to convince me to come to Portland and stay for a while. I was planning on making a life in North Harbor and that's what I want to do."

"I get that," Tim said. "But you don't have anywhere to live and you can't stay in Rose's apartment forever. I have a house. It just makes more sense to stay with me until you've figured out all the logistics."

"There's an apartment in Christine's building I could have," Debra said. "The building owner already offered."

I wasn't sure that was a good idea, but I knew it wasn't my place to say so and I didn't want Debra to feel ganged up on.

"Do you have to make a decision right now?" Mr. P. asked. "Is the building owner waiting for an answer?"

Debra shook her head. "No. She told me to take my time."

"So why not do that?" Mr. P. said. "Nothing has to be decided right now, so don't make a decision either way." He smiled. "As my mother—may she rest in peace—used to say, sit and have a cup of tea with it."

As usual, Alfred Peterson was the voice of reason. I saw a hint of a smile beginning on Debra's face and the tension seemed to be slipping off her shoulders. I looked at Tim. All of his focus was on Debra and all at once I realized he had more than a crush on her. His feelings ran a lot deeper. I felt a pang of empathy for him because everything I'd seen and heard her say told me that Debra didn't feel the same way.

"I like that idea, Alfred," Debra said to Mr. P. "And if Christine were here, she would be telling us to knock it off."

Tim nodded and I saw the first glimpse of a smile flit across his face even as the sadness couldn't seem to leave his eyes.

Mr. P. and I started to gather our things. "Rose

should be back in a couple of minutes," I said. "She's on a fact-finding mission."

He smiled. He knew what that meant.

I got Elvis's carrier bag from under the table and settled him inside. He yawned. "Being a show cat is an exhausting business," I said. He murped his agreement.

Mr. P. touched my arm and I turned around. "There was something else you wanted to talk to me about."

I nodded. "Is it all right if we wait until we're out in the car, where there's a bit more privacy? And I'd like to wait for Rose as well."

"Of course," he said. He pointed over my shoulder. "Here comes Rosie right now."

"So, did you learn anything useful?" I asked her. She looked pleased about something.

"All information is useful, Sarah," she said. "I think what you meant to ask is did I learn anything relevant?"

Once a teacher, always a teacher, as Liz liked to say. "I stand corrected," I said. "Did you learn anything relevant?"

"Perhaps. According to Junie, one of the judges is having an affair with one of the owners."

"That has to be against the rules."

"It is." Rose reached for her bag, which she'd stashed under the table. "The judges often know the owners—the cat show circuit is a small world, after all—but judging the cat of someone with whom you have a personal relationship is a no-no."

"Which judge is it, do you know?" Mr. P. asked. He

took the tote bag from her and began packing Elvis's dishes.

"James Hanratty."

"Wait a minute," I said. "He was Elvis's judge in the first round in the Searsport show, wasn't he? Mid-fifties, lots of white hair, glasses and a friendly smile. He said Elvis had a certain rakish charm."

In the bag, Elvis lifted his head and looked around. It seemed he wasn't too tired to hear a compliment.

Rose nodded. "Yes, that's Hanratty." She picked up one of the purple towels next to Elvis's crate and gave it a shake.

"So which owner is he involved with?"

"Junie didn't know," she said. She rolled the towel in a tight cylinder and handed it to Mr. P.

"But you think this might be important," I said. "Why?"

Rose reached for the other towel. "Maybe this is an innocent relationship. People do fall in love at the most unexpected times."

I saw Mr. P. smile at her words.

"But sometimes relationships have a little more mercenary component to them. And if someone were willing to canoodle with a judge to affect the outcome of the show then perhaps they'd be willing to resort to vandalism . . . or worse."

"So we may have a suspect to add to our list," Mr. P. said.

"Junie is keeping an ear to the ground," Rose said, handing him the second rolled towel.

"Jeffery Walker is off the list," I said.

Rose's eyes darted from me to Alfred. "It seems the two of you were busy while I was with Junie."

"I'll give you the details later," he said.

I looked around to see if there was anything we'd forgotten. There was a paper bag with recycling under the crate. I reached for it, but Mr. P. beat me to it. "I'll take this, Sarah," he said. "You have Elvis."

I smiled. "All right."

We headed for the entrance. Easily half the competitors, maybe more, had already left. I knew that when the building was empty, Memphis and Cleveland would do another security sweep.

Just before we reached the doors, I noticed Jacqueline Beyer hurrying in our direction and waving one arm. I put a hand on Mr. P.'s shoulder. "I think Jacqueline wants to talk to you," I said.

We stopped and waited for her to join us. She was wearing skinny black pants, leopard-print shoes and a black blazer over a jewel green blouse. Her hair was up in a bun, a few wisps framing her face.

"I'm glad I caught up with you before you left," she said. She was a little out of breath. "I've been doing damage control all afternoon, but unfortunately news about the two mice has spread."

"I can't say I'm surprised," Mr. P. said.

"The vendor is still upset, of course," Jacqueline continued. "Although you figuring out a better, more prominent location for their booth did help. I never would have thought of moving the booth with the visitor information closer to the door and getting one of the staff up on their feet to hand out maps and brochures so that Guardian could take that space."

Guardian Pet Security was the company that had been in the booth where the mice had been discovered.

Jacqueline gave Alfred a tight smile. "You saved the day." She seemed just a tiny bit jealous of his ability to solve the problem. It wasn't the first time I'd seen Mr. P. do something like that.

"I'm glad I could help."

Elvis had poked his head out of the top of the open carrier bag and was trying valiantly to get Jacqueline's attention.

"Stop," I told him firmly. "You'll make Jacqueline sneeze."

Her eyes were already a little red. "I'm sorry, Elvis," she said. "You're very handsome, but I'm already late taking my allergy meds." She self-consciously tugged at the sleeve of her blazer and sniffed a couple of times. "I know I should stay away from the cats, but they're so cute."

Elvis meowed his agreement and we all laughed.

"I've been trying on social media to defuse the story about the mice. Cleveland assured me they were pets and I've been using that, telling the show's followers on Twitter and Instagram that the pet expo is for more than just cats. They have products no matter if your furry family member is a cat, a dog or a rodent."

"Very creative," I said.

"Let's hope it helps." She smiled and held up one hand, her middle and index fingers crossed over each other. Her sleeve slipped back and I caught a quick glimpse of hives on her wrist. She really was very allergic. "Cleveland did a check of the entire building and there's no sign of any other mice or anything else. I think we weathered this pretty well."

"Thank you for all your hard work," Mr. P. said.

"It's my job," she said. "Have a good evening. You have my number if you need anything."

We got out to the SUV and I let Elvis out of the bag. He walked across the seat and climbed onto Rose's lap.

"Sarah has something to share about the Lilleys," Mr. P. said from the backseat.

I slid behind the wheel, turning sideways so I could see him and Rose. "I think this might be important, but I'm not sure."

"What is it?" Rose asked.

"Do you remember what Junie said to you about the disguises Suzanne and Paul Lilley were wearing?"

Elvis had settled happily on Rose's lap, his head on one paw. "She thought they were way too obvious."

I nodded. "That's right. And do you remember when we walked around the pet expo the other day and we saw the producer from last summer?"

A frown creased her forehead. "Are you trying to say those two things are connected?" she asked.

"I think they might be." I explained what I had learned from Glenn.

"You're thinking the Lilleys could be involved in this reality show idea," Mr. P. said.

I brushed my hair back behind one ear and rested my hand on the steering wheel. "I am, but I don't have any idea how to find out for sure."

"Well I don't see the Lilleys themselves being very

forthcoming. I can see what rumors are circulating online."

"There might be something on one of those entertainment blogs," I said.

Rose had been sitting silently staring off into space, one hand absently stroking Elvis's fur. She suddenly smiled. "Of course."

I glanced at Mr. P., who looked as confused as I felt. "Of course what?" I asked.

"Peter," she said as though that should make sense to me.

It didn't.

"Dad?"

"Yes. Your father has to have some kind of connection somewhere that can help us, either from his newspaper days or through his students."

I nodded. "That's actually a good idea."

"Well I do have my moments," Rose said with a smile.

"I'll wait to see what Peter comes up with before I start looking online," Mr. P. said. "There's no point in duplicating our efforts."

I turned around in my seat and fastened my seat belt. "I'll call Dad after supper."

I started the car and pulled out of the parking spot.

"What are your plans for the evening?" Rose asked.

"I'm going to a concert with Jess," I said. Elvis was sitting up now on Rose's lap, green eyes fixed on the windshield. "It's a group of British percussionists called Bangers and Smash. I have no idea what they're going to be like, other than loud." I sent a quick sideways glance Rose's way. "And before you ask, Mac is going to a hockey game—University of Maine Black Bears—in Bangor with Glenn and a couple of guys he sails with. Do you and Mr. P. have plans?"

"We're going out for dinner," Mr. P. said.

Rose smiled. "I'm looking forward to it. We're going to that little café with the dessert crepes."

"What about Debra?" I asked.

"She's joining Junie and some other people from the show for supper. I told her Socrates could have the full run of the apartment. He had a challenging day."

I smiled at the way Rose talked about the cat like he was a person, the way she talked about and to Elvis.

We said good night at the door. Once we were inside our own apartment, I picked up Elvis and gave him a big hug. "I'm proud of you," I said, acutely aware that I was talking to him like he was a person, too. "And I want you to have fun tomorrow, but if you happen to win, that would be okay, too." I kissed his head and set him on the floor. If anyone other than the cat show people had heard me they'd think I was nuts. I was starting to like the cat show people.

Elvis and I had supper—cat food with an extra treat for him and Mac's leftovers for me. I sent him a text to say how good it was.

I'm getting spoiled.

My phone buzzed less than a minute later.

Good. My plan to dazzle you with my cooking is working.

I laughed out loud.

Consider me dazzled. Have fun.

He sent a happy face back.

I decided I had time to call Dad before I left to get Jess. Gram answered the phone.

"It's so good to hear your voice," she said. "What's going on?"

I tucked my legs up underneath me and leaned against the back of the sofa. "Rose convinced me to put Elvis in a cat show. It's for a case and he's in second place at the moment."

"He is an exceptional cat," Gram said. "I'm not the slightest bit surprised. I want all the details when I get home."

"I miss you," I said, suddenly realizing how true that was. John and Gram had gone on a very extended honeymoon after they got married and now that they were back in North Harbor, I'd gotten used to having her close by.

"I miss you too, sweet girl."

One of the things I loved the most about my grandmother was her huge heart. When Mom fell in love with Peter Kennelly and married him, Gram welcomed both him and Liam into her family. She was as much Liam's grandmother as she was mine and since Liam had no living biological grandparents Gram was especially important to him. She was the only one who had enough patience to teach both of us to drive, which probably explained why we both had a bit of a lead foot.

"What have you and John been doing?"

"Your mother and I have been haunting old bookstores, and Peter's teaching John how to make a mortise and tenon joint. They're building a little table."

"How's that going?" Dad was a good carpenter but not so good at breaking down how he did things. John, on the other hand, was the kind of person who liked an ordered list of steps before he started a project.

"The table has four legs and everyone has their fingers so far."

I laughed. "Is Dad around?" I asked. "I need to talk to him."

"He is," Gram said. "I love you and I'll see you soon."

"Love you, too," I said.

"How's my favorite daughter?" The sound of Dad's voice made me smile, the way it always did.

"I'm your only daughter," I said.

"Isn't that great the way things worked out?" he said. "I talked to your brother about half an hour ago." I wondered if my dad was in the kitchen, elbows propped on the counter.

"How's the trade show going?"

"It sounded like Liam was learning a lot."

I checked the time. I needed to get to the point. "Dad, I need a favor."

"Sure," he said. "What is it?"

I explained what I'd learned from Glenn and that I wanted to know more. "Do you have any contacts through your writing or your teaching who could help?"

"My Dad Spidey Sense says this has something to do with one of the Angels' cases."

"There's no such thing as Dad Spidey Sense."

He laughed. "See? My Dad Spidey Sense told me you would say that."

I'm sure he knew I was making a face. "Okay," I

said. "Can your Spidey Sense think of any way to help?"

His voice became serious then. "I have a former student who works for one of the networks. He's involved in developing reality programming. There's a good chance he'd know what's going on. I can give him a call. Is there anything specific you want to know?"

One foot had gone to sleep. I stuck out my leg and gave it a shake. "The main thing I'm trying to find out is whether Suzanne and Paul Lilley are connected to the project."

"*Y* or *E-Y*?" he asked.

"*E-Y*," I said, "and two *L*s."

"What kind of case have Rose and the others taken on now?"

"It involves some vandalism at a cat show. I don't want to see any cats get hurt." I wasn't saying anything about Christine's death. Technically it was a separate case. "Elvis has become a show cat, at least temporarily."

Dad laughed. "Good for Elvis. How's he doing?"

"He's holding steady in second place. Final judging is tomorrow."

"I'm crossing everything."

"I'm sure Elvis will appreciate that," I said.

"I'll make some calls first thing in the morning and see what I can find out."

I suddenly realized how happy I'd be to see them at Thanksgiving. "Thanks, Dad," I said. "I have to go. Give Mom a hug from me."

"I will," he said. "I love you, sweetiebug."

"Love you, too. Good night."

I ended the call and set my phone on the coffee table. "Dad says he's crossing everything for you," I said to Elvis. His response was to wave one paw in the air.

I'd texted Jess before I left and she was waiting at the curb when I pulled up. She fastened her seat belt, flipped her hair over one shoulder and grinned at me. "This is going to be so much fun."

"This is going to be so much loud," I said.

She made a face. "What are you, eighty?" Before I could answer she waved a hand in the air. "No, wait; it can't be an age thing since Alfred Peterson is almost eighty and he was the one who told me about this group."

"Mr. P. suggested this concert?" I said.

Out of the corner of my eye, I saw Jess nod. "He did. He's a fascinating little man. He knows a ton about music."

"I know a ton about music," I said. I realized I sounded a little defensive, but I had worked in radio for several years.

"You know a ton about old rock and roll. Alfred knows about a lot of different musical genres and he says this concert is going to be great." She adjusted the multicolored scarf at her neck. "So how did the furball do today?"

The subject had been changed. "He's sitting very comfortably in second place. His main competition is a cute little calico cat that Rose insists is wearing mascara on her whiskers."

"Is that actually a thing?" Jess asked. "I wouldn't think it would be good for the cat."

"Me neither," I said. "But I can tell you that some show people are very competitive."

I started looking for somewhere to park. Jess was doing the same thing. "Up there," she suddenly said, pointing to the corner. "Someone just pulled out."

We snagged the parking spot before anyone else did and then started down the sidewalk to the theater. "Jess, remember when that reality show was being filmed over the summer?"

"I do," she said. "A couple of those people are in town, you know."

I nodded. "Rose and I saw one of the producers at the pet expo." I stuffed my hands in my pockets, wishing I'd remembered to bring my gloves.

"Probably the same guy I saw outside Sam's a couple of days ago."

"Was he by himself?" I asked.

Jess shook her head. "No. Well, he might have been, but he was talking to a woman when I saw him."

"What did she look like?"

She frowned at me. "Why are you asking?"

"Can you just tell me without me answering that question?" I said.

She eyed me for a moment before the frown was replaced with a smile. "All right," she said. "The woman was probably in her forties. Very fashionable. She was wearing a fitted black wool jacket, sort of punk-looking with some leather and metal details. She had to be at least six feet tall, plus the boots she was wearing gave her three or four more inches, and she had the kind of perfect posture that dancers always seem to have. Does that help?"

Jess had just described Chloe Hartman. Why had *she* been talking to that reality show producer?

"Yeah, maybe," I said. "Thank you for not pushing. I owe you."

She looped her arm through mine as we joined the crowd heading toward the door of the theater. "I know," she said. "I like it when people owe me."

The concert was fantastic and we came out of the theater buzzing with energy. "How can they make so much incredible music with just garbage cans, brooms and a few wooden poles?" I said.

"I have no idea," Jess said, "but it's going to change how I look at garbage day from now on!"

I was too energized to sleep when I got home, so I surfed around until I found one of my favorite movies on TV and I curled up on the sofa with Elvis and some popcorn. We were about twenty minutes into the movie when I got a text from Nick.

You up?

I'm watching The Goodbye Gurl. Rats! I mean Girl.

I counted to four. My phone rang. "Hi," I said. "Tell me you're not still working."

"I was, but I'm home now."

"What's up?"

"I talked to Michelle and to Tom Manning." He let out a breath. "I jumped to a conclusion about the way the fire started and I'm sorry."

I picked up the remote and muted the sound on the TV. "I appreciate the apology. And as Mr. P. would say, I've had a burr under my saddle about the fire.

I've been pushing hard because I liked Christine. So we both haven't been at our best."

"Thanks," he said. I heard him yawn.

"May I say something?" I asked.

"If I say no, will that stop you?"

"It won't."

"Go ahead then."

I sat up a little straighter, which got me a glare from Elvis. "I hope you won't take this the wrong way, but you work way too much and you have no personal life."

"Oh c'mon," Nick said. "I'm not that bad." I could hear doors opening and closing, which told me he was in his kitchen looking for something to eat.

"How many paramedic shifts have you taken in the last month?"

"I don't know. I'd have to look at the calendar." He was hedging.

"And as for your personal life, when was the last time you did something fun?"

"I was at the jam on Thursday with you and Jess, so ha." He sounded more than a little self-righteous.

"Besides that," I said, "and ha back at you."

"Oh c'mon, Sarah, I'm busy." I heard the crinkle of a popcorn bag being opened.

I laughed. "And you just made my point. All you do is work, and you're eating popcorn for supper."

"Not that long ago all you did was work, and I know you've had popcorn for supper more than once."

"Guilty as charged," I said. "And it's not a good way to live. You need someone in your life, Nick."

He groaned. "Please don't tell me you're going to join forces with Rose and my mother and play match-maker."

"I just might have to." I reached for my own popcorn and discovered I'd eaten it all. How had that happened? When had that happened?

"I'm changing the subject," Nick said. "Do the Angels have any leads on who started the fire?"

"Not really. No one seems to know of any enemies Christine might have had." I sighed. "I know it's an overused word, but she was a nice person."

"From what Michelle said, no one had a motive to hurt the woman. Her classmates liked her. Her former students and colleagues liked her. She even stayed close to her late husband's family."

I stretched both arms over my head, which seemed to annoy Elvis. He jumped down and headed for the bedroom. "I know I'm the one who's probably jumping to conclusions now, but I can't shake the feeling Christine's death is connected to the show."

"Gut feeling or something else?" he asked.

"Both," I said. I explained what Christine had said about the vandalism at the shows being personal. "I didn't think any more about her words at the time and now I can't stop thinking about them. And you don't have to tell me that I sound like Rose, because I know I do."

Nick cleared his throat. "If you tell Rose I said this I will egg your house, but her gut feelings often turn out to be right. So don't dismiss your own. And you know what I'm going to say next, don't you?"

I laughed. "Be careful. Don't do anything stupid."

"Yes. And call me or Michelle if you or your . . . tribe come up with anything."

"I will," I said.

We said good night and I put the phone on the couch beside me. I laced my fingers behind my head and leaned back against the cushions. A new thought was rolling around in my head.

If Christine was right and the vandalism at the shows wasn't about the shows themselves, then what was it about?

Chapter 16

Rose was waiting in the hallway in the morning. She was wearing the scarf she'd gotten from Steven Tyler. Rose always claimed it was her good-luck charm.

"How were the crepes?" I asked.

"Delicious does not begin to describe them," she said as we walked outside. "I had one with a fruit and cream cheese filling and another with chocolate and crushed hazelnuts."

"They both sound good," I said as I lifted Elvis onto the front seat of the SUV. He was starting to like being picked up.

"You could take Mac there. The atmosphere is very romantic."

I laughed. "Is that why you took Mr. P. there?"

Rose gave me a sly smile. "It never hurts to stoke the flames a little."

"Really sorry I asked that question," I said. From the corner of my eye, I could see her grinning.

"So how was the concert?" she asked after a few moments' silence.

I was grateful for the change of subject. "Loud and wild and wonderful. Jess said Mr. P. recommended the group."

"He does have very wide-ranging tastes in music. Alfred is a Renaissance man."

It seemed like an odd way to describe a little old man who wore his pants up under his armpits, but it was accurate.

Liz's car pulled into the parking lot ahead of us.

"Oh good, she's on time," Rose said.

I looked over at her. "You called a meeting."

"I did."

"Why didn't you tell me?"

"I'm telling you now," she said.

"And you're going to do something you think I won't be in favor of."

Rose looked thoughtful for a moment, a small frown pulling her eyebrows together and her lips pursed. "Well, yes, there is that, too," she said.

"So are you going to tell me what that something is?" I asked. I tried to sound stern, but the effect is lost on someone who once changed your diapers.

She nodded. "Of course. At the meeting."

She was out of the SUV before I could say anything else. She moved fast.

I scooped up Elvis, who could not be expected to walk across the parking lot on his big day.

We all trooped inside. Mr. P. had walked. His cheeks were rosy from the cool morning air. Liz had brought Charlotte and Avery with her.

I could smell coffee as soon as we were in the workroom. Mac was coming toward us carrying a tray with cups and napkins.

"The tea and coffee are all made as per your instructions," Mac said to Rose.

She beamed at him. "Thank you so much. It's a busy day and we don't have a lot of time." She looked around at the rest of us. "Take a seat, everyone. The clock is ticking."

We filed in and took our places around the table. I got myself a cup of coffee.

"Pour one of those for me, please," Liz said.

I reached for a cup. Avery frowned at us. "You don't need coffee, Nonna," she said.

"I most decidedly do, child," Liz replied. "I need something to get rid of that foul concoction you made me drink for breakfast."

Avery was unfazed. She put her hands on her hips and smiled at her grandmother. "A green juice every morning will boost your immune system. It's much healthier than a cup of coffee." She glanced at me. "No offense, Sarah."

"None taken," I said, leaning around her to hand Liz her coffee.

Charlotte had taken off her coat and hung it on the back of a chair. Now she set a large rectangular tin on the table and took the top off. I could smell apples and cinnamon. "Applesauce muffins?" I asked.

Charlotte nodded.

I reached for one, thinking Rose was pulling out all the stops.

Once we all had tea or coffee and one—or two—of

Charlotte's muffins Rose got to her feet. "Are we waiting for Nick?" I asked.

She shook her head. "Not this time."

So Nick wouldn't like what she had planned, either.

Rose looked around the table. "I've been thinking
about what Christine said to Sarah the day we had
lunch, about the vandalism at the shows—maybe it
didn't have anything to do with the cats, maybe it was
more personal. Well, what could be more personal
than having an affair?"

I suddenly had a feeling I knew what Rose wanted
to do.

She explained briefly about what she'd learned
from Junie. "I want to watch James Hanratty to see
who he hooks up with. It's Saturday night and I can't
believe he won't be connecting with his paramour.
He'll be heading home tomorrow. So we're going to
watch the Rosemont Inn, where he's staying, and see
if he goes anywhere or if anyone comes to see him."

"What do you mean by 'watch him'?" I asked as I
reached for the coffee.

"I mean exactly that. Watch where he goes, watch
who comes to see him. Take photographs. That's it. I
think if we cover the time between six o'clock and
midnight that should be enough."

It struck me that if Nick were there his face would
be red and he'd be sputtering objections.

Rose looked at me. "Sarah, you and Charlotte have
the first shift from six until eight."

"All right," I said.

She waited for a moment as if she expected me to
say something else, but I just took a sip of my coffee.

"Liz and I will take the second shift from eight until ten."

Liz didn't seem surprised, which told me Rose had already run this part past her.

"And me," Avery said.

"No," Liz said.

Avery turned to look at her grandmother. "Why not? There's nothing dangerous about being in the car with you and Rose except for maybe how fast you drive." She reminded me so much of Liz. She had the same challenge in her eyes, the same matter-of-fact tone to her voice.

One perfectly shaped eyebrow rose just a fraction. "You're not helping your case," Liz said.

"I can keep you both awake."

"Still not helping," Liz retorted.

Avery leaned back in her chair and crossed her arms over her chest. It made me think of an old Western with the young upstart going toe-to-toe against the grizzled veteran. "I have an iPhone with night mode that will let me take photos in the dark."

Liz picked up her coffee cup. "No green drink and no speeches about how people with pets live longer."

"Fine," Avery said.

Round one to the upstart.

"And Alfred and Mac will take the last shift from ten until midnight," Rose said. Mac looked surprised. Mr. P. didn't.

"What if Mr. Hanratty leaves the inn?" Charlotte asked.

"Follow him," Rose said. "This isn't downtown

Boston. It shouldn't be a problem doing that without being seen. However, I suspect he'll stay in."

It occurred to me then that I hadn't told Rose—or anyone else—about what Jess told me about seeing the producer with whom I was certain was Chloe Hartman. I was about to say something when my phone buzzed. I checked the screen. It was Dad.

I excused myself and went out into the workroom. "Hi, Dad, that was fast," I said.

"I realized that my former student was in California so I called last night," he said. "You were right. The producers of the treasure hunt show are pitching a project based on the cat show circuit. Now whether a pilot will get made is still up in the air."

"What about the Lilleys?"

"They're attached to the project as consultants at the moment, along with a woman named Chloe Hartman."

I hadn't been expecting that.

"Does this help at all?" Dad asked.

"It helps a lot," I said. "Thank you."

"Anytime," he said. "I'll see you soon."

I put my phone in my pocket again and went back into the Angels' office. Rose and Mr. P. were standing by his desk. Charlotte was talking to Avery and Mac and Liz were deep in conversation about who knew what.

"That was Dad," I said to Rose.

"And?" Mr. P. prompted.

"And Suzanne and Paul Lilley are connected with the cat show project as consultants."

"It doesn't make the case for either of them having

anything to do with the sabotage or the fire," Mr. P. said. "If the cat shows are cancelled, there's no reality show."

Rose nodded. "I agree."

"So do I," I said. "I'm not sure they were ever really viable suspects, anyway."

"Maybe we'll learn something tonight," she said.

"There is one more interesting piece of information I learned from Dad."

"What is it?" Mr. P. asked, a gleam of curiosity in his eyes.

"Suzanne and Paul aren't the only consultants attached to this project."

Rose was already smiling. She'd made the connection.

"So is Chloe Hartman."

Mr. P. made a face. "I should have guessed that one."

"You did," I said to Rose. "How?"

"Chloe is a self-made woman. Her father died when she was barely a toddler, leaving her mother with seven children and no family to help her."

I shook my head. "That's awful."

"I have no doubt it was. Everything Chloe has today has come from hard work. *Her* hard work. I don't see her saying no to an opportunity that has the possibility of making her money, not to mention leading to other opportunities."

I rubbed the back of my neck with one hand. I needed to go for a run. A long one. "I hope we do find out something tonight."

"You can be at the Rosemont by six o'clock?" Rose asked.

"I can," I said. "I'll get Charlotte to bring her camera. She's better at taking pictures than I am."

Rose patted my arm. "Thank you, dear," she said.

"I take it we're not sharing this little side project with Nick?"

"I would never ask you to lie to Nicolas." She gave me a smile.

"But I don't have to bring the subject up, either."

The smile got wider. "Exactly."

I leaned over and kissed the top of her head. She smelled like lavender. "Leave in about forty-five minutes?" I asked.

Mr. P. nodded. "That will be fine, Sarah," he said. "Thank you."

I walked over to join Charlotte and Avery. "Want me to go open up?" Avery asked.

"Please," I said.

She grabbed the last muffin and headed for the front.

"So we're Cagney and Lacey tonight?" Charlotte said with a smile. She had introduced me to the '80s TV show. I'd binged on all seven seasons the previous winter.

"It seems we are," I said. "Could you bring your camera, please? You're just better in general at taking photos than I am."

Charlotte nodded. "Of course I can."

I put my arms around her shoulders. "Will this stakeout involve cookies?" I told myself if I was going for a long run then I could have a cookie or two tonight.

"You do know that we're just going to sit in your

SUV for two hours, don't you?" she asked. "Rose has taken the middle shift because she thinks that's when the action will be."

"All the more reason for cookies," I said, tilting my head to one side and batting my eyelashes at her like I was Elvis trying to wheedle a bit of bacon.

Charlotte laughed. "Child, you are single-minded. How about this? You're probably not going to have time for supper. I'll bring sandwiches and a cookie for dessert."

I held up two fingers.

"Fine," she said. "Two. Now unhand me. I have to go find my apron."

I dropped off Rose, Elvis and Mr. P. at the show, giving the cat a kiss for good luck. Mac was out in the garage workshop looking at a vanity table and a matching stool when I got back.

"The answer is oxblood," he said, "assuming your question was 'What *is* that color?'"

"It was," I said. Both the table and stool had been stained the same shade as a bottle of red wine. "My second question is, where did they come from?"

"Teresa pulled in maybe two minutes after you left. I bought a galvanized milk container and a glass shade that I'm about fifty percent certain will work on that old lamp that's been in the workroom for the last six months." He gestured at the furniture. "As for this, I traded that oak barrel that we ended up with when we cleaned out the house that belonged to Alfred's poker buddy."

"You mean the bat house," I said, rubbing my

wrist. I had sprained it chasing a bat out of the house with a broom. Mr. P.'s poker buddy had run off to Mexico with a woman he'd met online. It wasn't one of those younger woman/older man things. The woman was actually five years older than he was and had lots of money.

"It seemed she liked the cut of Rodney's jib," Mr. P. had said in an incredulous tone. Rodney—at least in his photographs—was about the same size as Mr. P. He wore a bad toupee that Rose insisted the man had bought from a late-night infomercial. But he had a warm smile and a devilish glint in his eye and I hoped he and his lady friend were living it up south of the border.

We'd been hired to clear the house to the walls, sell what could be sold, dispose of what couldn't and hand the keys over to Rodney's real estate agent. What Rodney had forgotten to mention was that he hadn't lived in the house in six months. I'd (eventually) taken care of the bat. Elvis had dealt with the rest of the squatters. The only thing we hadn't been able to find a home for was an oak barrel.

"Rodney was going to make whiskey with that," Mr. P. had said. "Or maybe a table."

"So Teresa wanted the barrel?" I said. I walked around the vanity. It looked like it was in good shape other than a few loose joints. Painted a soft cream or some other pale color, it would be perfect for a girl's bedroom.

Mac nodded. "I felt like I was taking advantage of her, but the funny thing is, when we made the trade I had the feeling she thought she might be taking advantage of me."

I smiled at him. "That's the best kind of deal. Both sides feel as though they got the upper hand." My hands were cold and I stuffed them in my jacket pockets. "I need your opinion on something."

"I have opinions," he said. "What is it?"

"I'm thinking about closing the shop at one o'clock so we can all go to the show and cheer for Elvis. What do you think?"

"I think you should do it."

"I will, then." I hated to keep dumping all the work on him and Charlotte and it would be fun to have all of us there rooting on Elvis and Debra and Socrates. I reached over and pulled a bit of dried leaf off of his quilted jacket. "I'm sorry you're not going to be my stakeout partner tonight."

Mac smiled. "Me, too, but I think you'd be way too distracting. I mean no disrespect to Alfred, but you're a lot cuter."

I took a step closer to him. "In the interest of fair play, I should remind you that he'll probably bring some of Rose's coffee cake. She would never send the two of you out into the field without supplies."

His forehead furrowed and he pulled his mouth to one side. "Rose's coffee cake. That does change things. Just think about it: cinnamon, brown sugar, butter."

I closed the gap between us, put one hand on his chest and kissed him. Then I turned and headed for the main building.

"Still thinking about cake?" I called over my shoulder.

"Not even a little bit," he replied.

I didn't think so.

*   *   *

At one o'clock, I put a large sign on the door telling any potential customers that we were closed for the day but would be open again on Monday morning. I had never closed the store early like this before. There were no bus tours with stops planned for North Harbor as far as I knew, so I was hoping we wouldn't annoy too many customers.

Charlotte and I headed over to the arena. Mac left with Avery to pick up her friend Greg. "Avery knows how to find Elvis's staging area," I said.

"Okay," Mac said. "I'll see you there."

I had to circle the parking lot twice before Charlotte spotted a place to park. "All these cars have to be a good thing," she said as we walked toward the main doors.

"I think they are," I said. "This place has been packed every day."

She smiled. "There are a lot of cat people."

"According to Rose, slightly more cat owners than dog owners."

"I think Elvis has turned all of us into cat people."

It was my turn to smile. "I had no idea when Sam set me up to take him that I'd ever be taking part in a cat show—and having so much fun."

Charlotte nudged me with her hip. "So you're saying Rose was right about entering Elvis in these two shows?"

I looked askance at her. "Well, not out loud," I said.

She laughed. "Your secret is safe with me!"

Chapter 17

Charlotte bought a ticket, I showed my participant badge and we made our way to Elvis's station. "Hi," Debra said. "Rose and Alfred just took Elvis over to be judged. If you hurry, you'll be able to watch."

I looked at Charlotte. She nodded.

Debra pointed over to the right. "They're at area number four," she said.

We headed through the crowd. We seemed to be going in the opposite direction from pretty much everyone else and I was beginning to think we weren't going to be able to find the judging area when Charlotte grabbed my arm. "I think I see them," she said.

I followed her and as we pushed past a large man with a very petite Siamese I finally caught sight of Mr. P. getting Elvis set up in the judging cage. Rose was standing next to a tall man in a patterned gray and blue sweater vest. He wore black-framed glasses with round lenses and a tuft of gray hair stood up on each side of his head. He looked like a friendly owl.

I tapped on Rose's shoulder. She turned around

and her expression was a mix of surprise and delight. "What are you two doing here?" she asked.

"We came to watch Elvis," I said.

"But who's working at Second Chance?"

"Sarah closed the shop for the afternoon," Charlotte said. She slipped off her coat and folded it over her arm.

"I wanted to be here to cheer for Elvis and Mr. P. and it didn't seem fair to expect everyone else to work." I felt my cheeks getting red.

Rose hugged my arm. "I'm so glad you came. Elvis is your cat. You should be here to see his victory."

Her certainty that Elvis was going to be top cat in his category was rubbing off on me. I looked at his competitors in the other cages. None of them seemed as engaged as Elvis was and I did agree with James Hanratty that he had a rakish charm.

Mr. P. joined us then. "Sarah, Charlotte, I'm glad you made it in time for the judging," he said.

"How did you know we were coming?" I asked as I undid my jacket. It was warm in the arena.

"Mac sent me a text." He glanced at the owlish man still standing next to Rose. "Has Rose introduced you to Henry?" he asked.

"Good gracious, no I haven't," Rose said, putting a hand to her chest. "Henry, I apologize for my terrible manners." She quickly introduced Charlotte and me. Henry had a warm smile and a deep rich voice.

"Henry is a judge," Mr. P. explained. "He's been telling us some of the ways owners have tried to influence his rankings over the years."

"Let me guess," Charlotte said. "Cookies?"

Henry nodded. "And pie, a surprising number of times. And meatloaf twice."

I frowned. "Meatloaf?"

He shrugged. "I guess word got around that I'm a meat-and-potatoes kind of guy."

"Have you ever been offered money?" Charlotte asked.

"I haven't, but I have been offered just about everything else—wine, beer, tequila, concert tickets." Henry held up one hand. "The judging is about to start."

The judge was a woman in her early sixties with gray hair in a chin-length bob and cat's-eye glasses on a chain around her neck. The first cat to be judged was an elegant tuxedo with a slightly aloof manner.

"Elvis has more personality," Rose whispered.

Cat number two was a calico with part of her left ear missing. She was cute and playful and the judge seemed taken with her personality.

"Too wiggly," Rose said.

As far as she was concerned, none of the other cats came even close to having Elvis's mix of personality and good looks. He was the second to last cat to be judged. I found myself squeezing my arm with the opposite hand, my fingernails digging into my skin.

After the judge had finished inspecting all the cats, she studied her notes for a moment. Rose put a hand on my arm and I covered it with one of my own. Finally the judge took off her glasses and picked up the ribbons for first, second and third place.

The third-place winner was the adorable little calico. The judge moved down the line, the second place rosette in her hand. I held my breath. Second place went to the big ginger tabby we'd first seen in Searsport.

"He's going to win," Rose whispered. And then the judge put the first-place ribbon on Elvis's cage.

We might have gone just a little crazy. Rose and I held on to each other and jumped up and down. Mr. P. and Charlotte high-fived. Henry grinned and so did several other people around us.

I went to collect Elvis. He was sitting up, head held high as though he understood exactly what had just transpired. I lifted him out of the judging cage and gave him a hug. He nuzzled my chin. "Good job!" I said. I picked up the first-place ribbon and Elvis put a paw on top of it. He definitely understood what had happened.

I felt a hand touch my shoulder. I turned to see the judge's smiling face. "You must be Sarah Grayson," she said.

I smiled. "I am."

"I'm Amanda Niles. I just wanted to tell you what a charming cat Elvis is."

"Thank you," I said. "This is his first win. To tell the truth, it's kind of exciting."

She reached over to pet the top of the cat's head and he began to purr. "He deserved to win. He's healthy and well taken care of and he has the most wonderful disposition."

I couldn't stop smiling. "I can take some of the credit for the first two, but his personality is all Elvis."

"There are quite a few pet food companies here because of the expo next door. A couple have asked about Elvis. May I give them your contact information?"

"Mrrr," Elvis said with a fair amount of enthusiasm.

"Yes from both of us," I said.

"It was a pleasure to meet you both," Amanda said. "Good luck at your next show."

Our next show? Were we going to do this again or just retire on top? I was sure Rose would have an opinion.

Mac had just arrived with Avery and Greg as we got back to the staging area. "Well?" Avery said. "Did he win?"

Rose gave her head a toss and patted her hair with one hand. "Did I call it or what?" she asked.

Avery gave a squeal of delight. She threw her arms around Greg and hugged him tightly. He looked a little startled and a lot happy. Then she bounced over to me and scooped Elvis out of my arms and kissed the top of his furry head.

Mac came over to me and put one arm around my shoulders. "How does it feel to be a winner?" he asked.

"I'm not the winner," I said. "Elvis is."

"You took him off the street and gave him a home."

I ducked my head, suddenly and inexplicably emotional. "Sam kind of tricked me into that; and anyway, if I hadn't taken Elvis in, someone else would have."

He leaned his head against mine. "Someone else didn't. You did. Take the compliment."

Charlotte took charge then, corralling Avery and Greg to go with her for coffee and tea for everyone. "We'll have coffee and donuts to celebrate," she said.

"They don't sell donuts," I said. "Just coffee, tea and hot chocolate."

"Mac stopped for donuts," Charlotte said, pointing at the box on the table next to Elvis's crate. He would have been trying to get at them if Mr. P. hadn't given him a tiny dish of chicken-flavored cat crackers.

"You brought donuts," I said with a grin, slugging his arm like we were in grade school.

He smiled. "What's a celebration without donuts?"

"Not nearly as much fun," Rose said, standing up on tiptoe to kiss his cheek.

"Did you learn anything interesting from Henry?" I asked Rose, leaning back against the table. "Other than that pie is a good bribe."

Mac looked confused.

"Former cat show judge," I said by way of explanation.

"As a matter of fact, we did," Rose said. "You heard Henry say that the vast majority of participants are not trying to influence him. They want to win fair and square."

"But he's run into the odd person who wants to win at any cost."

"Or who just wants the competition to be a little more exciting." Rose exchanged a look with Mr. P., but she didn't say anything else.

It took me a moment to fit the pieces together in my mind. "Are you saying the Hartmans tried to bribe a judge at one of their own shows?"

"I'm saying that Henry very strongly implied that one of the Hartmans tried to influence his final decision." One eyebrow went up slightly.

"I'm guessing she didn't offer to make him a pie," I said.

Mac's lips twitched.

"No, she didn't," Mr. P. said.

I laced my fingers on top of my head. "But I thought we'd decided the Hartmans couldn't be behind the sabotage."

"I don't think they are," Mr. P. said. He plucked a bit of Elvis's hair from his shirt.

"So you don't think there's a connection between the fire and the vandalism?" Mac asked.

Had we been going in the wrong direction all this time?

"I think the connection *is* the shows."

"I don't understand," I said.

Mr. P. nudged his glasses up his nose. "Just about everyone who knew Christine knew that she was supposed to be in class, plus her car wasn't in the parking lot and the apartment was most likely in darkness."

I nodded.

"We've been thinking that Christine's comment to you—that maybe the sabotage was personal—meant that she had figured out who the saboteur was and that person had tried to frighten her into silence."

"And now you think that's not the case?" I dropped my hands into my lap, trying not to let my frustration show.

"Just that maybe there's another possibility," Rose said. "What if someone was trying to influence the judging, trying to play up the competition among the top three cats in the purebred categories?"

"You mean up the drama?" Mac said.

Mr. P. nodded. "Exactly. Debra's Socrates, Jeffery's

Nikita and Kimber's Basil are all at the top of the standings, all just a few points apart. At this point no one knows which cat will be the regional champion, let alone the national winner. I happen to know that website traffic is up twenty-two percent and all the New England cat shows have had increased traffic, including this one."

I shifted my attention to Rose. "That's what tonight's about. You think that judge, James Hanratty, is having an affair with Chloe Hartman."

She smiled. It was all the confirmation I needed. "I think she's the most likely suspect and nothing I heard from Henry has changed my mind."

"What pointed you in that direction?" I asked. I could see Charlotte making her way back with Greg and Avery and I knew this conversation was just about over.

"Junie said that women loved Mr. Hanratty," Rose said as she cleared a place on the table. Elvis had finished his crackers and was sniffing in the direction of the donuts. "She said Chloe had told several of them to knock it off, they were so blatant, but she also said Chloe was just as bad as anyone else. I started to wonder who would benefit from an affair with the judge and it seemed Chloe would as much as anyone." She looked up at me. "Sarah, you know if we find out that James Hanratty and Chloe are involved it doesn't necessarily mean she started the fire that killed Christine."

I nodded. "I get that," I said. I also knew it didn't necessarily mean she hadn't, either.

We celebrated Elvis's win the way we celebrated

everything—with coffee, tea and food. Avery and Greg went to wander around and look at the cats. Charlotte and Rose headed over to the other building to check out the pet expo. Mr. P. went to check in with Cleveland, which left Mac and me with Elvis. I told him what Amanda Niles had said about the pet food companies' possible interest in Elvis.

"What are you going to do if you hear from one of them?" he asked.

"I don't know," I said, taking a sip from the dregs of my coffee. "Can you picture Elvis's face on a bag of cat food?"

He looked over at the enclosure where Elvis was stretched out on his side, almost asleep. Being cute and charming was apparently very tiring work. "Actually I can."

I smiled and leaned against his shoulder. "I can, too."

"You're still thinking about what Rose said, aren't you?"

I nodded. "I just don't see Chloe Hartman sneaking into Christine's apartment and setting it on fire to scare her. I don't exactly know the woman, but from what I've seen and heard about her, it doesn't seem like her style."

"People have more than one side to them," Mac said.

"What if we never figure out who started that fire?"

Mac turned his head to look at me. "Not going to happen. First of all, I have faith in Michelle and in Nick. They're both good at what they do and they are not going to give up. But most of all, I have faith in

Rose. Do you remember what you once said to me about her?"

I straightened up and hunched my shoulder to work out a kink. "I've said a lot of things about Rose."

"Well this particular time you said she's a pit bull with sensible shoes and a tote bag full of cookies. And you were right. The Angels are not conventional detectives, but their crime-solving methods have worked in the past. And I know deep down inside they're going to work this time, too."

"You're always the voice of reason," I said. "Which sometimes is really annoying."

He grinned.

"What would I do without you?"

Mac leaned sideways and planted a kiss on my cheek. "Lucky for you, you don't have to find out."

When it was time for the trophy presentation, I insisted Mr. P. go up on stage with Elvis.

"You're the one who did all the work," I said. "You deserve a share of the accolades." I looked over at Rose, who was giving Debra a little pep talk. Socrates had come in second to Nikita. "Don't make me go get Rose." I shook a finger at him.

"You win, my dear," he said with a smile.

We were a rowdy bunch when Elvis and Mr. P. accepted the trophy. I glanced sideways to see Liz standing next to Avery with Channing Caulfield on her other side. He smiled and raised a hand in acknowledgment.

I kept my eyes fixed on Liz until she looked my way and I grinned at her. And winked. I probably should have skipped the wink, but in my defense Mac had let me eat two donuts. Liz shot back a look that told me I would be very sorry if I said anything in Channing's presence. I pressed my lips together and mimicked zippering them closed. Then I turned back to the stage. I could feel her glaring at me. I half expected my hair to start smoking.

And then it was over, aside from taking apart our station on Sunday. Debra was going out with some of her friends. She was still in the running for both the regional and national titles, but not coming first had left her sad.

"I'm sorry Socrates didn't win," I said.

"He was off his game," Debra said. "He misses Christine. And the ironic thing is if she were here, she'd be dancing around singing that Taylor Swift song 'Shake It Off' and telling me to move on."

I smiled. "I can picture that." I reached over to stroke Socrates's fur. His dense gray coat reminded me of a teddy bear. "Rose says you're going to stay for a couple more days," I said.

She nodded. "And after that I may take Tim up on his offer to spend some time in Portland after all." She looked across the arena. Tim had gone to get her a cup of tea. "You know, don't you, that he has feelings for me?"

I shrugged. "I guessed."

"I saw you watching him the other day and I thought you had." She played with a button on the sleeve of her gray-striped sweater. "Rose told me to tell him the truth. I'm glad he's my friend, but I don't feel the way he does. I'm going to let him decide if he still wants me to stay with him." She ducked her head for a moment and then looked up at me with a bit of an embarrassed smile. "She also said to tell him about the potato chips."

I nodded because that sounded like Rose. "I've known Rose all my life," I said. "She likes to occasionally point out that she changed my diapers."

Debra smiled.

"She's given me advice over the years and I haven't always listened to it, but I've never been sorry when I did."

Avery and Greg left with Liz and Channing. Liz would be picking up Rose just before eight for their turn at the stakeout. Charlotte went with Mac. He had already arranged when and where he'd get Mr. P. I'd told Charlotte I'd get her at quarter to six, which would give us lots of time to get in place outside the inn.

Rose had gone to talk to a couple of people before we left and Mr. P. was checking in with Memphis one last time. I stayed behind with Elvis and the massive trophy.

"Where are we going to put that?" I said to him. He cocked his head to one side and wrinkled his whiskers as though he was trying to figure that out.

"Congratulations!" a voice said.

I turned to see Jacqueline Beyer walking toward me, a big smile on her face. "I have some good shots of Elvis from the trophy ceremony," she said. "I'll text them to Alfred tonight."

"Thank you," I said. "Tomorrow or even next week is fine."

"It's no trouble," she said. "I have some things I have to send out for Chloe because she has plans tonight."

Chloe had plans. Maybe Rose was right about her and the show judge.

Elvis reached a paw out in Jacqueline's direction. "No," I said. "You'll make her sneeze."

Elvis turned his paw over and studied it as if trying to figure out how it was going to do that.

Jacqueline smiled at the cat. "I just took my allergy medicine about an hour ago, so I'm not too bad right now." She looked at me. "Have you always been a cat person, Sarah?" she asked.

I laughed. "No. I wasn't a cat person. I wasn't a pet person at all."

"How did you end up with Elvis, then?"

"The short version of the story is that a friend of mine has a business downtown. Elvis had been hanging around and he didn't seem to belong to anyone. Sam—my friend—kind of tricked me into taking Elvis, and here we are."

Jacqueline grinned back at me. "Ta-da! You're a cat person."

"Pretty much," I said, shifting Elvis to my other side so he was a bit farther away from her. "What about you? How did you end up working around cats when you're allergic to them?"

A strand of hair had come loose from her high ponytail and she brushed it back from her face. Her smile was gone, like a cloud blocking the sun. "My mother loves cats. She worked as a veterinary assistant for years. And she invented a padded vest-slash-safety harness system for cats and dogs, but nothing came of that. I grew up with cats. I wasn't always allergic. That just developed in the past year or so."

She looked at Elvis and her smile returned. "I hope you and Alfred are going to keep showing Elvis. You know, there are opportunities and money for the companion cats as well as the purebreds. Elvis doesn't just have the King's name, he also has some of his charisma."

"It's actually been a lot of fun. Maybe we will," I said.

"I'm glad I got to meet you," Jacqueline said. She fished a business card out of her pocket. "This is my card in case Elvis ever needs a social media person." She handed it to me. JACQUELINE ARIANNE BEYER, SOCIAL MEDIA AND PROMOTION, it read. "And I'll make sure Alfred gets those photos."

Elvis was getting restless and I shifted him again so he could people watch over my shoulder. "I'm glad I got to meet you, too. And I should have told you earlier how much I like the banners with the cat sayings on them. I heard they were your idea."

"I got a lot of them from my mom." Jacqueline looked at the one over our head that read CURIOSITY KILLED THE CAT BUT SATISFACTION BROUGHT IT BACK. "I'll tell her you liked them."

Jacqueline left to get back to work and I gave up on a wriggling Elvis and set him in the carrier bag where he grumbled and made a sulky face.

Mr. P. came back as I was debating whether or not to eat the last donut.

"How's the pet expo?" I asked.

"Things are going very well," he said. He removed his glasses, took out his lint-free cloth and began his glasses-cleaning ritual. "The uproar over the mice seems to have had no effect on visitors and everything is still on track for a record number of people at the expo. The vendors all seem to be happy, even Guardian."

"What about the Hartmans?" I said. "How do they feel?"

He folded the little cloth and put it away again. "The Hartmans are happy, but I'm not. We haven't caught the culprit."

I nodded. I felt the same way. "I know Rose doesn't think they could be behind the vandalism because it might cause the shows to lose money and that's something Chloe would never risk, but do you think she could be wrong? Maybe they were trying to generate a little turmoil to help sell the reality show idea."

"I thought of that but there was a very small window when the vandalism to the enclosures happened and both of the Hartmans were at a fund-raising dinner for a no-kill shelter at that time. That's one thing they're not guilty of." He smiled. "I'm not giving up, my dear," he said. "Not on finding out who's been sabotaging these shows or who started the fire that killed Christine. I will get answers."

Rose was coming our way carrying a large cardboard box and he hurried over to intercept her.

I looked up once more at the banner over my head. CURIOSITY KILLED THE CAT BUT SATISFACTION BROUGHT IT BACK. I wondered if that was a sign and if it was a good one.

Chapter 18

We were on the way home less than ten minutes later. "All you have to do is take pictures," Rose reminded me. "There isn't any need to confront anyone."

I nodded, hoping she would remember her own advice. "Don't worry," I said. "Charlotte is bringing her camera. We'll see you at eight."

I got Elvis some supper, changed my clothes, washed my face and headed out to get Charlotte. I grabbed the two plaid throw blankets from the sofa before I left. It was drizzling outside and I had a feeling it was going to be a cold stakeout.

I pulled into Charlotte's driveway at exactly quarter to six. She was waiting, wearing her navy raincoat and carrying her small red and white cooler. She climbed in and set the cooler at her feet.

"Did you bring your camera?" I asked.

She patted the small bulge in the front of her coat. "Right here," she said.

We found a place to park on the street on the opposite side, one house before the inn. We had a good view of the verandah, the path to the front steps and the sidewalk.

"What if the judge isn't here?" I said to Charlotte as I unfastened my seat belt.

"Then we've spent two hours sitting at the curb when we could have been out on a hot date."

"I didn't actually have a hot date planned—or any date planned for that matter."

"Speak for yourself," Charlotte said with a grin as she reached for the cooler.

I stared at her, wide-eyed. "Charlotte Elliot, are you seeing someone?" I asked.

She gave an elaborate shrug. "Maybe."

There was just enough illumination from the streetlight that I could see a flush of pink on her cheeks. I jabbed a finger in her direction. "Details."

She took the lid off the cooler, set it on the seat between us and covered it with a red-and-white-checked napkin. "There isn't that much to tell. It's very new."

"Is this someone you've known for a long time? Is it someone new? Is he older?" I waggled my eyebrows at her. "Is he younger? Did he ask you out or did you ask him?"

Charlotte had a bemused look on her face and she was shaking her head. "Good gracious! Were we all like this when we were trying to get you and Nicolas together? Do I sound like this to Nicolas now?"

"Yes and yes," I said. "I'd like to point out my dental health was mentioned more than once, along with the thickness of Nick's hair."

Laughing, she put two sandwiches on the makeshift table. "I'm sorry. Really I am."

I held up a finger. "One question. Are you having fun?"

She nodded. "I am."

"Good," I said. I reached for my sandwich. "I'm tabling the rest of my questions. *For now,* not forever."

"Duly noted," Charlotte said.

The sandwich was roast beef on sourdough bread with spicy mustard, dill pickles and sunflower sprouts.

"Can you teach me how to make sourdough bread?" I asked, wiping a bit of mustard from the edge of my lip.

"I believe I can," she said.

Once again I'd forgotten I'd asked the question of a teacher. "Would you teach me? Please?"

She smiled. "I would be happy to. You've made a lot of progress when it comes to cooking."

"That's because you and Rose are such good teachers. Mom says you two had way more patience than she did when she was trying to teach me how to cook."

Charlotte had also brought a thermos of hot chocolate for the two of us to share and she took a sip of hers before she answered. "In your mom's defense, she was trying to teach two teenagers how to cook at the same time."

"But Liam picked it up so easily," I said.

Charlotte cleared away the beeswax wraps from our sandwiches and set a glass container of cookies in their place. "Your brother was motivated," she said. "He figured if he could cook it would impress the heck out of women."

"It worked all through high school. Heck, it's still

working now." I reached for a cookie. As usual they were delicious—crispy on the edges, chewy and chocolatey in the middle.

"And once you were motivated you learned as well."

I realized Charlotte was right. I'd gotten tired of scrambled eggs, take-out pizza and mooching off of Gram. But she and Rose had been infinitely patient, too. I'd always thought that a tiny bit of Rose's motivation in teaching me to cook was because she hoped someday there would be little people that shared my teeth and Nick's hair running around and that I'd be able to feed them.

We sat in companionable silence for a couple of minutes before Charlotte spoke. "I shouldn't have asked you to find someone for Nick. I need to stay out of his personal life."

"I couldn't think of anyone," I said. "I did tell him he needs a personal life, though."

"How did that go?" she asked.

I shrugged. "About how you'd expect. I love Nick like he's my other brother, but he is stubborn."

Charlotte nodded, brushing cookie crumbs off the front of her rain jacket. "I don't know where he got that from."

I stared at her without speaking until she laughed. Then suddenly she leaned forward. "Wait a minute. Is that him?"

"Nick's here?" I said. Not a good thing.

"No," Charlotte said. "James Hanratty. A car just went around back to the parking area. Is that him coming around the side of the inn?" She was already reaching for the camera, which she'd set on the seat when we began eating.

I looked at the man coming from the parking lot in back, walking down the driveway of the building, headed for the main entrance. The drizzle had stopped, but he had the collar of his dark-colored raincoat turned up and he was wearing a snap-brim fedora.

"That's him," I said. Charlotte started snapping photos. I wasn't really sure if or why we needed them, but I didn't see how it could hurt.

Once the judge had gone inside, Charlotte set the camera down. "Are we following him if he leaves?"

"I think we should."

She picked up the empty cookie container and set it in the cooler. "Do you know what Mr. Hanratty drives?" she asked.

"According to Mr. P., a silver Subaru."

Charlotte folded the checked napkin and set it inside the cooler as well. Then she put the lid back on, straightened up and looked at me. "Do you have any idea how to follow the man without getting caught?"

"Not a clue," I said. "I don't think Rose planned for that."

Charlotte looked over at the inn. "Let's just cross our fingers that we don't have to."

And luckily we didn't. James Hanratty didn't come out again and no one else showed up. Maybe he had no assignation planned for the evening. Maybe he was going to eat chips and watch Netflix.

At five to eight, Liz pulled up behind us.

"I feel as though we should be handing off night-vision goggles or something similar," Charlotte said.

I shot her a look.

She gave me a cheeky smile. "I know. I don't have the right attitude for a stakeout."

"But you did have cookies," I said. "I'm going to talk to Rose. I'll be right back."

I slipped out of the SUV and climbed in the backseat of Liz's car next to Avery. Rose was in the front-passenger seat. "Has anything happened?" she asked.

"Hanratty got here a bit more than an hour ago. He's been here ever since and no one else has come or gone." I held up a hand. "Before you ask, yes, I'm certain it was him."

"Good job," Rose said. "You and Charlotte can go."

"If you need anything, call me."

"We'll be fine, dear," she said.

I got back into the truck and fastened my seat belt. "We've been dismissed," I said.

I dropped Charlotte at her house and drove home. Elvis was sitting on the sofa. He looked at me and then looked at the TV. "You need to learn how to use the remote," I said.

He looked blankly at me with his green eyes as if to say, *that's what I have you for.*

I pulled out my phone and called Mac.

"Hey, how was the stakeout?"

"Good," I said. "Charlotte brought cookies."

"I take it Natasha Fatale didn't show up," he said, referring to the baddie from the Rocky and Bullwinkle cartoons.

"She did not. Want to come over after your shift?"

"It'll be after midnight," Mac said.

"I promise I won't turn into a pumpkin," I teased.

"I'll be there," he said, and it seemed I could feel his smile coming through the phone.

I surfed through the TV listings and discovered *The Goodbye Girl* was about to start again. We'd missed a chunk near the beginning because Nick had called. Well, I had. Elvis had seen it.

I changed the channel, propped my feet on the coffee table since there was no one other than the cat to see me and settled that cat on my lap. He lifted his head and looked in the direction of the kitchen. "We don't need popcorn," I said. "I had two donuts and two cookies and you had I don't know how many of those chicken crackers. We don't need popcorn."

Elvis made a sound like a sigh and laid his head on one paw.

We were just about at the point in the movie where Nick had called on Thursday when my phone buzzed. I had a text from Avery. Two words.

Come back

There was no way that meant anything good. I put on my shoes, grabbed my jacket and bag and decided I'd leave the TV on for Elvis.

Less than ten minutes later, I pulled up behind Liz's car. I walked up beside it and tapped on the driver's window even though I knew Liz had seen me coming.

She lowered the window halfway. "To what do we owe the pleasure?" she asked.

"I just wondered what was going on," I said. "Anything interesting happen so far?"

Liz shook her head. She tapped a switch on the

armrest and I heard the car doors unlock. "Get in," she said.

I slid into the back next to Avery. Liz turned in her seat and looked at her granddaughter. "You called Sarah."

"I did not," Avery said.

"Then you texted or Facebooked or waved a flag or something."

"I texted," Avery said. She went back to looking out the window, watching the inn across the street.

"Somebody tell me what's going on," I said.

Rose was watching the building as well. I realized she had a pair of binoculars in her lap. She turned her head to look at me. "We—I think Mr. Hanratty's paramour is over there right now."

"Nonna said we should just go confront the strumpet," Avery said.

I looked at Liz. "Strumpet?"

"I had an excellent education," she said. "I know a lot of words."

"I thought we weren't going to confront anyone?"

"I was thinking more of just having a conversation than actually confronting the woman," Rose said.

"Did you get any photos?" I asked.

Avery handed me her phone without taking her eyes away from the car window.

There were half a dozen images of a woman in a dark raincoat heading for the front door of the inn. The hood of the coat was up and I couldn't see her face. I studied the photographs, but I couldn't tell who the woman was. I did know who she wasn't, though.

"That's not Chloe Hartman," I said, putting the phone back in Avery's hand.

Rose turned to look at me again. "Why do you say that?" she asked.

"Chloe Hartman is taller than whoever that woman is," I said. "In one of the photos she's at the bottom of the steps and the top of the newel post is about level with her waist. The post looks exactly the same as the ones on our front steps, which means they're forty inches high. That makes the woman in the photos about five foot four. Even without her heels Chloe Hartman is taller than that. It's not her."

Avery extended her hand over the front seat. Rose took the phone. She scrolled through the photographs, stopping at the one of the woman about to go up the steps. She stared at it for a long time. Finally she handed the phone back to Avery. "You're right," she said. "I think I had my mind set on our mystery woman being Chloe Hartman and I saw what I wanted to see."

"What do you want to do now?" I said.

"Whoever it is, she's coming back out right now," Avery said from the backseat.

Rose leaned forward to look through the windshield and I shifted so I could look through the passenger-side window. The woman in the black raincoat was standing on the verandah, the hood of the coat pulled up so we couldn't see her face. She wore a small cross-body bag and a pair of tall rubber boots with some sort of pattern I couldn't make out. As she started down the steps the boots caught my eye. The design was reflective, and in the light from the two fixtures at the top of the steps I recognized it: cats. Cartoon cats. Big ones and small ones. I'd seen those boots before.

Rose had come to the same conclusion. "That's Kimber Watson," she said slowly.

"I know," I said. It had never occurred to me that Kimber would have been sleeping with James Hanratty, although now I remembered what she'd said to me when I wished her good luck: *I make my own luck.*

"Enough of this," Rose suddenly said. She opened the car door and started across the street.

Confrontation or conversation: It was about to happen. I muttered a word I probably shouldn't have used in front of Avery and scrambled out after her.

Kimber had just reached the driveway when Rose called her name. She went rigid for a moment before she turned around and pushed back the hood of her coat. "Is there something I can do for you?" she asked.

"Are you having an affair with James Hanratty?" Rose asked.

"That's none of your business," Kimber said. She looked annoyed but not the slightest bit embarrassed or guilty.

"Are you the person responsible for what happened at the pet expo? Did you put those two mice in the Guardian booth?"

"I can't believe you're asking me that question." Anger flashed in her dark eyes. "No. I didn't."

"Did you have any problems with Christine Eldridge?" Rose asked.

"I don't have to talk to you and I'm not," Kimber

said. She pushed past Rose and walked down the driveway toward the parking area.

For a moment I thought that Rose was going to follow her, but saner heads prevailed. We walked back to the car.

"I really did expect to see Chloe," she said, "not Kimber Watson, of all people."

I nodded. "I know." I wasn't really sure whom I thought we'd see or if we'd see anyone; but I hadn't expected Kimber, either.

I heard Rose sigh. "We haven't done a good job on this case," she said.

"That's not true."

She gave me a halfhearted smile. "Thank you. But it is. However, now that I know better, I'm going to do better."

I wasn't sure I liked the sound of that. We had reached the car by then. Rose climbed in the front-passenger side. Avery slid over and I climbed in the back next to her.

I propped one arm on the back of the front seat. "What do you mean, you're going to do better?" I asked.

Kimber's car was just pulling out of the driveway across the street.

Rose half turned. "Do you remember what Michelle said? If we found out anything to call her?"

I nodded.

"I'm going to call her. I don't know if Kimber is responsible for the vandalism or for the fire, but Michelle will be able to find out."

"I think that's a good idea," I said.

"You can teach an old dog new tricks," she said with a smile. She looked at Liz then. "We're done."

"Are you sure?" Liz asked.

Rose nodded. "I'm confident that Kimber is the one having the affair with James Hanratty. He's the only guest at the inn at the moment. The others have already checked out. Michelle can handle this one."

Liz raised an eyebrow but didn't say anything.

"So the stakeout is over?" Avery said.

"Yes," I said. "Would you make sure Mr. P. gets the best five or six photos, please?"

"No probs," she said, bending her head over her phone.

"You did the right thing when you texted Sarah," Rose said. "I might possibly have been overreacting."

I smiled at her. "You? Never."

I glanced at Liz. "Don't look at me," she said. "I think I reacted appropriately."

I made a face at her and then I fished a twenty out of my wallet and handed it to Avery. "Take Greg out for pizza."

She looked at the money, then she looked at me, eyes narrowed. "Because I finked out Rose and Nonna?"

"No," I said. "Because you gave up part of your Saturday night to help."

She thought for a moment, then she stuffed the twenty in her pocket. "Okay, thanks," she said.

My phone rang then. I pulled it out of my pocket. It was Mr. P. "I'm sorry to trouble you," he said. "There's been a small problem at the arena. Mac and I are on the way over. Could you cover the first part of our shift at the inn?"

"It's not necessary," I said. "I'm with Rose and we know who the judge is involved with. It's not Chloe. It's Kimber Watson."

"My goodness," Mr. P. said. "That's not what we were expecting."

"Rose and I will meet you at the arena and explain when we see you."

"Thank you, my dear," he said.

I ended the call.

"That was Alfred," Rose said.

I nodded and stuffed my cell back in my pocket. "He said there's a problem at the arena. He and Mac are headed there and you heard me say you and I will meet them there."

Rose nodded. "All right."

I leaned over the back of the front seat and kissed Liz on the cheek. "Thank you for being part of the stakeout," I said. "Give Channing my love."

She tried to swat me with one hand, but I leaned back out of her way and opened the car door.

"You can be replaced with a self-driving car and a talking parrot," Liz said.

"You'd miss me," I said. "Thank you," I mouthed to Avery, tipping my head in Rose's direction as I got out of the car.

"Like a toothache," Liz retorted. "Like one of those wretched green drinks for breakfast.

I laughed as I headed for the truck. "I love you," I called over my shoulder.

Liz waved one hand out of the window and I knew what was coming next. "Yeah, yeah, everybody does."

Chapter 19

I turned the SUV around in a nearby driveway and we drove toward the arena. "I need to let the Hartmans know about Kimber and Mr. Hanratty," Rose said.

"I think you do," I said.

"Did Alfred say what the problem was at the arena?"

I shook my head and glanced over at her. "Do you think it's more vandalism?"

She was frowning. "I don't know, but if it is, that seems to let Kimber off the hook."

"I know," I said. "I was thinking the same thing."

When I pulled into the parking lot, I spotted Mac waiting by the doors to the building where the pet expo had been held. I parked and we walked over to him.

"What happened?" Rose asked after he'd let us in.

"There was a problem with the sprinklers," he said. "Memphis managed to get them shut off fairly quickly so there isn't much damage and it's contained to three booths. He used a Shop-Vac to get up most of the water. Right now it's just a matter of drying things and seeing what—if any—damage there is."

We started walking toward the second set of doors. "Was it accidental or did someone set off the sprinklers on purpose?" Rose asked.

"Cleveland seems to think it was deliberate."

Rose and I exchanged glances. "That eliminates Kimber," I said.

Mac frowned. "Kimber?"

"Owns a Bengal named Basil. Came in third after Socrates and Nikita, the white Persian. Turns out she's the one, not Chloe Hartman, who's sleeping with James Hanratty."

"Got it. I think," he said.

We found Cleveland and Mr. P. spreading out a large blue plastic tarp. Mac moved to take the end Mr. P. was holding. "Let me do that while you bring Sarah and Rose up to date," he said.

Mr. P. joined us and we moved several steps away.

"How much damage is there?" Rose asked, concern pulling at the lines around her mouth.

"Most things are just damp," he said. "Cleveland is going to set up a couple of fans, which will help. One of the booths is a pet food company. Some of their small sample bags are ruined; but other than that, things look all right."

"Mac said this wasn't an accident," I said.

Mr. P. shook his head. "Both Cleveland and Memphis agree. The only sprinkler that went off is the one up there." He pointed above our heads. "Memphis was able to go into the system and override that particular sprinkler head. That's why there's so little damage."

"There don't seem to be many people here," I said.

"Takedown is Sunday morning, so there aren't very many people around, just a few vendors who need to get out of here tonight."

"So the culprit was in the building?" Rose said.

Mr. P. smoothed one hand over his hair. "Not necessarily. According to Memphis, the system could have been hacked from anywhere. And from what I've seen, the arena doesn't have a very robust firewall."

Mac and Cleveland were spreading things on the plastic tarp. "Was the Guardian booth one of the three that got wet?" I asked.

"Yes, it was," Mr. P. said. "Along with Colorado Pet Food and a company that makes dog coats and footwear."

"I'm going to give those guys a hand," I said, gesturing over my shoulder at Mac and Cleveland. "Rose will tell you what happened over at the inn." I looked across the huge space and saw Jacqueline headed in our direction. The social media maven probably wanted to do some damage control once again even though the expo and the show were over.

Rose nodded. "And we need to talk to the Hartmans."

Mac and Cleveland had set a couple of large boxes on the edge of the tarp and were removing what looked to be some kind of padded vests. I realized they were part of Guardian's vehicle restraint systems for cats and dogs. I'd been thinking about getting one for Elvis. I went to help the guys.

"Hey, Cleveland," I said. "Does all of this just need to dry out?"

"Hi, Sarah," he said. "As far as I can see, all that's wrong with this stuff is that it's damp. Looks like this booth got the worst of the water. The sprinkler head is right above us."

I'd started taking the vests from the box. I realized Cleveland was right. There was no real damage done to anything.

He straightened up. "I'm going to get a couple of fans," he said. "Be right back."

I kept working, but I couldn't stop thinking about the fact that this was the second time that Guardian's booth had been the victim of vandalism. I realized Mac was watching me.

"What?" I said.

"I can see the wheels turning in your head. Something is bothering you."

I sat back on my heels. "This is the same vendor where Cleveland found those mice."

"I know you don't like the word, but it could be a coincidence," Mac said, rolling up his left sleeve.

"It could be."

"But you don't think it is."

I got to my feet. "I . . . give me a minute."

Jacqueline had stopped to speak to Memphis. Rose and Mr. P. still had their heads together. I walked over to them. Mr. P. smiled at me. "Did Cleveland go to get the fans?" he asked.

I nodded. "I have a question about the vandalism at the earlier shows," I said.

"What is it?" Rose said.

"Someone tampered with the sprinklers before, right?"

"That's right," Mr. P. said.

"Was there more damage that time, or less?"

"Based on the photos I saw, more. In that case it took longer to get the sprinklers turned off."

"So things haven't escalated?"

Mr. P. looked thoughtful. "I can't say that. They could have. The perpetrator wouldn't have known how easy it was for Memphis to shut the sprinkler off."

I looked over at the tarp covered with Guardian products. "How many booths had water damage the last time?" I asked.

"Five," he said.

"Do you remember who the vendors were?"

A frown knotted Rose's forehead. "Why all the questions?"

I shook my head. "I don't know. I just have this niggling feeling that I'm missing something. I'm probably just tired."

"Don't dismiss a gut feeling," Rose said.

I smiled at her. "Sometimes it's hard to tell the difference between a gut feeling and the fact that I ate too many cookies."

"You have very good intuition, Sarah," Mr. P. said. "To answer your question, those five vendors were two pet food manufacturers—major supermarket brands—a company that made pet beds out of recycled materials; a custom dog house manufacturer; and Safe Paws, a business that sells leashes, harnesses and restraint systems. Does that help?"

"No," I said, raking a hand back through my hair.

"I think I'm just looking for connections that aren't there."

I rejoined Mac. "Figure anything out?" he asked.

"No," I said. I stood there weighing my options and then I pulled my phone out of my pocket. "I just need to look up one thing." I did a quick online search and found Safe Paws. I was way out on a limb. I hoped I wasn't about to end up crashing to the ground.

Safe Paws, it turned out, didn't manufacture their own products like a lot of the other vendors I'd seen at the pet expo. They were a source for a variety of products including Guardian Pet Security's restraint systems. So damage to the Safe Paws booth indirectly was damage to Guardian.

"Did you find something?" Mac asked.

I held up a finger but kept my eyes on the phone screen. "Maybe," I said.

I went to Guardian's website. They actually had a page about their participation in cat shows across the country. It seemed they did almost half of their business through the pet expos that ran in conjunction. Half their business. That was a lot of money.

I looked at Mac. "I think I know what Christine meant when she said maybe the vandalism had nothing to do with the shows. Maybe it was personal. I think someone is after this company." I pointed at the tarp covered in harnesses. "Guardian Pet Security's products were targeted in three instances. There's something fishy going on."

Mac nodded. "Once is happenstance. Twice is coincidence. Three times is enemy action. Ian Fleming."

"All I have to do is figure out who's behind that

enemy action." I looked around, wishing a clue would somehow appear out of nowhere. All I saw was Cleveland approaching, pushing a cart holding two large black fans. Mac went to help him just as Jacqueline joined Rose and Mr. P.

I started unpacking the closest box. The straps and harnesses in this one were barely damp. They wouldn't take long to dry, especially with those oversized fans. The guys got the fans set up and plugged in.

"I'll turn them on once we have everything spread out," Cleveland said, putting another box next to the one I already had half emptied. His sleeves were pushed back and I could see what looked like hives on his right wrist. He noticed my gaze and smiled. "At least I won't get a rash from cleaning up this mess."

"Are you allergic to cats?" I asked, thinking of all the times he'd picked up Elvis.

"No," he said. "That's not hives. It's papular urticaria—hypersensitivity to fleas. I've had it before; one of the drawbacks of crawling around a lot of abandoned buildings. Lots of critters."

"So it's because of the mice?"

Cleveland nodded. "Probably."

"Are you sure they were pets?"

"Yeah, they were too tame not to be."

I was still holding one of the padded vests.

"Don't you wish you invented that?" Cleveland asked as he pulled three more out of the box he'd just set down. "It made millions for the company last year."

"Really?" I said. I turned the vest over in my hands.

Mesh and nylon over memory foam padding with adjustable straps that attached to a car's seat belt system with a tether; it was simple but ingenious.

"Oh yeah," he said. "That harness system is the company's best-selling product." He tipped his head toward a large, and droopy from the water, poster hanging in the Guardian booth.

I stared at Cleveland, who was feeling the sides of the box, probably trying to see if it was damp. I felt as though I was putting a puzzle together, studying pieces, turning them, trying them in different configurations. Suddenly they were snapping together where they hadn't before, making a picture.

It can't be so simple, I thought. But it was. All the little pieces fit. I got to my feet. Mac was untangling a knot of leashes. He glanced up at me and smiled. Then did a double take when the expression on my face registered. "What's wrong?" he said.

"I know who did it." I gestured at the tarp. "This and the mice and all the rest of it at the other shows." I pointed at Jacqueline across the room talking to Mr. P. and Rose. "It was her."

"The social media person?" Mac looked confused. I didn't blame him.

"Did you notice the rash Cleveland has on his arm?" I asked.

He nodded. "He said one of the mice must have had fleas."

"Jacqueline has the same rash. I thought it was because she's allergic to cats."

"Okay," he said. "But how do you get from a rash to her being behind the vandalism?"

I rested one arm on the top of my head. "When the two mice got into this booth, Jacqueline thought Guardian was upset enough that they were leaving the pet expo show, but Mr. P. saved the day. He found a better location for their booth. She didn't seem completely happy about that. I thought she was a bit jealous because she hadn't found a solution and Mr. P. had. But what if she didn't want a solution?"

"Because?"

"Jacqueline told me that her mother had invented a padded pet harness, but nothing came of it." I held out the padded vest still in my hand.

"You think the company stole her idea?"

I pulled out my phone again. "Let me know if she starts to leave." I went online and googled Guardian's name and the word "lawsuit."

Nothing.

I closed my eyes and took a couple of deep breaths. *Think*, I said to myself.

I looked up the company's history. I wasn't even sure exactly what I was looking for and then I found it. The company's name had changed when one company merged with a second one six years earlier. I put the first company's name and lawsuit into a search engine. Once again, nothing. But I hit pay dirt on the second name. An Arianne Flynn had sued them over a design for a pet restraint system she claimed they stole from her. I pictured the business card Jacqueline had given to me earlier. Her middle name was Arianne.

I looked at Mac. "I have it," I said.

Rose and Mr. P. were still talking to Jacqueline. I couldn't put this off. I couldn't take some time to think about it. I'd looked for answers. I'd found them. Liz would say, *Be careful what you wish for.*

"Are you all right?" Mac asked. I could see the concern in his eyes.

"No," I said. "Come with me?"

He nodded. "Of course."

Rose smiled as I joined them. "Jacqueline has some good news," she said. "*USA Today* is doing an article on the increasing interest in regional cat shows. They're sending a photographer to take photos of some of the cats, including Elvis."

"That is good," I said. I didn't sound at all enthusiastic. I didn't feel it.

Mr. P. frowned at me. "What is it?" he said.

I studied Jacqueline. I was certain she was behind the vandalism at this show and the others. Could she have set the fire that killed Christine? "Guardian stole your mother's idea," I said.

Jacqueline didn't say anything, but her face flooded with color. Rose frowned.

Mr. P.'s eyes moved from me to her and back again. "Sarah, what's going on?" he asked.

Mac gave my hand a squeeze. "Jacqueline damaged the sprinkler system," I said. "She brought the mice into the show. She's behind the vandalism at the other shows. For all I know, maybe she started the fire that killed Christine."

"I didn't start that fire," Jacqueline said, anger flashing in her eyes. "I can't believe you could think I would do something like that."

"You did this." I held out both hands.

Her chin came up. "It's not the same."

"Because Christine was a person and this"—I waved one hand in the direction of the Guardian booth—"this is a company."

"A company that cheats people," she said. "A company that steals other people's work." I could hear the bitterness in her voice.

"They cheated your mother," I said. Part of me felt sorry for her, I realized.

"You were the one who tried to sabotage the shows?" Mr. P. said. He was frowning as though none of what he'd just heard made sense.

"I'm sorry, Alfred," Jacqueline said. "I'm sorry I lied to you. I didn't have any other alternative. Nothing else worked." She looked almost defiant, shoulders squared, hands clasped in front of her.

"Why did you damage the cages?" I asked. "Guardian doesn't make those."

"I wanted everyone to think someone was trying to sabotage the shows, not one of the businesses. I didn't mean for any of the cats to get hurt. I swear." I saw her swallow a couple of times. "Guardian makes a huge amount of money from the pet expos and the cat shows. Their restraint system was my mother's design. They stole it. I wanted to drive them away. I wanted to drive them out of business."

She didn't see how futile her efforts were. More people were shopping online than ever before. If the cat shows weren't bringing in enough sales, it would just push Guardian into doing more business online.

Jacqueline turned to me. "What did I do wrong?" she asked. "How did you figure it out?"

I pointed at her arm. "That rash. It's not hives from

a cat allergy. It's a reaction to a flea bite. Cleveland has the same thing."

Rose hadn't said a word. She looked . . . sad more than anything else. "Did you start that fire?" she asked. "The truth."

Jacqueline was shaking her head before Rose finished the question. "I swear I didn't."

I wanted to believe her, but she'd fooled me up to this point.

"Christine knew who my mother was, that she'd tried to sue over her design. She'd taken a business course and it was one of the case studies—just a fluke. I told her I didn't want people to know. She promised not to tell anyone and she'd kept her promise, but I think she might have been starting to get suspicious."

That would explain Christine's comment to me about the vandalism being personal. For Jacqueline it was.

Jacqueline looked around the arena. "I can prove I didn't start the fire," she said. She pointed at Memphis, who was wheeling out another fan. "That was the night before the pet expo opened. I was over in the other building supervising the banners being hung. Memphis was there checking the security cameras. Ask him."

No surprise, Memphis confirmed Jacqueline's alibi.

"I have to call the Hartmans," Mr. P. said.

Jacqueline nodded. "I know you do. Go ahead. I'm not going to try to take off."

He stared at her for a moment then stepped away and pulled out his phone.

Jacqueline looked at me. "I was afraid I'd slipped

up when I mentioned my mother to you," she said. A strand of hair had slipped free of her ponytail and I wanted to brush it back off of her face. It struck me that she wasn't much older than Avery.

"It was just one of the pieces," I said.

She smiled then. "And I meant what I said before. Elvis deserved to win. I really did want the show—all of the shows—to be a success. I just wanted Guardian to suffer a little."

Mr. P. wasn't on the phone very long. He walked back over to us, his expression unreadable. "The Hartmans don't want to call the police because they don't want the bad publicity," he said to Jacqueline. "But you are fired and they won't give you a reference."

"I . . . I understand," she said.

I wondered if Mr. P. had had anything to do with the decision not to call the police.

"You're angry and I would never tell you not to be, but in the end the only person it will destroy is you."

She nodded, her eyes suddenly bright with tears. She took the lanyard with her ID card from around her neck and handed it to Mr. P. As she turned to go, Rose stepped in front of her. She handed Jacqueline a business card. "This is an honest lawyer who will tell you the truth about whether your mother has grounds for another lawsuit. Whatever he says, think carefully about what you decide to do next."

Jacqueline swiped at her cheek with one hand. "Thank you," she whispered. She started for the main doors.

I put my arm around Rose. "You gave her Josh

Evans's card," I said. It wasn't a question. Josh was the best lawyer I knew. We'd been friends since we were kids and he'd gotten the Angels out of a tight spot more than once.

"I did," Rose said. "I suppose I'm a foolish old lady."

"No, you're not," I said, leaning my head against hers. "You're the best person I know."

Chapter 20

I went for a run in the morning. It was cold and windy, it had been windy all night, and I felt like I was fighting the gusts no matter which direction I was headed. Mac was waiting for me when I got home, sitting in his truck in front of the house.

"How about we go out for breakfast before we head over to the arena?" he said.

"Yes," I said. "I need coffee and pancakes. Lots and lots of coffee. My cheeks are frozen."

He pulled me to him and kissed me. "Still frozen?" he asked.

I nodded. "I think you're going to have to do that again."

Rose poked her head around her apartment door when we stepped inside.

"We're going out for breakfast," I said, "but we'll be back in lots of time to get over to the arena."

"There's no need to hurry," she said. "The power is out in that part of town. We won't be able to get into the arena until this afternoon because even with the backup generators there isn't enough light to work."

Mac and I went to a little diner just on the edge of town. I had blueberry pancakes. Mac had sausage and eggs with fried tomatoes. I swiped half a sausage. We were lingering over a third cup of coffee when my phone rang.

I looked down. "It's Michelle," I said. "Maybe she's talked to Kimber." I swiped the screen.

It turned out Michelle had talked to Kimber and to James Hanratty. "I'm sorry, Sarah," she said. "They both have an alibi for the time of the fire. They were together in a motel in Rockport. They had dinner in the dining room. The charge is on the judge's credit card."

"That's not too smart considering Hanratty wears a wedding ring," I said.

"To use an old-fashioned word, he seems besotted with Ms. Watson." I could hear the smile in her voice. "I'm not sure I get it. She's a . . . prickly person."

"Rose would say there's someone out there for everyone. Liz would say there's probably five or six someones."

Michelle laughed. "I like the way Liz thinks."

I looked at Mac sitting across the table, watching me over his coffee cup, a hint of a smile playing across his face. I liked the way Rose thought.

"There's also security video of Hanratty and Ms. Watson walking to his room. I'm sorry you didn't get the answers you all were looking for. We're still investigating."

I leaned back in my chair. "I know you are," I said. "Thanks for . . . everything."

"You're welcome," she said. "It wasn't a big deal. I can't believe Rose was actually willing to step back for once, though."

It was my turn to laugh. "Yeah, well, don't get used to it."

We said good-bye and I promised to let her know when we had anything else to share.

Debra's car was gone when we got back. I knocked on Rose's door to see if she'd heard whether the power was back on.

"It's not," she said. Socrates was happily curled up on her lap.

"I think you've made a friend," I said.

Rose smiled. "I'm going to hate to say good-bye. I've been trying to convince Debra to stay a bit longer, but she says she needs to get settled in her own place. She's gone to look at an apartment in a different building owned by Christine's landlord. I offered to go with her, but she wanted to go alone."

"Has she talked to Tim?" Socrates lifted his head and looked up at me. I reached down to scratch the top of his head. He gave a happy little sigh.

"She says she's going to do that when he comes to help her pack up."

"He seems to think if he just hangs around long enough she'll change the way she feels," I said.

"If that worked, then your last name would be Mc-Namara and Clayton would be your grandfather because he tried that on Isabelle," Rose said.

I shrugged. "But in Clayton's defense, he was only six."

"And he still took the hint a lot quicker than Tim Grant has."

"Well, Gram has never been the type of person to beat around the bush," I said. "Can you imagine her spending years eating potato chips she doesn't even like just to spare someone's feelings?"

Rose shook her head. "No slight intended to Debra, but I can't imagine anyone doing that."

It was late afternoon when the power was restored to the arena and the surrounding area. Both Elvis and Socrates went with us. The photographer for *USA Today* was meeting us there. Jeffery was waiting with Nikita. The beautiful white Persian looked regal and elegant as would befit a potential national champion.

I also got to talk to and take a photo with the owner of the big ginger tabby who had come in second to Elvis. She was somewhere in her midtwenties, with a warm smile and an even better laugh. She wore a sparkly cat ear headband and a T-shirt with a cartoon cat on the front and the caption: *I did the math. We can't afford the dog.*

The photo session took longer than I expected, but we finally got our staging area taken apart and everything packed up. There was almost no one around by the time we were done.

Debra had pulled Tim aside to talk to him. Rose glanced in their direction. "That doesn't seem to be going well," she said. Based on Tim's body language, he wasn't very happy with the conversation.

"Do you want to take the tent home or to the shop?" Mr. P. asked.

"I was thinking about the shop," I said. "It could either go up in my office or maybe even in yours. I know Elvis spends time out there with you."

"He's very good at internet searches," Mr. P. said with a completely straight face.

Mac was taking Mr. P. home and dropping some of the boxes at the shop. Rose was coming with me and we had everything else.

Socrates had stayed with us, eating liver-flavored cat treats and watching us pack things up with the typical bored indifference of a cat, while Debra talked to Tim.

"Do you want us to hang around?" Mac asked.

I looked over at Debra and Tim again. Debra's arms were folded and she'd taken a step back. She was pretty much done. "No, go ahead," I said.

They had only been gone for a couple of minutes before Debra headed back toward Rose and me. Her shoulders were rigid, her lips pressed tightly together.

Socrates lifted his head to look at her and she reached over and stroked the top of his head.

"Are you all right?" Rose asked, gently.

Debra hesitated then nodded. "I am. Could you do me a big favor and take Socrates home with you? Please? I want to go take a second look at that apartment."

"Of course I can," Rose said. "Take all the time you need."

Debra gave her a quick hug. "Thank you," she said. She headed for the door and I watched Tim watch her.

Part of me felt a little sad for him and part of me thought he should have moved on a long time ago.

We were partway home when out of the corner of my eye I saw Rose patting her pockets.

"What did you lose?" I asked, glancing over at her.

She squeezed her eyes closed for a brief second. "I left my phone behind," she said. "I remember setting it on the table to get the carrier for Socrates and now I don't have it."

"Not a problem," I said, looking for somewhere to turn around.

Rose let out a breath. "I'm sorry. I'm acting like a doddering old lady today."

There was a small convenience store ahead on the left. I pulled in, turned and started back to the arena.

"You do not dodder," I said. I didn't actually know what the word meant, but it seemed to imply being old and feeble and Rose was neither. "You could text Mac for me so he knows I'm running a little late."

"I can do that," she said. "And I'll call Cleveland so we can get in. He should still be there."

Cleveland met us at the main doors into the show space. We had both cats with us. It didn't seem like a good idea to leave them in the car.

Rose thanked him profusely. "Hey, don't worry about it," he said. "You probably don't wanna know some of the places I've left my cell."

My phone rang just as we stepped out onto the floor. With close to half the tables down, the space looked even larger.

"It's Nick," I said to Rose. "I better take this."

She patted the side of the carrier bag slung over her shoulder. "Socrates and I will go find my phone."

"Hi, Nick," I said. "What's up?"

"I just wanted to be the first to tell you that the state fire marshall's office will officially rule in the morning that the fire that killed Christine Eldridge was arson. It's a formality, but I wanted you to know."

"Thanks," I said.

"We'll find out who did this. They won't get away with it."

"I hope you're right." I heard someone call his name in the background.

"I gotta go," he said. "And I am right. We'll get him—or her. I hate that someone used an old light-bulb and a handful of ketchup-flavored potato chips, of all things, to end someone's life."

I wasn't sure I'd heard him right.

I heard a voice in the background again. "Nick, what do you mean—" I didn't get to finish the sentence.

"I'll talk to you soon," he said and was gone.

I stood there with a buzzing sound in my ears. *An old lightbulb and a handful of ketchup-flavored potato chips.* I hadn't heard Nick wrong. I looked around for Rose, but the first person I spotted was Tim. He was folding and stacking tables on a wheeled cart. I remembered Debra mentioning that he and Christine had always helped with the takedown after a show.

Tim started the fire that killed Christine. *Tim.* I stared at him. I couldn't seem to look anywhere else. As if he could somehow feel my gaze fixed on him, he turned around and looked in my direction. I should have looked away, but I didn't.

And then something changed in his face. I saw a brief glimpse of . . . awareness. He knew I had figured it all out.

Rose was looking under a table halfway between us. I couldn't leave her there. I started toward her even as Tim did the same. His legs were longer, but he was trying to make his movements look casual. I, on the other hand, didn't care how frantic I looked and I was just a few feet closer than he was.

I got to Rose first and grabbed her arm. "I found it," she said, holding up her phone.

"We have to get out of here." I pulled her toward me.

She frowned. "Sarah, what's going on?" she asked.

Tim closed the last of the distance between us. He seemed bigger than the last time I'd seen him. "Go ahead. Tell her what's going on," he said. His expression was anything but friendly.

I put Rose and Socrates behind me. "Rose is going to go now," I said. "She doesn't know anything." I was surprised that my voice didn't shake. I could feel my knees trembling.

"I'm not going anywhere," Rose said in her best teacher voice. "One of you tell me what's happening."

"Just go, Rose. Please just go," I said, keeping my eyes locked on Tim.

He was bigger, but I could charge him. He wouldn't be expecting that and it would give Rose time to run.

Suddenly his hand darted out and he tried to grab my arm. I managed to twist out of the way and push

Rose backward. It put a bit more space between us and Tim. Elvis hissed and showed his claws.

"Tim started the fire," I said.

Rose was stunned into silence for a minute. "No," she said. "That doesn't make any sense."

"He did it."

"But . . . but why?" she asked. "Christine was your friend."

He clenched his jaw. "I didn't mean for Christine to die," he said.

I took two more steps backward, which moved Rose back as well. If I could manage three or four more steps without him noticing I could push Rose in one direction and lead Tim off in the other.

"All I wanted to do was damage Christine's apartment so Debra couldn't stay there. If she just spent more time with me I know she'd love me the way I love her." He held up one hand. "I know she said we're just friends, but that will change if I just have time to work on her. That's all I was trying to do when I started the fire. Christine wasn't even supposed to be home."

I moved us back two more steps. I knew I had to make Tim mad enough to chase me and not Rose.

"Debra isn't going to love you," I said. "First of all, you killed her best friend. And second, you can't make people love you. They either do or they don't and if they don't you suck it up and move on." I took one more step backward.

"You don't know what you're talking about," Tim said. His body almost seemed to vibrate with suppressed anger.

"Debra doesn't love you." Where had everyone gone? If I screamed, would anyone hear me?

He shook his head. "That's not true."

"She doesn't and she's never going to, Tim. Just give it up!" I tried to sound disdainful instead of scared.

"No! No! No!" His voice kept getting louder each time he said the word. He pulled his hand back and in a split second of focus I knew two things: I knew he was going to hit me and I knew no one was coming to save us.

"Run!" I yelled at Rose, giving her a push to one side.

She stumbled, but she scrambled around the side of the closest table. Instead of slapping me Tim shoved me hard against the table. The edge of it cracked hard against the back of my skull as I went over and I slid to the floor like my legs had been kicked out from under me. Elvis jumped out of my arms. And Tim went after Rose.

My stomach pitched. Tiny flashes of light, like fireflies, danced around the edge of my vision.

Rose kept the table between her and Tim.

"Hurting Sarah and me won't help anything," she said to him.

I struggled to get to my feet. For some reason all of a sudden the floor kept tilting down to the left. And there was blood on the table. Where had that come from?

"Christine was supposed to be in class," Tim said stubbornly. "Every Tuesday night she goes to a class."

"I know that," Rose said.

How did she manage to sound so calm?

Tim hauled a hand back over his hair. "Why didn't she just go and study at the library like a normal person?" He moved forward and Rose slipped behind another table.

Elvis was nudging my leg as though urging me to stand up. I couldn't. It was impossible to stand up when the floor had such a dramatic slant. How were Rose and Tim managing to stay upright?

I started to crawl toward them. If Tim went after Rose again I'd sink my teeth into his leg, I decided. The idea struck me as both brilliant and hilariously funny. I had to bite the inside of my cheek so I wouldn't laugh and clue in Tim that I was coming to get him.

Tim was telling Rose about the first time he saw Debra back in high school. Rose still had a table between them. I kept crawling. As I closed the space between us, I saw that he was wearing heavy jeans and a pair of lace-up Timberland boots. How was I going to bite him?

I needed another plan. I grabbed the edge of the table closest to me and pulled myself upright. The floor seemed to wobble as though we were on a ship out at sea in a storm.

I looked around. There was a metal garbage can maybe two steps away. Elvis had jumped onto the tabletop at some point and Socrates was out of his carrier, sitting next to Rose's elbow, fur fluffed up, tail lashing through the air. I thought I saw the cats exchange a look and wondered if maybe I had a concussion. Tim turned around, realizing that I was behind him then. Both cats launched themselves at him, claws barred, yowling.

Tim yelled, flailing his arms at them. I grabbed the lid from the garbage can and swung it with all the strength I had left. I caught him right across the back of the head. He swayed like a spindly birch tree in a windstorm and went down, unconscious. My legs gave out and I dropped to the floor, still clutching the lid of the trash can.

Rose rushed over, crouching beside me on the floor while both cats climbed on top of me.

"I took out the trash," I said to her. That seemed even funnier than the idea of biting Tim had so I said it again.

Then I passed out.

I didn't find out until much later what happened next. Rose called 911 and Cleveland. The latter rushed in and restrained Tim with his belt before he came to. The police came, along with Mac and Mr. P. An ambulance took me to the hospital.

It turned out I'd been right. I did have a concussion. They kept me all night. Mac slept in a chair on one side of the bed and Rose in one on the other. I woke up sometime after midnight and tried to send them home, but they wouldn't go and I fell asleep again halfway through arguing with them.

I was trying to convince Mac to get me a cup of coffee and Rose to get me my clothes the next morning when Liz breezed in with Charlotte and Avery.

"Good morning, toots," she said. "You're being discharged and you're going to stay with Charlotte."

I opened my mouth to tell her I wanted to go home.

She pointed one finger at me. "Don't bother wasting what little brain function you have at the moment arguing."

"Make Rose go home and get some rest," I said. I knew Liz was the one person who could make that happen.

"She'll be coming home with me," Liz said.

"I'm all right," Rose said, pulling herself upright in her chair. She wasn't fine. She had dark circles under her eyes and lines I'd never noticed before around her mouth.

Liz was unfazed. "Rose Jackson, I am perfectly capable of tucking you under my left arm and carrying you like a baby pig. Don't make me prove that to everyone."

Rose looked away first. "Fine," she said. "There's no need to make a fuss."

Avery looked at me. "Did you really whack a guy with a garbage can lid?" she asked.

"Yes, she did," Rose said. "She saved both of us—and Elvis and Socrates."

I reached out a hand and caught one of hers, giving it a squeeze. "Rose distracted Tim and so did Socrates and Elvis. It wasn't just me." I suddenly realized I didn't know where the cats were.

"Debra is looking after both of them," Mac said as though he had read my mind or more likely the look on my face. "They're fine."

"How is she?" I asked.

Rose looked away for a moment. "Heartbroken," she finally said.

The nurse came in then with my paperwork. Charlotte helped me get dressed and Mac pushed the wheelchair the nurse—and Liz—insisted I needed.

Mac reached for my hand before we pulled out of the parking lot. "I was so scared when Rose called."

"I'm sorry," I said. I had to swallow down the lump in my throat before I could speak.

He shook his head. "You don't have anything to apologize for," he said. He almost smiled. "I can't believe you hit Tim over the head with a garbage can lid."

I did smile. "It worked out better than my first plan probably would have."

"Which was?"

I laid my head back against the seat. "Biting his ankle."

He looked at me, unsure whether to laugh. "And you changed your mind because?"

"He was wearing boots."

His eyes were suspiciously bright. He leaned over and wrapped his arms around me. "I don't even want to think about what I would have done if anything had happened to you."

"Nothing is going to happen to me," I said, my head settled on his shoulder. He felt so warm. "I've been hanging around Rose so much, my head is as hard as hers."

"Remind me to thank her," he said.

It struck me there was a lot I needed to thank Rose for, too.

Mac drove me to Charlotte's house, holding my hand all the way. Everyone else went with Liz.

When we got to Charlotte's, Mr. P. and Jess were waiting. Jess had brought clean clothes and Elvis.

"I'm so glad you're okay," she said, pulling me into a hug. "How about from now on you spend Sunday watching Netflix and eating takeout like the rest of us?"

"Thank you for taking care of Rosie," Mr. P. said. He took hold of both of my hands and kissed my cheek.

"She took care of me, too," I said. "We're kind of a team."

He smiled. "And a very good one, too."

Mr. P. and Avery made pancakes. We all gathered around Charlotte's dining room table to eat. I was hungry. Apparently you can work up an appetite swinging a garbage can lid and getting concussed.

"Next time Bangers and Smash are in town, you should audition," Jess teased.

I pointed at her with my fork. "You joke," I said, "but I had a certain finesse with that garbage can lid."

Every time I even looked for something Avery jumped to her feet. She brought me another pancake and a second cup of coffee and syrup *and* a fork after I dropped mine.

"You don't have to wait on me," I said.

To my surprise, she flung her arms around me. "Thank you for saving Rose," she whispered against my hair, "and thank you for saving you."

After we'd eaten, Liz looked around the table. "Go home," she said. "All of you." She fixed her gaze on Mac. "Including you. Because if you're here Sarah will stay up making gooey eyes at you. Plus you look like hell."

Mac kissed me in front of everyone. "I'll be back," he said.

"Love you," Jess mouthed, and went with him.

Mr. P. gave my arm a squeeze.

Rose took my face in her hands. "I am so glad you're in the world," she said softly.

"Back at you," I said.

Avery was already in the kitchen, likely doing the dishes on her grandmother's instructions. Charlotte had just gotten Elvis a second bowl of what looked like chopped roast beef.

"Whatever you need, just say the word," Liz said.

I nodded very aware of how much love there was around me.

"Wagons ho," she said to Rose and Mr. P. Then she looked back over her shoulder at me. "Love you."

I grinned at her. "Yeah, yeah, everybody does," I said.

Chapter 21

Debra and Socrates came to see me after lunch. Socrates climbed onto my lap and nudged my hand with his head. I scratched behind his right ear. "You were fantastic," I told him.

"Mrrr," he said, then started to purr.

"I'm so sorry," Debra said. Her eyes were red and her voice was raspy.

I shook my head. "No. None of this is your fault. Not what happened to Rose and me and the furballs, and not what happened to Christine."

"If I'd made it clear to Tim a lot sooner that I didn't feel about him the way he felt about me, none of this would have happened."

Having seen the man's obsessiveness up close I didn't believe that. I put my hand on her arm. "Don't do that," I said. "Don't pick up other people's stuff. You have enough of your own to carry around. The only one responsible for what Tim did is Tim."

*   *   *

A few days later, everyone arrived for Thanksgiving. Gram was in charge of the meal, but we gathered at Charlotte's because there was more room.

Gram, Rose and Charlotte continued with the conceit that Jess and Liam were a serious couple. And it was kind of funny to watch Liam try to play the attentive boyfriend and Jess try to look adoringly at him whenever one of them was around. Mostly she looked gassy.

Nick was sitting beside me on the couch. "He sucks at this," he said.

I grinned. "I know."

"Don't you feel even a little bit guilty about not telling them that Mom and the others know?"

I made a show out of thinking about his question, wrinkling my nose and twisting my mouth to one side. "Nope, not really," I said with a shake of my head. "What about you? Do you feel guilty?"

"You just told me five minutes ago," Nick retorted.

"Well, it wasn't that much fun sitting here watching them by myself."

Just then Liam draped his arm awkwardly around Jess's shoulders. A look passed between Gram and Rose.

Nick saw it as well. He poked me with his elbow. "This is going to be good."

It turned out Jess had seen the look, too. She twisted out from underneath Liam's arm. "They know," she said, taking care to enunciate both words.

I leaned my head toward Nick. "Busted," I said out of the corner of my mouth.

Jess came across the room, dropped onto the sofa beside me and slugged my arm. "How long have you known?" she asked.

I put a hand to my head. "My memory is fuzzy. I had a concussion not that long ago."

Over by the table, Liam had draped his arms around Gram's shoulders. "You tricked me," I heard him say.

She smiled. "And you deceived me. I think we're even."

He leaned in and kissed her cheek.

"For the record, I think Jess made a wonderful fake girlfriend," Gram said, raising her voice so Jess would hear her.

"For the record, you made a wonderful fake possible grandmother-in-law," Jess said, blowing her a kiss.

I looked around the room. Dad, Mac, John and Avery seemed to be building something with what looked like saltines and cream cheese. Gram and Rose were clearly talking up Jess's attributes to Liam. They kept looking in her direction and smiling. Liz and Mr. P. were watching something on her tablet. Charlotte was eyeing the tablecloth as though she was about to whip it out from under the dishes. Elvis was sitting on the footstool like some kind of furry royalty. And Mom had just opened the front door to Michelle, who was carrying a huge bottle of mayonnaise and a package of tube socks. Mom seemed very happy to get both gifts.

All the people I loved most in the world were close enough to touch.

"You are a weird group of people," Jess said.

"First of all, there is no 'you,'" Nick said. "There's only us, which means you're part of the weird. And second, we don't call it 'weird.'" He raised an eyebrow at me. "Right, Sarah?"

I grinned. "Right. We just call it 'family.'"

Acknowledgments

Thanks to my agent, Kim Lionetti, my editor, Jessica Wade, and assistant editor Miranda Hill, whose hard work has helped make Sarah, Elvis and the Angels a success. Thanks as well go to all the readers who made suggestions for the different "cat sayings" quoted in this book. I had so much fun reading all your ideas.

This book and every book in the Second Chance Cat series has benefitted from the talents of many people behind the scenes at Berkley, especially Dache Rogers and Elisha Katz. Thank you all!

A special thank-you to the cat show people who answered all my questions and shared their love of all things feline with me.

And as always, thank you to Patrick and Lauren. Love you both!

Love Elvis the cat?
Then meet Hercules and Owen!
Read on for an excerpt of the first book in
the Magical Cats series.

CURIOSITY THRILLED THE CAT

by Sofie Kelly. Available now!

The body was smack in the middle of my freshly scrubbed kitchen floor. Fred the Funky Chicken, minus his head.

"Owen!" I said, sharply.

Nothing.

"Owen, you little fur ball, I know you did this. Where are you?"

There was a muffled "meow" from the back door. I leaned around the cupboards. Owen was sprawled on his back in front of the screen door, a neon yellow feather sticking out of his mouth. He rolled over onto his side and looked at me with the same goofy expression I used to get from stoned students coming into the BU library.

I crouched down next to the gray-and-white tabby. "Owen, you killed Fred," I said. "That's the third chicken this week."

The cat sat up slowly and stretched. He padded over to me and put one paw on my knee. Tipping his head to one side he looked up at me with his golden eyes. I sat back against the end of the cupboard. Owen climbed onto my lap and put his two front paws on my chest. The feather was still sticking out of his mouth.

I held out my right hand. "Give me Fred's head," I said. The cat looked at me unblinkingly. "C'mon, Owen. Spit it out."

He turned his head sideways and dropped what was left of Fred the Funky Chicken's head into my hand. It was a soggy lump of cotton with that lone yellow feather stuck on the end.

"You have a problem, Owen," I told the cat. "You have a monkey on your back." I dropped what was left of the toy's head onto the floor and wiped my hand on my gray yoga pants. "Or maybe I should say you have a chicken on your back."

The cat nuzzled my chin, then laid his head against my T-shirt, closed his eyes and started to purr.

I stroked the top of his head. "That's what they all say," I told him. "You're addicted, you little fur ball, and Rebecca is your dealer."

Owen just kept on purring and ignored me. Hercules came around the corner then. "Your brother is a catnip junkie," I said to the little tuxedo cat.

Hercules climbed over my legs and sniffed the remains of Fred the Funky Chicken's head. Then he looked at Owen, rumbling like a diesel engine as I scratched the side of his head. I swear there was disdain on Hercules' furry face. Stick catnip in, on or near anything and Owen squirmed with joy. Hercules, on the other hand, was indifferent.

The stocky black-and-white cat climbed onto my

lap, too. He put one white paw on my shoulder and swatted at my hair.

"Behind the ear?" I asked.

"Meow," the cat said.

I took that as a yes, and tucked the strands back behind my ear. I was used to long hair, but I'd cut mine several months ago. I was still adjusting to the change in style. At least I hadn't given in to the impulse to dye my dark brown hair blonde.

"Maybe I'll ask Rebecca if she has any ideas for my hair," I said. "She's supposed to be back tonight." At the sound of Rebecca's name Owen lifted his head. He'd taken to Rebecca from the first moment he'd seen her, about two weeks after I'd brought the cats home.

Both Owen and Hercules had been feral kittens. I'd found them, or more truthfully they'd found me, about a month after I'd arrived in town. I had no idea how old they were. They were affectionate with me, but wouldn't allow anyone else to come near them, let alone touch them. That hadn't stopped Rebecca, my backyard neighbor, from trying. She'd been buying both cats little catnip toys for weeks now, but all she'd done was turn Owen into a chicken-decapitating catnip junkie. She was on vacation right now, but Owen had clearly managed to unearth a chicken from a secret stash somewhere.

I stroked the top of his head again. "Go back to sleep," I said. "You're going cold turkey . . . or maybe I should say cold chicken. I'm telling Rebecca no more catnip toys for you. You're getting lazy."

Owen put his head down again, while Hercules used his to butt my free hand. "You want some attention, too?" I asked. I scratched the spot, almost at the top of his head, where the white fur around his mouth and up the bridge of his nose gave way to black. His green eyes narrowed to slits and he began to purr, as well. The rumbling was kind of like being in the service bay of a Volkswagen dealership.

I glanced up at the clock. "Okay, you two. Let me up. It's almost time for me to go and I have to take care of the dearly departed before I do."

I'd sold my car when I'd moved to Minnesota from Boston, and because I could walk everywhere in Mayville Heights, I still hadn't bought a new one. Since I had no car, I'd spent my first few weeks in town wandering around exploring, which is how I'd stumbled on Wisteria Hill, the abandoned Henderson estate. Everett Henderson had hired me at the library.

Owen and Hercules had peered out at me from a tumble of raspberry canes and then followed me around while I explored the overgrown English country garden behind the house. I'd seen several other full-grown cats, but they'd all disappeared as soon as I got anywhere close to them. When I left, Owen and Hercules followed me down the rutted gravel driveway. Twice I'd picked them up and carried them back to the empty house, but that didn't deter them. I looked everywhere, but I couldn't find their mother. They were so small and so determined to come with me that in the end I'd brought them home.

There were whispers around town about Wisteria Hill and the feral cats. But that didn't mean there was anything unusual about my cats. Oh no, nothing unusual at all. It didn't matter that I'd heard rumors about strange lights and ghosts. No one had lived at the estate for quite a while, but Everett refused to sell it or do anything with the property. I'd heard that he'd grown up at Wisteria Hill. Maybe that was why he didn't want to change anything.

Speaking of not wanting change, Hercules was not eager to relinquish his prime spot on my lap. But after some gentle prodding, he shook himself and got off. Owen yawned a couple of times, stretched and took twice as long to move.

I got the broom and dustpan from the porch and swept up the remains of Fred the Funky Chicken. Owen and Hercules sat in front of the refrigerator and watched. Owen made a move toward the dustpan, like he was toying with the idea of grabbing the body and making a run for it.

I glared at him. "Don't even think about it."

He sat back down, making low, grumbling meows in his throat.

I flipped open the lid of the garbage can and held the pan over the top. "Fred was a good chicken," I said solemnly. "He was a funky chicken and we'll miss him."

"Meow," Owen yowled.

I flipped what was left of the catnip toy into the garbage. "Rest in peace, Fred," I said as the lid closed.

I put the broom away, brushed the cat hair off my shirt and washed my hands. I looked in the bathroom mirror. Hercules was right. My hair did look better tucked behind my ear.

My messenger bag with a towel and canvas shoes for tai chi class was in the front closet. I set it by the door and went back through the house to make sure the cats had fresh water.

"I'm leaving," I said. But both cats had disappeared and I didn't get any answer.

I stopped to grab my keys and pick up my bag. Locking the door behind me, I headed out, down Mountain Road.

The sun was yellow-orange, low on the sky over Lake Pepin. It was a warm Minnesota evening, without the sticky humidity of Boston in late July. I shifted my bag from one shoulder to the other. I wasn't going to think about Boston. Minnesota was home now—at least for the next eighteen months or so.

The street curved in toward the center of town as I headed down the hill, and the roof of the library building came into view below. It sat on the midpoint of a curve of shoreline, protected from the water by a rock wall. The brick building had a stained-glass window that dominated one end and a copper-roofed cupola, complete with its original wrought-iron weather vane.

The Mayville Heights Free Public Library was a Carnegie library, built in 1912 with money donated by the industrialist and philanthropist Andrew Carnegie. Now it was being restored and updated to celebrate its centenary. That was why I had been in town for the last several months. And why I'd be here for the next year and a half. I was supervising the restoration—which was almost finished—as well as updating the collections, computerizing the card catalogue and setting up free Internet access for the library patrons. I was slowly learning the reading history of everyone in town. It made me feel like I knew the people a little, as well.

ABOUT THE AUTHOR

Sofie Ryan is a writer and mixed-media artist who loves to repurpose things in her life and in her art. She is the author of *Claw Enforcement, No Escape Claws* and *The Fast and the Furriest* in the *New York Times* bestselling Second Chance Cat Mysteries. She also writes the *New York Times* bestselling Magical Cats Mysteries under the name Sofie Kelly.

CONNECT ONLINE

SofieRyan.com